Praise for the reigning queen of romance,

DIANA PALMER

"Palmer's talent for character development and ability to fuse
heartwarming romance with nail-biting suspense shine in *Outsider.*"
—*Booklist*

"A gentle escape mixed with real-life menace
for fans of Palmer's more than 100 novels."
—*Publishers Weekly* on *Night Fever*

"The ever-popular and prolific Palmer has penned another sure hit."
—*Booklist* on *Before Sunrise*

"Nobody does it better."
—*New York Times* bestselling author Linda Howard

"Palmer knows how to make sparks fly...heartwarming."
—*Publishers Weekly* on *Renegade*

"Sensual and suspenseful."
—*Booklist* on *Lawless*

"Diana Palmer is a mesmerizing storyteller
who captures the essence of what a romance should be."
—*Affaire de Coeur*

"Nobody tops Diana Palmer when it comes to delivering pure,
undiluted romance. I love her stories."
—*New York Times* bestselling author Jayne Ann Krentz

DIANA PALMER

MAN OF THE HOUR

HQN™

HQN™

ISBN-13: 978-0-373-77327-5
ISBN-10:   0-373-77327-7

MAN OF THE HOUR

Copyright © 2008 by Harlequin Books S.A.

The publisher acknowledges the copyright holder of the individual works as follows:

NIGHT OF LOVE
Copyright © 1993 by Diana Palmer

SECRET AGENT MAN
Copyright © 1993 by Diana Palmer

Printed in U.S.A.

CONTENTS

NIGHT OF LOVE

PROLOGUE

Steven Ryker paced his office at Ryker Air with characteristic energy, smoking a cigarette that he hated while he turned the air blue in quiet muttering. A chapter of his life that he'd closed the door on four years past had reopened, leaving his emotional wounds bare and bleeding.

Meg was back.

He didn't recognize his own fear. It wasn't a condition he'd ever associated with himself. But things had changed. He'd gone through a period of mourning when Meg had walked out on him to begin a balletic career in New York. He'd consoled himself with woman after willing woman. But in the end, he'd been alone with the painful memories. They hurt, and because they still hurt, he blamed Meg. He wanted her to suffer as he had. He wanted to see her beautiful blue eyes fill with tears, he wanted to see pain on that exquisite face framed by soft blond hair. He wanted consolation for the hell she'd put him through by leaving without a word when she'd promised to be his wife.

He put out the cigarette. It was a habit, like loving Meg. He hated both: cigarettes and the blond memory from his past. He'd never had a woman jilt him. Of course, he'd never asked a woman to marry him, either. He'd been content to live alone, until Meg had kissed him in gratitude for the present he'd given her when she turned eighteen. His life had turned over then.

Their fathers, hers and his, had become business partners when Meg was fourteen and her brother, David, just a little older. The families had developed a closeness that tied their lives together. Meg had been a sweet nuisance that Steven had tolerated when he and David had become best friends. But the nuisance grew up into a beautiful, regal woman who'd melted the ice around his hard heart. He'd given everything he was, everything he had, to Meg. And it hadn't been enough.

He couldn't forgive her for not wanting him. He couldn't admit that his obsession with her had all but cost him his sanity when she left. He wanted vengeance. He wanted Meg.

There would be a way to make her pay, he vowed. She'd hurt her leg and couldn't dance temporarily. But that ballet company she worked for was in real financial straits. If he played his cards right, he might yet have that one magical night in Meg's arms that he'd dreamed of for years. But this time, it wouldn't be out of love and need. It would be out of vengeance. Meg was back. And he was going to make her pay for what she'd made of him.

1

Meg was already out of humor when she went to answer the phone. She'd been in the middle of her exercises at the bar, and she hated interruptions that diverted her concentration. An injury had forced her into this temporary hiatus at her family home in Wichita, Kansas. It was hard enough to do the exercises in the first place with a damaged ligament in her ankle. It didn't help her mood when she picked up the receiver and found one of Steven Ryker's women on the other end of the line.

Steven, the president of Ryker Air, had been playing tennis all afternoon with Meg's brother, David. He'd obviously forwarded his calls here. It irritated Meg to have to talk to his women friends at all. But then, she'd always been possessive about Steven Ryker; long before she left Wichita for New York to study ballet.

"Is Steve there?" a feminine voice demanded.

Another in a long line of Steve's corporate lovers, no doubt, Meg thought angrily. Well, this one was going to become a lost cause. Right now.

"Who's calling, please?" Meg drawled.

There was a pause. "This is Jane. Who are you?"

"I'm Meg," she replied pertly, trying not to laugh.

"Oh." The voice hesitated. "Well, I'd like to speak to Steve, please."

Meg twirled the cord around her finger and lowered her voice an octave. "Darling?" she purred, her lips close to the receiver. "Oh, darling, do wake up. It's Jane, and she wants to speak to you."

There was a harsh intake of breath on the other end of the line. Meg stifled a giggle, because she could almost read the woman's mind. Her blue eyes twinkled in her soft oval face, framed by pale blond hair drawn into a disheveled bun atop her head.

"I have *never...!*" An outraged voice exploded in her ear.

"Oh, you really should, you know," Meg interrupted, sighing theatrically. "He's so *marvelous* in bed! Steven, darling...?"

The phone was slammed in her ear loud enough to break an eardrum. Meg put a slender hand over her mouth as she replaced the receiver in its cradle. Take that, Steven, she thought.

She turned and walked gingerly back into the room David had converted from the old ballroom into a practice room for his sister. It didn't get a lot of use, since she was in New York most of the year now, but it was a wonderfully thoughtful extravagance on her brother's part. David, like Meg, had shares in Ryker Air. David was a vice president of the company as well. But the old family fortune had been sacrificed by their late father in an attempt to take over the company, just before his death. He'd lost, and the company had very nearly folded. Except for the uncanny business acumen of Steven Ryker, it would have. Steve pulled the irons out of the fire and made the company solvent. He owned most of it now. And he should, Meg thought charitably. Heaven knew, he'd worked hard enough for it all these years.

As she exercised, Meg felt wicked. She shouldn't have caused Steve problems with his current love. They hadn't been engaged for four years, and she'd long ago relinquished the right to feel possessive about him.

Pensively she picked up her towel and wrapped it around her long, graceful neck, over the pink leotard she wore with her leg warmers and her pitiful-looking toe shoes. She stared down at them ruefully. They were so expensive that she had to wear her old ones for practice, and anyone seeing her in them would be convinced that she was penniless. That was almost the truth. Because despite the shares of stock she held in Ryker Air—the company that Steven's father and Meg and David's father had founded jointly—Meg *was* practically destitute. She was only a minor dancer in the New York ballet company she'd joined just a year ago, after three years of study with a former prima ballerina who had a studio in New York. She had yet to perform her first solo role. Presumably when she passed that landmark, she'd be higher paid, more in demand. Unless she missed a jump, that was, as she had a week ago. The memory was painful, like her ankle. That sort of clumsiness wasn't going to get her any starring roles. And now she had the added worry of getting her damaged tendon back in shape. The exercise, recommended and outlined by a physical therapist, was helping. But it was torturously slow, and very painful, to exercise those muscles. It had to be done carefully, too, so that she wouldn't damage them even further.

She went back into her disciplined exercises with a determined smile still on her face. She tried to concentrate on fluidity of movement and not the inevitable confrontation when Steve found out what she'd said to his girlfriend. Her whole life seemed to have been colored by him, since she was fourteen and their fathers had become business partners. Her father had worshiped Steven from the beginning. So had David. But Meg had hated him on sight.

For the first few years, she'd fought him tooth and nail, not bothering to hide her animosity. But on the eve of her eighteenth birthday, things had changed between them quite suddenly. He'd given her a delicate pearl necklace and she'd kissed him for it, a little shyly. Except that she'd missed his lean cheek and found his hard, rough mouth instead.

In all fairness, he'd been every bit as shocked as Meg. But instead of pulling away and making a joke of it, there had quite suddenly been a second kiss; one that couldn't be mistaken for anything but a passionate, almost desperate exchange. When it ended, neither of them had spoken. Steven's silver eyes had flashed dangerously and he'd left the room abruptly, without saying a single word.

But that kiss had changed the way they looked at each other. Their relationship had changed, too. Reluctantly, almost helplessly, Steven had started taking her out on dates and within a month, he proposed marriage. She'd wanted ballet so much by that time that despite her raging desire and love for Steve, she was torn between marriage and dancing. Steven, apparently sensing that, had turned up the heat. A long bout of lovemaking had almost ended in intimacy. Steven had lost control and his unbounded ardor had frightened Meg. An argument had ensued, and he'd said some cruel things to her.

That same evening, after their argument, Steven had taken his former mistress, Daphne, out on the town very publicly, and an incriminating photo of the couple had appeared in the society column of the daily newspaper the next day.

Meg had been devastated. She'd cried herself to sleep. Rather than face Steven and fight for a relationship with him, she'd opted to leave and go to New York to study ballet.

Like a coward, Meg had run. But what she'd seen spoke for itself and her heart was broken. If Steven could go to another woman that quickly, he certainly wasn't the type to stay faithful after he was married. Steven had been so ardent that it was miraculous she was still a virgin, anyway.

All of those facts raised doubts, the biggest one being that Steven had probably only wanted to marry her to keep all the stock from the partnership in the family. It had seemed quite logical at the time. Everyone knew how ambitious Steven was, and he and his father hadn't been too happy at some of the changes Meg's father had wanted to make at the time of the engagement.

Meg had gone to New York on the first plane out of Wichita, to be met by one of her mother's friends and set up in a small apartment near the retired prima ballerina with whom she would begin her studies.

Nicole, meanwhile, met Steve for coffee and explained that Meg had left town. Afterward, Meg heard later, Steven had gotten roaring drunk for the first, last and only time in his life. An odd reaction for a man who only wanted to marry her for her shares of stock, and who'd thrown her out of his life. But Steven hadn't called or written, and he never alluded to the brief time they'd spent as a couple. His behavior these days was as cold as he'd become himself.

Steve hadn't touched her since their engagement. But his eyes had, in a way that made her knees weak. It was a good thing that she spent most of her time in New York. Otherwise, if she'd been around Steven very much, she might have fallen headlong into an affair with him. She wouldn't have been able to resist him, and he was experienced enough to know that. He'd made sure that she kept her distance and he kept his. But the lingering passion she felt for him hadn't dimmed over the years. It was simply buried, so that it wouldn't interfere with her dreams of becoming a prima ballerina. She'd forced herself to settle; she'd chosen not to fight for his love. Her life since had hardly been a happy one, but she told herself that she was content.

Steve still came to the Shannon house to see David, and the families got together at the annual company picnics and benefits. These days, the family meant Steven and his mother and Meg and her brother David, because the older Shannons were dead now.

Mason Ryker, Steven's father, and John and Nicole Shannon had died in the years since Meg went to New York; Mason of a heart attack, and John and Nicole in a private-plane crash the very year Meg had left Wichita. Amy Ryker was as protective of Meg as if she'd been her mother instead of Steve's, but she lived in West Palm Beach now and only came home when she had to. She and Steven had never really been able to bear each other's company.

Steven had women hanging from the chandeliers, from what Amy told Meg on the occasions when she came to New York to watch Meg dance. He was serious about none of them, and there had never been a whisper of a serious commitment since his brief engagement to Meg.

Meg herself had become buried in her work. All she lived and breathed was the dance. The hours every day of grueling practice, the dieting and rigid life-style she lived made relationships difficult if not impossible. She often thought she was a little cold as a woman. Since Steven, she'd never felt her innocence threatened. Men had dated her, of course, but she was too conscious of the dangers to risk the easy life-styles some of the older dancers had once indulged in. These days, a one-night stand could be life-threatening. Besides, Meg thought sadly, only Steven had ever made her want intimacy. Her memories of him were devastating sometimes, despite the violent passion he'd shown her the last time they'd been together.

She stretched her aching muscles, and her mind wandered back to the mysterious Jane who'd telephoned. Who the hell was Jane? she wondered, and what did Steven want with someone who could speak that haughtily over the phone? She pictured a milky little blonde with a voluptuous figure and stretched even harder.

It was time to take off the lean roast and cottage potatoes she was cooking for supper by the time David walked in the door, still in his tennis outfit, looking as pleasant and jovial as ever. He had the same coloring his sister had, but he was shorter and a little broader than she.

He grinned at her. "Just thought I might mention that you're in it up to your neck. Steve got a call while we were at his house, and your goose is about to be cooked."

She stopped dead in the hall as Steven Ryker walked in behind her brother. Steve was a little over six feet tall, very dark and intimidating. He reminded her of actors who played mobsters, because he had the same threatening look about him, and even a deep scar down one cheek. It had probably been put there by some jealous woman in his checkered past, she thought venomously, but it gave him a rakish look. Even his eyes were unusual. They were a cross between ice blue and watered gray, and they could almost cut the skin when they looked as they did at the moment. The white shorts he was wearing left the muscular length of his tanned, powerful legs bare. A white knit shirt did the same for his arms. He was incredibly fit for a man on the wrong side of thirty who sat at a desk all day.

Right now he looked very casual, dressed in his tennis outfit, and that was the most deceptive thing about him. He was never casual. He always played to win, even at sports. He was also the most sensuous, sexy man she'd ever known. Or ever would. Just looking at him made her weak-kneed. She hid her reaction to him as she always had, in humor.

"Ah, Steven." Meg sighed, batting her long eyelashes at him. "How lovely to see you. Did one of your women die, or is there some simpler reason that we're being honored by your presence?"

"Pardon me while I go out back and skin a rock," David mumbled with a grin, diving quickly past his sister in a most ungentlemanly way to get out of the line of fire.

"Coward!" she yelled after him as the door slammed.

"You wouldn't need protection if you could learn to keep your mouth shut, Mary Margaret," Steven said with a cool smile. "I'd had my calls forwarded here while I was playing tennis. Jane couldn't believe what she'd heard, so she telephoned my home again and got me. It so happened David and I had stopped back by the house to look at a new painting I'd bought. I canceled the call forwarding just in time—or I might have been left in blissful ignorance."

She glared at him. "It was your own fault. You don't have to have your women telephone you here!"

The glitter in his eyes got worse. "Jealous, Meg?" he taunted.

"Of you? God forbid," she said as casually as she could, and with a forced smile. "Of course I do remember vividly the wonderful things you can do with your hands and those hard lips, darling, but I'm quite urbane these days and less easily impressed."

"Careful," he warned softly. "You may be more vulnerable than you realize."

She backed down. "Anyway," she muttered, "why don't you just take Jane Thingamabob out for a steak and warm her back up again?"

"Jane Dray is my mother's maiden aunt," he said after a minute, watching her reaction with amusement. "You might remember her from the last company picnic?"

Meg did, with horror. The old dowager was a people-eater of the first order, who probably still wore corsets and cursed modern transportation. "Oh, dear," she began.

"She is now horrified that her favorite great-nephew is sleeping with little Meggie Shannon, who used to be such a sweet, innocent child."

"Oh, my God," Meg groaned, leaning against the wall.

"Yes. And she'll more than likely rush to tell *your* great-aunt Henrietta, who will feel obliged to write to my mother in West Palm Beach and tell her the scandalous news that you are now a scarlet woman. And my mother, who always has preferred you to me, will naturally assume that I seduced you, not the reverse."

"Damn!" she moaned. "This is all your fault!"

He folded his arms over his broad chest. "You brought it on yourself. Don't blame me. I'm sure my mother will be utterly shocked at your behavior, nevertheless, especially since she's taken great pains to try to make up for the loss of your own mother years ago."

"I'll kill myself!" she said dramatically.

"Could you fix supper first?" David asked, sticking his head around the kitchen door. "I'm starved. So is Steve."

"Then why don't the two of you go out to a restaurant?" she asked, still reeling from her horrid mistake.

"Heartless woman." David sighed. "And I was so looking forward to the potatoes and roast I can smell cooking on the stove."

He managed to look pitiful and thin, all at the same time. She glared at him. "Well, I suppose I can manage supper. As if you need feeding up! Look at you!"

"I'm a walking monument of your culinary skills," David argued. "If I could cook, I'd look healthy between your vacations."

"It isn't exactly a vacation," Meg murmured worriedly. "The ballet company I work for is between engagements, and when there's no money to pay the light bill, we can't keep the theater open. Our manager is looking for more financing even now."

"He'll find it," David consoled her. "It's an established ballet company, and he's a good finance man. Stop brooding."

"Okay," she said.

"Do we have time to shower and change?" David asked.

"Sure," she told him. "I need to do that myself. I've been working out all afternoon."

"You push yourself too hard," Steve remarked coolly. "Is it really worth it?"

"Of course!" she said. She smiled outrageously. "Don't you know that ballerinas are the ideal ornament for rich gentlemen?" she added, lying through her teeth. "I actually had a patron offer to keep me." She didn't add that the man had adoption, not seduction, in mind, and that he was the caretaker at her apartment house.

Incredibly Steve's eyes began to glitter. "What did you tell him?"

"That I pay my own way, of course." She laughed. She held on to the railing of the long staircase and leaned forward. "Tell you what, Steve. If you play your cards right, when I get to the top of the ladder and start earning what I'm really worth, I'll keep *you*."

He tried not to smile, but telltale lines rippled around his firm, sculptured mouth.

"You're impossible." David chuckled.

"I make your taciturn friend smile, though," she added, watching Steve with twinkling eyes. "I don't think he knew how until I came along. I keep his temper honed, too."

"Be careful that I don't hone it on you," he cautioned quietly. There was something smoldering in his eyes, something tightly leashed. There always had been, but when he was around her, just lately, it threatened to escape.

She laughed, because the look in those gunmetal-gray eyes made her nervous. "I won't provoke you, Steven," she said. "I'm not quite that brave." He scowled and she changed the subject. "I'm sorry about Aunt Jane," she added with sincere apology. "I'll call her and explain, if you like."

"There's no need," he said absently, his gaze intent on her flushed face. "I've already taken care of it."

As usual. She could have said it, but she didn't. Steven didn't let grass grow under his feet. He was an accomplished mover and shaker, which was why his company was still solvent when others had gone bankrupt. She made a slight movement with her shoulders and proceeded up the staircase. She felt his eyes on her, but she didn't look back.

When Meg had showered and changed into a lacy white pantsuit, she went back downstairs. She'd left her long blond hair in a knot, because she knew how much Steven disliked it up. Her blue eyes twinkled with mischief.

Steve had changed, too, and returned from his house, which was barely two blocks away. He was wearing white slacks with a soft blue knit shirt, and he looked elegant and unapproachable. His back was broad, his shoulders straining against the expensive material of his shirt. Meg remembered without wanting to how it had felt all those years ago to run her hands up and down that expanse of muscle while he kissed her. There was a thick pelt of hair over his chest and stomach. During their brief interlude, she'd learned the hard contours of his body with delight.

He could have had her anytime during that one exquisite month of togetherness, but he'd always drawn back in time. She wondered sometimes if he'd ever regretted it. Secretly she did. There would never be anyone else that she'd want as she had wanted Steve. The memories would have been bittersweet if they'd been lovers, but at least they might fill the emptiness she felt now. Her life was dedicated to ballet and as lonely as death. No man touched her, except her ballet partners, and none of them excited her.

She'd always been excited by Steven. That hadn't faded. The past two times she'd come home to visit David, the hunger she felt for her ex-fiancé had grown unexpectedly, until it actually frightened her. *He* frightened her, with his vast experience of women and his intent way of looking at her.

He turned when he heard her enter the room, with a cigarette in his hand. He quit smoking periodically, sometimes with more success than others. He was restless and high-strung, and the cigarette seemed to calm him. Fortunately, the house was air-conditioned and David had, at Meg's insistence, added a huge filtering system to it. There was no smell of smoke.

"Nasty habit," she muttered, glaring at him.

He inclined his head toward her with a mocking smile. "Doesn't your great-aunt Henrietta dip snuff…?"

She sighed. "Yes, she does. You look very much as your father used to," she murmured.

He shook his head. "He was shorter."

"But just as somber. You don't smile, Steve," she said quietly, and moved gracefully into the big front room with its modern black and white and chrome furniture and soft honey-colored carpet.

"Smiling doesn't fit my image," he returned.

"Some image," she mused. "I saw one of your vice presidents hide in a hangar when he spotted you on the tarmac. That lazy walk of yours lets everyone know when you're about to lose your temper. So slow and easy—so deadly."

"It gets results," he replied, indicating that he was aware of the stance and probably used it to advantage with his people. "Have you seen a balance sheet lately? Aren't you interested in what I'm doing with your stock?"

"Finance doesn't mean much to me," she confessed. "I'm much more interested in the ballet company I'm working with. It really is in trouble."

"Join another company," he said.

"I've spent a year working my way up in this one," she returned. "I can't start all over again. Ballerinas don't have that long, as a rule. I'm going on twenty-three."

"So old?" His eyes held hers. "You look very much as you did at eighteen. More sophisticated, of course. The girl I used to know would have died before she'd have insinuated to a perfect stranger that she was sharing my bed."

"I thought she was one of your women," Meg muttered. "God knows, you've got enough of them. I'll bet you have to keep a computer file so you won't forget their names. No wonder Jane believed I was one of them without question!"

"You could have been, once," he reminded her bluntly. "But I got noble and pushed you away in the nick of time." He laughed without humor. "I thought we'd have plenty of time for intimate discoveries after we were married. More fool me." He lifted the cigarette to his mouth, and his eyes were ice-cold.

"I was grass green back then," she reminded him with what she hoped was a sophisticated smile. "You'd have been disappointed."

He blew out a soft cloud of smoke and his eyes searched hers. "No. But you probably would have been. I wanted you too badly that last night we were together. I'd have hurt you."

It was the night they'd argued. But before that, they'd lain on his black leather sofa and made love until she'd begged him to finish it. She hadn't been afraid, then. But he hadn't. Even now, the sensations he'd kindled in her body made her flush.

"I don't think you would have, really," she said absently, her body tingling with forbidden memories as she looked at him. "Even so, I wanted you enough that I wouldn't have cared if you hurt me. I was wild to have you. I forgot all my fears."

He didn't notice the implication. He averted his eyes. "Not wild enough to marry me, of course."

"I was eighteen. You were thirty and you had a mistress."

His back stiffened. He turned, his eyes narrow, scowling. "What?"

"You know all this," she said uncomfortably. "My mother explained it to you the morning I left."

He moved closer, his lean face hard, unreadable. "Explain it to me yourself."

"Your father told me about Daphne," she faltered. "The night we argued, she was the one you took out, the one you were photographed with. Your father told me that you were only marrying me for the stock. He and your mother cared about me—perhaps more than my own did. When he said that you always went back to Daphne, no matter what, I got cold feet."

His high cheekbones flushed. He looked...stunned. "He told you that?" he asked harshly.

"Yes. Well, my mother knew about Daphne, too," she said heavily.

"Oh, God." He turned away. He leaned over to crush out his cigarette, his eyes bleak, hopeless.

"I knew you weren't celibate, but finding that you had a mistress was something of a shock, especially when we'd been seeing each other for a month."

"Yes. I expect it was a shock." He was staring down into the ashtray, unmoving. "I knew your mother was against the engagement. She had her heart set on helping you become a ballerina. She'd failed at it, but she was determined to see that you succeeded."

"She loved me..."

He turned, his dark eyes riveting to hers. "You ran, damn you."

She took a steadying breath. "I was eighteen. I had reasons for running that you don't know about." She dropped her eyes to his broad chest. "But I think I understand the way you were with me. You had Daphne. No wonder it was so easy for you to draw back when we made love."

His eyes closed. He almost shuddered with reaction. He shook with the force of his rage at his father and Meg's mother.

"It's all water under the bridge now, though," she said then, studying his rigid posture with faint surprise. "Steve?"

He took a long, deep breath and lit another cigarette. "Why didn't you say something? Why didn't you wait and talk to me?"

"There was no point," she said simply. "You'd already told me to get out of your life," she added with painful satisfaction.

"At the time, I probably meant it," he replied heavily. "But that didn't last long. Two days later, I was more than willing to start over, to try again. I came to tell you so. But you were gone."

"Yes." She stared at her slender hands, ringless, while her mind fought down the flood of misery she'd felt when she left Wichita. The fear had finally defeated her. And he didn't know…

"If you'd waited, I could have explained," he said tautly.

She looked at him sadly. "Steve, what could you have said? It was perfectly obvious that you weren't ready to make a real commitment to me, even if you were willing to marry me for your own reasons. And I had some terrors that I couldn't face."

"Did you?" he asked dully. He lifted the cigarette to his chiseled mouth and stared into space. "Your father and mine were involved in a subtle proxy fight about that time, did anyone tell you?"

"No. Why would they have needed to?"

"No reason," he said bitterly. "None at all."

She hated the way he looked. Surely what had happened in

the past didn't still bother him. His pride had suffered, though, that might explain it.

She moved closer, smiling gently. "Steve, it was forever ago," she said. "We're different people now, and all I did really was to spare us both a little embarrassment when we broke up. If you'd wanted me that badly, you'd have come after me."

He winced. His dark silver eyes caught hers and searched them with anguish. "You're sure of that."

"Of course. It was no big thing," she said softly. "You've had dozens of women since, and your mother says you don't take any of them any more seriously than you took me. You enjoy being a bachelor. If I wasn't ready for marriage, neither were you."

His face tautened. He smiled, but it was no smile at all. "You're right," he said coldly, "it was no big thing. One or two nights together would have cured both of us. You were a novelty, you with your innocent body and big eyes. I wanted you, all right."

She searched his face, looking for any trace of softening. She didn't find it. She hated seeing him that way, so somber and remote. Impishly she wiggled her eyebrows. "Do you still? Feel like experimenting? Your bed or mine?"

He didn't smile. His eyes flashed, and one of them narrowed a little. That meant trouble.

He lifted the cigarette to his lips one more time, drawing out the silence until she felt like an idiot for what she'd suggested. He bent his tall frame to put it out in the ashtray, and she watched. He had beautiful hands: dark and graceful and long-fingered. On a woman's body, they were tender magic...

"No, thanks," he said finally. "I don't like being one in a queue."

Her eyebrows arched. "I beg your pardon?"

He straightened and stuck his hands deep into his pockets, emphasizing the powerful muscles in his thighs, his narrow hips and flat stomach. "Shouldn't you be looking after your roast? Or do you imagine that David and I don't have enough charcoal in our diets already?"

She moved toward him gracefully. "Steve, I dislike very much what you've just insinuated." She stared up at him fearlessly, her eyes wide and quiet. "There hasn't been a man. Not one. There isn't time in my life for the sort of emotional turmoil that comes from involvement. Emotional upsets influence the way I dance. I've worked too hard, too long, to go looking for complications."

She started to turn away, but his lean, strong hands were on her waist, stilling her, exciting her.

"Your honesty, Mary Margaret, is going to land you in hot water one day."

"Why lie?" she asked, peering over her shoulder at him.

"Why, indeed?" he asked huskily.

He drew her closer, resting his chin on the top of her blond head, and her heart raced wildly as his fingers slid slowly up and down from her waist to her rib cage.

"What if I give in to that last bit of provocation?" he whispered roughly.

"What provocation?"

His teeth closed softly on her earlobe, his warm breath brushing her cheek. "Your bed or mine, Meg?" he whispered.

2

Meg wondered if she was still breathing. She'd been joking, but Steve didn't look or sound as if he were. "Steve…" she whispered.

His eyes fell to her mouth as her head lay back against his broad chest. His face changed at the sound of his name on her lips. His hands on her waist contracted until they bruised and his face went rigid. "Mouth like a pink rose petal," he said in an oddly rough tone. "I almost took you once, Meg."

She felt herself vibrating, like drawn cord. "You pushed me away," she whispered.

"I had to!" There was anger in the silvery depths of his eyes. "You blind little fool." He bit off the words. "Don't you know why even now?"

She didn't. She simply stared at him, her blue eyes wide and clear and curious.

He groaned. "Meg!" He let out a long, rough breath and

forcibly eased the grip of his lean hands and pushed her away. He shoved his hands into his pockets and stared for a long time into her wide, guileless eyes. "No, you don't understand, do you?" he said heavily. "I thought you might mature in New York." His eyes narrowed and he frowned. "What was that talk about some man wanting to keep you, then?"

She smiled sheepishly. "He's the caretaker of my apartment house. He wanted to adopt me."

"Good God!"

She rested her fingers on his arms, feeling their strength, loving them. She leaned against him gently with subdued delight that heightened when his hands came out of his pockets and smoothed over her shoulders. "There really isn't room in my life for complications," she said sadly. "Even with you. It wouldn't be wise." She forced a laugh from her tight throat. "Besides, I'm sure you have all the women you need already."

"Of course," he agreed with maddening carelessness and a curious watchfulness. "But I've wanted you for a very long time. We started something that we never finished. I want to get you out of my system, Meg, once and for all."

"Have you considered hiring an exorcist?" she asked, resorting to humor. She pushed playfully at his chest, feeling his heartbeat under her hands. "How about plastering a photo of me on one of your women...?"

He shook her gently. "Stop that."

"Besides," she said, sighing and looping her arms around his neck, "I'd probably get pregnant and there'd be a scandal in the aircraft community. My career would be shot, your reputation would be ruined and we'd have a baby that neither of us wanted." Odd that the threat of pregnancy no longer terrified her, she thought idly.

"Mary Margaret, this is the twentieth century," he murmured on a laugh. "Women don't get pregnant these days unless they want to."

She turned her head slightly as she looked up at him, wide-eyed. "Why, Mr. Ryker, you sound so sophisticated. I suppose you keep a closetful of supplies?"

He burst out laughing. "Hell."

She smiled up at him. "Stop baiting me," she said. "I don't want to sleep with you and ruin a beautiful friendship. We've been friends for a long time, Steve, even if cautious ones."

"Friend, enemy, sparring partner," he agreed. The smile turned to a blank-faced stare with emotion suddenly glittering dangerously in his silver eyes. His chest rose and fell roughly and he moved a hand into the thick hair knotted at her nape and grasped it suddenly. He held her head firmly while he started to bend toward her.

"Steve..." she protested uncertainly.

"One kiss," he whispered back gruffly. "Is that so much to ask?"

"We shouldn't," she whispered at his lips.

"I know..." His hard mouth brushed over hers slowly, suggestively. His powerful body went very still and his free hand moved to her throat, stroking it tenderly. His thumb tugged at the lower lip that held stubbornly to its mate and broke the taut line.

Her hands pressed at his shirtfront, fascinated by warm, hard muscle and a heavy heartbeat. She couldn't quite manage to push him away.

"Mary Margaret," he breathed jerkily, and then he took her mouth.

"Oh, glory...!" she moaned, shivering. It was a jolt like diving into ice water. It burned through her body and through her veins and made her go rigid with helpless pleasure. He was far more expert than he'd been even four years ago. His tongue gently probed its way into the warm darkness of her mouth and she gasped at the darting, hungry pressure of its invasion. He tasted of smoke and mint, and his mouth was rough, as if he'd gone hungry for kisses.

While she was gathering up willpower to resist him, he reached down and lifted her in his hard arms, crushing her into the wall of his chest while his devouring kisses made her oblivious to everything except desire. At the center of the world was Steve and his hunger, and she was suddenly, shockingly, doing her very best to satisfy it, to satisfy him, with her arms clinging helplessly around his neck.

He lifted his mouth to draw in a ragged breath, and she hung there with swollen lips, wide-eyed, breathing like a distance runner.

"If you don't stop," she whispered unsteadily, "I'll tear your clothes off and ravish you right here on the carpet!"

Despite his staggering hunger, the humor broke through, as it always had with her, only with her. There had never been another woman who could make him laugh, could make him feel so alive.

"Oh, God, why can't you shut up for five minutes?" he managed through reluctant laughter.

"Self-defense," she said, laughing, too, her own voice breathless with traces of passion. "Oh, Steve, can you kiss!" she moaned.

He shook his head, defeated. He let her slide down his body to the floor, close enough to feel what had happened to him.

"Sorry," she murmured impishly.

"Only with you, honey," he said heavily, the endearment coming easily when he never used them. He held her arms firmly for a minute before he let her go with a rueful smile and turned away to light another cigarette. "Odd, that reaction. I need a little time with most women. It was never that way with you."

She hadn't thought about it in four years. Now she had to, and he was right. The minute he'd touched her, he'd been capable. She'd convinced herself that he never wanted her, but her memory hadn't dimmed enough to forget the size and power of him in arousal. She'd been a little afraid of him the first time it had happened, in fact, although he'd assured her that they were compatible in every way, especially in that one. She didn't like remembering how intimate they'd been, because it was still painful to remember how it had all ended. Looking back, it seemed impossible that he could have gone to Daphne after they argued, unless…

She stiffened as she remembered how desperately he'd wanted her. Had he been so desperate that he'd needed to spend his desire with someone else?

"Steve," she began.

He glanced at her. "What?"

"What you said, earlier. Was it difficult for you," she said slowly. "Holding back?"

"Yes." His face changed. "Apparently that didn't occur to you four years ago," he said sarcastically.

"A lot of things didn't occur to me four years ago," she said. She felt a dawning fear that she didn't want to explore.

"Don't strain your memory," he said with a mocking smile. "God forbid that you might have to reconsider your position. It's too damned late, even if you did."

"I know that. I wouldn't...I have my career."

"Your career." He nodded, but there was something disconcerting in the way he said it, in the way he looked at her.

"I'd better see about the roast," she murmured, retreating.

He studied her face with a purely masculine appreciation. "Better fix your lipstick, unless you want David making embarrassing remarks."

"David is terrified of me," she informed him. "I once beat him up in full view of half our classmates."

"So he told me, but he's grown."

"Not too much." She touched her mouth. It was faintly sore from the pressure of his hard kisses. She wouldn't have expected so much passion from him after four years.

"Did I hurt?" he asked quietly. "I didn't mean to."

"You always were a little rough when we made love," she recalled with a wistful smile. "I never minded."

His eyes kindled and before he could make the move his expression telegraphed, she beat a hasty retreat into the kitchen. He was overwhelming at close range, and she couldn't handle an affair with him. She didn't dare try. Having lived through losing him once, she knew she'd never survive having to go through it again. He still wanted her, but that was all. She was filed under unfinished business, and there was something a little disturbing about his attitude toward her. It wasn't quite unsatisfied passion on his part, she thought nervously. It was more like a deeply buried, long-nurtured vendetta.

It was probably a good thing that she was going back to New York soon, she thought dimly. And not a minute *too* soon. Her knees were so wobbly she could barely walk, and just from one kiss. If he turned up the heat, as he had during their time together, she would never be able to resist him. The needs she felt were overpowering now. She was a woman and she reacted like one. It was her bad luck that the only man who aroused her was the one man she daren't succumb to. If Steve really was holding a grudge against her for breaking off their engagement, giving in to him would be a recipe for disaster.

Supper was a rather quiet affair, with Meg introspective and Steven taciturn while David tried to carry the conversation alone.

"Can't you two say something? Just a word now and again while I try to enjoy this perfectly cooked pot roast?" David groaned, glancing from one set face to the other. "Have you had another fight?"

"We haven't been fighting," Meg said innocently. "Have we, Steve?"

Steven looked down at his plate, deliberately cutting a piece of meat without replying.

David threw up his hands. "I'll never understand you two!" he muttered. "I'll just go see about dessert, shall I? I shall," he said, but he was talking to himself as he left the room.

"I don't want any," she called after him.

"Yes, she does," Steve said immediately, catching her eyes. "You're too thin. If you lose another two or three pounds, you'll be able to walk through a harp."

"I'm a dancer," she said. "I can't dance with a fat body."

He smiled gently. "That's right. Fight me." Something alien glittered in his eyes and his breathing quickened.

"Somebody needs to," she said with forced humor. "All that feminine fawning has ruined you. Your mother said that lines of women form everywhere you go these days."

His eyes contemplated his coffee cup intensely and his brow furrowed. "Did she?" he asked absently.

"But that you never take any of them seriously." She laughed, but without much humor. "Haven't you even thought about marrying?"

He looked up, his expression briefly hostile. "Sure. Once."

She felt uncomfortable. "It wouldn't have worked," she said stiffly. "I wouldn't have shared you, even when I was eighteen and naive."

His eyes narrowed. "You think I'm modern enough in my outlook to keep a wife and a mistress at the same time?"

The question disturbed her. "Daphne was beautiful and sophisticated," she replied. "I was green behind the ears. Totally uninhibited. I used to embarrass you…"

"Never!"

There was muted violence in the explosive word.

She glanced up at him curiously. "But I did! Your father said that's why you never liked to take me out in public…"

"My father. What a champion." He lifted the cold coffee to his lips and sipped it. It felt as cold as he did inside. He looked at Meg and ached. "Between them, your mother and my father did a pretty damned good job, didn't they?"

"Daphne was a fact," she replied stubbornly.

He drew in a long, weary breath. "Yes. She was, wasn't she? You saw that for yourself in the newspaper."

"I certainly did." She sounded bitter. She hated having given her feelings away. She forced a smile. "But, as they say, no harm done. I have a bright career ahead of me and you're a millionaire several times over."

"I'm that, all right. I look in the mirror twice a day and say, 'lucky me.'"

"Don't tease."

He turned his wrist and glanced at the face of the thin gold watch. "I have to go," he said, pushing back his chair.

"Are you off to a business meeting?" she probed gently.

He stared at her without speaking for a few seconds, just long enough to give him a psychological advantage. "No," he said. "I have a date. As my mother told you," he added with a cold smile, "I don't have any problem getting women these days."

Meg didn't know how she managed to smile, but she did. "The lucky girl," she murmured on a prolonged sigh.

Steve glowered at her. "You never stop, do you?"

"Can I help it if you're devastating?" she replied. "I don't blame women for falling all over you. I used to."

"Not for long."

She searched his hard face curiously. "I should have talked to you about Daphne, instead of running away."

"Let the past lie," he said harshly. "We're not the same people we were."

"One of us certainly isn't," she mused dryly. "You never used to kiss me like that!"

He cocked an eyebrow. "Did you expect me to remain celibate when you defected?"

"Of course not," she replied, averting her eyes. "That would have been asking the impossible."

"Fidelity belongs to a committed relationship," he said.

She was looking at her hands, not at him. Life seemed so empty lately. Even dancing didn't fill the great hollow space in her heart. "Being in a committed relationship wouldn't have mattered," she murmured. "I doubt if you'd have been capable of staying faithful to just one woman, what with your track record and all. And I'm hardly a raving beauty like Daphne."

He stiffened slightly, but no reaction showed in his face. He watched her and glowered. "Nice try, but it doesn't work."

She glanced up, surprised. "What doesn't?"

"The wounded, downcast look," he said. He stretched, and muscles rippled under his knit shirt. "I know you too well, Meg," he added. "You always were theatrical."

She stared at him without blinking. "Would you have liked it if I'd gone raging to the door of your apartment after I saw you and Daphne pictured in that newspaper?"

His face hardened to stone. "No," he admitted, "I loathe scenes. All the same, there's no reason to lie about the reason you wanted to break our engagement. You told your mother that dancing was more important than me, that you got cold feet and ran for it. That's all she told me."

Meg was puzzled, but perhaps Nicole had decided against mentioning Daphne's place in Steven's life. "I suppose she decided that the best course all around was to make you believe my career was the reason I left."

"That's right. Your *mother* decided," he corrected, and his eyes glittered coldly. "She yelled frog, and you jumped. You always were afraid of her."

"Who wasn't?" she muttered. "She was a world-beater, and I was a sheltered babe in the woods. I didn't know beans about men until you came along."

"You still don't," he said flatly. "I'm surprised that living in New York hasn't changed you."

"What you are is what you are, despite where you live," she

reminded him. She looked down again, infuriated with him. "I dance. That's what I do. That's all I do. I've worked hard all my life at ballet, and now I'm beginning to reap the rewards for it. I like my life. So it was probably a good thing that I found out how you felt about me in time, wasn't it? I had a lucky escape, Steve," she added bitterly.

He moved close, just close enough to make her feel threatened, to make her aware of him so that she'd look up.

He smiled with faint cruelty. "Does your good fortune compensate?" he asked with soft sarcasm.

"For what?"

"For knowing how much other women enjoy lying in my arms in the darkness."

She felt her composure shatter, and knew by the smile that he'd seen it in her eyes.

"Damn you!" she choked.

He turned away, laughing. "That's what I thought." He paused at the doorway. "Tell your brother I'll call him tomorrow." His eyes narrowed. "I hated you when your mother handed me the ring you'd left with her. You were the biggest mistake of my life. And, as you said, it was a lucky escape. For both of us."

He turned and left, his steady footsteps echoing down the hall before the door opened and closed with firm control behind him. Meg stood where he'd left her, aching from head to toe with renewed misery. He said he'd hated her in the past, but it was still there, in his eyes, when he looked at her. He hadn't stopped resenting her for what she'd done, despite the fact that he'd been unfaithful to her. He was in the wrong, so why was he blaming Meg?

"Where's Steve?" her brother asked when he reappeared.

"He had to go. He had a hot date," she said through her teeth.

"Good old Steve. He sure can draw 'em. I wish I had half his... Where are you going?"

"To bed," Meg said from the staircase, and her voice didn't encourage any more questions.

Meg only wished that she had someplace to go, but she was stuck in Wichita for the time being. Stuck with Steven always around, throwing his new conquests in her face. She limped because of the accident, and the tendons were mending, but not as quickly as she'd hoped. The doctor had been uncertain as to whether the damage would eventually right itself, and the physical therapist whom Meg saw three times a week was uncommunicative. Talk to the doctor, she told Meg. But Meg wouldn't, because she knew she wasn't making much progress and she was afraid to know why.

Besides her injury, there was no work in New York for her just now. Her ballet company couldn't perform without funds, and unless they raised some soon, she wouldn't have a job. It was a pity to waste so many years of her life on such a gamble. She loved ballet. If only she were wealthy enough to finance the company herself, but her small dividends from her stock in Ryker Air wouldn't be nearly enough.

David didn't have the money, either, but Steve did. She

grimaced at just the thought. Steve would throw the money away or even burn it before he'd lend any to Meg. Not that she'd ever ask him, she promised herself. She had too much pride.

She'd tried not to panic at the thought of never dancing again. She consoled herself with a small dream of her own, of opening a ballet school here in Wichita. It would be nice to teach little girls how to dance. After all, Meg had studied ballet since her fourth birthday. She certainly had the knowledge, and she loved children. It was an option that she'd never seriously considered before, but now, with her injury, it became a security blanket. It was there to keep her going. If she failed in one area, she still had prospects in another. Yes, she had prospects.

The next morning, it was raining. Meg looked out the front window and smiled wistfully, because the rain pounding down on the sprouting grass and leafing trees suited her mood. It was late spring. There were flowers blooming and, thank God, no tornadoes looming with this shower. The rain was nice, if unexpected.

She did her exercises, glowering at the ankle that was still stiff and painful after weeks of patient work. David was at the office and no doubt so was Steve—if he wasn't too worn out from the night before, she thought furiously. How dare he rub his latest conquest in her face and make sarcastic and painful remarks about it?

He wasn't the person she'd known at eighteen. That Steve had been a quiet man without the cruelty of this new man who used women and tossed them aside. Or perhaps he'd always been like this, except that Meg had been looking at him through loving eyes and missed all his flaws.

She didn't expect to see him again after his harshness the night before, but David telephoned just before he left the office with an invitation to dinner from Steve.

"We've just signed a new contract with a Middle-Eastern potentate. We're taking his representative out for dinner and Steve wants you to come with us."

"Why me?" she asked with faint bitterness. "Am I being offered as a treat to his client or is he thinking of selling me into slavery on the Barbary Coast? I understand blondes are still much in demand there."

David didn't catch the bitterness in her voice. He laughed uproariously, covered the mouthpiece and mumbled something. "Steve says that's not a bad idea, and for you to wear a harem outfit."

"Tell him fat chance," she mumbled. "I don't know if I want to go. Surely Steven has plenty of women who could help him entertain his business friends."

"Don't be difficult," David chided. "A night out would do you good."

"All right. I'll be ready when you get home."

"Good."

She hung up, wondering why she'd given in. Steven had probably invited one of his women and was going to rub Meg's face in his latest conquest. She herself would no doubt be tossed to the Arab for dessert. Well, he was due for a surprise if he thought she'd go along with his plotting!

By the time David opened the front door, Meg was dressed in an outfit she'd bought for a Halloween party in New York: a black dress that covered her from just under her ears to her ankles, set off by a wide silver belt and silver-sprayed flat shoes. It was impossible to wear high heels just yet, and even though her limp wasn't pronounced, walking was difficult enough in flats. Her hair was in its neat bun and she wore no makeup. She didn't realize that her fair beauty made makeup superfluous anyway. She had an exquisitely creamy complexion with a natural blush all its own.

"Wow!" David whistled.

She glowered at him. "You aren't supposed to approve. I'm rebelling. This is a revolutionary outfit, not debutante dressing."

"I know that, and so will Steve. But——" he grinned as he took her arm and herded her out the door "——believe me, he'll approve."

3

David's remark made sense until he escorted Meg into the restaurant where Steve—surprisingly without a woman in tow—and a tall, very dark Arab in an expensive European suit were seated. The men stood up as Meg and David approached. The Arab's gaze was approving. The puzzle pieces as to why Steve would be happy with her outfit fell into place.

"Remember that the Middle East isn't exactly liberated territory," David whispered. "You're dressed very correctly for this evening."

"Oh, boy," she muttered angrily. If she'd thought about it, she'd have worn her backless yellow gown....

"Enchanté, mademoiselle," the foreigner said with lazy delight as he was introduced to her. He smiled and his black mustache twitched. He was incredibly handsome, with eyes that were large and almost a liquid black. He was charming without being

condescending or offensive. "You are a dancer, I believe? A ballerina?"

"Yes," Meg murmured demurely. She smiled at him. "And you are the representative of your country?"

He quirked an eyebrow and glanced at Steve. "Indeed, I am."

"Do tell me about your part of the world," she said with genuine interest, totally ignoring Steve and her brother.

He did, to the exclusion of business, until Steve sat glowering at her over dessert and coffee. She shifted a little uncomfortably under that cold look, and Ahmed suddenly noticed his business colleague.

He chuckled softly. "Steven, my friend, I digress. Forgive me. But *mademoiselle* is such charming company that she chases all thought of business from my poor mind."

"No harm done," Steve replied quietly.

"I'm sorry," Meg said genuinely. "I didn't mean to distract you, but I do find your culture fascinating. You're very well educated," Meg said.

He smiled. "Oxford, class of '82."

She sighed. "Perhaps I should have gone to college instead of trying to study ballet."

"What a sad loss to the world of the arts if that had been so, *mademoiselle*. Historians are many. Good dancers, alas, are like diamonds."

Her cheeks flushed with flattery and excitement.

Steven's fingers closed around his fork and he stared at it. "About these new jets we're selling you, Ahmed," he persisted.

"Yes, we must discuss them. I have been led astray by a lovely face and a kind heart." He smiled at Meg. "But my duty will not allow me to divert my interests too radically from my purpose in coming here. You will forgive us if we turn our minds to the matter at hand, *mademoiselle?*"

"Of course," she replied softly.

"Kind of you," Steven murmured, his dagger glance saying much more than the polite words.

"For you, Steven, anything," she replied in kind.

The evening was both long and short. All too soon, David found himself accompanying the tall Arab back to his suite at the hotel while Steven appropriated Meg and eased her into the passenger seat of his Jaguar.

"Why is it always a Jaguar?" she asked curiously when he was inside and the engine was running.

"I like Jaguars."

"You would."

He pulled the sleek car out into traffic. "Leave Ahmed alone," he said without preamble.

"Ah. I'm being warned off." She nodded. "It's perfectly obvious that you consider me a woman of international intrigue, out to filch top-secret information and sell it to enemy agents." She frowned. "Who is the enemy these days, anyway?"

"Mata Hari, you aren't."

"Don't insult me. I have potential." She struck a pose, with her hand suspended behind her nape and her perfect facial profile toward him. "With a little careful tutoring, I could be devastating."

"With a little careful tutoring, you could be concealed in an oil drum and floated down the river to Oklahoma."

"You have no sense of humor."

He shrugged. "Not much to laugh about these days. Not in my life."

She leaned her cheek against the soft seat and watched him as he controlled the powerful car. It was odd that she always felt safe with him. Safe, and excited beyond words. Just looking at him made her tremble.

"What are you thinking?" he asked.

"That I'm sorry you never made love to me," she said without thinking.

The car swerved and his face tautened. He never looked at her. "Don't do that."

She drew in a slow breath, tracing patterns in the upholstery. "Aren't you, really?"

"You might have been addictive. I don't like addiction."

"That's why you smoke," she agreed, staring pointedly at the glowing cigarette in his lean, dark hand.

He did glance at her then, to glare. "I'm not addicted to nicotine. I can quit anytime I feel like it."

"What's wrong with right now?"

His dark eyes narrowed.

"What's wrong? Are you afraid you can't do without it?" she coaxed.

He pressed the power window switch, then threw the cigarette out when there was an opening. The window went back up again.

Meg grinned at him. "You'll be shaking in seconds," she predicted. "Combing the floor for old cigarette butts with a speck of tobacco left in them. Begging stubs from strangers."

"Unwise, Meg."

"What is? Taunting you?"

"I might decide to find another way to occupy my hands," he said suggestively.

She threw her arms out to the sides and closed her eyes. "Go ahead!" she invited theatrically. "Ravish me!"

The car slammed to a halt and Meg's eyes opened as wide as cups. She stared at him, horrified.

He lifted an eyebrow as her arms clutched her breasts and a blush flamed on her face.

"Why, Meg, is anything wrong?" he asked pleasantly. "I just stopped to let the ambulance by."

"What amb—"

Sirens and flashing red lights swept past them and vanished quickly into the distance. Meg felt like sinking through the floorboard with embarrassment.

Steven's eyes narrowed just a little. He looped one long arm over the back of her seat and studied her in the darkened car.

"All bluff, aren't you?" he chided. "Didn't I warn you that playing games with me would get you into trouble?"

"Yes," she said. "But you've done nicely without me for four years."

He didn't answer. His hand lowered to her throat and he toyed with a wisp of her hair that had come loose from her bun, teasing her skin until her pulse began to race and her body grew hot in the tense silence.

"Steven, don't," she whispered huskily, staying his hand.

"Let me excite you, Meg," he replied quietly. He moved closer, easing her hand aside. His mouth poised over hers and he began all over again, teasing, touching, just at her throat while his coffee-scented breath came into her mouth and made her body ache. "It was like this the first night I took you out. Do you remember?" His voice was a deep, soft caress, and his hand made her shiver with its tender tracing. "I parked the car in your own driveway after we'd had dinner. I touched you, just like this, while we talked. You were more impulsive then, much less inhibited. Do you remember what you did, Meg?"

She was finding it difficult to talk and breathe at the same time. "I was very...young," she said, defending herself.

"You were hungry." His lips parted and brushed her mouth open, softly nibbling at it until he heard the sound she made deep in her throat. "You unbuttoned my shirt and slid your hand inside it, right down to my waist."

She shivered, remembering what that had triggered. His mouth had hit hers like a tidal wave, with a groan that echoed in the silence of the car. He'd lifted her, turned her, and his hand had gone down inside the low bodice of her black dress to cup her naked breast. She'd come to her senses all too soon, fighting the intimacy. He'd stopped at once, and he'd smiled down at her as she lay panting in his arms, on fire with the first total desire she'd ever felt in her life. He'd known. Then, and now...

"You were so innocent," he said quietly, remembering. "You had no idea why I reacted so violently to such a little caress. It was like the first time I let you feel me against you when I was fully aroused. You were shocked and frightened."

"My parents never told me anything, and my girlfriends were just as stupid as I was, they made sure of it," she said hesitantly. "All the reading in the world doesn't prepare you for what happens, for what you feel when a man touches you intimately."

His hand smoothed over the shoulder of her black dress, back to the zipper. Slowly, gently, he eased it down, controlling her panicked movement with careless ease.

"It's been four years and you want it," he said. "You want me."

She couldn't believe that she was allowing him to do this! She felt like a zombie as he eased the fabric below the soft, lacy cup of her strapless bra and looked at her. His big, lean hand, darkly tanned, stroked her collarbone and down, smoothing over the swell of her breasts while he looked at her in the semidarkness.

His mouth touched her forehead. His breath was a little unsteady. So was hers.

"Let me unhook it, Meg. I want you in my mouth."

This had always been his sharpest weapon, this way of talking to her that made her body burn with dark, wicked desires. Her forehead rested against his chin while his fingers quickly disposed of three small hooks. She felt the cool air on her body even as he moved her back and looked down, his posture suddenly stiff and poised, controlled.

"My God." It was reverent, the way he spoke, the way he looked at her. His hands contracted on her shoulders as if he were afraid that she might vanish.

"I let you look at me...that last night," she whispered unsteadily. "And you went to her!"

"No. No," he whispered, bending his head. "No, Meg!"

His mouth fastened on her taut nipple and he groaned as he lifted her, turned her, suckling her in a silence that blazed with tension and promise.

Her fingers gripped his thick hair and held on while his mouth gave her the most intense pleasure she'd ever known. He'd tried to kiss her this way that long-ago night and she'd fought him. It had been too much for her already overloaded senses and, coupled with his raging arousal and the sudden determination of his weight on her body, she'd panicked. But she was older now, with four years of abstinence to heighten her need, strip her nerves raw. She was starved for him.

His mouth fed on her while his fingers traced around the firm softness he was enjoying. She felt his tongue, his teeth, the slow suction that seemed to draw the heart right out of her body. She shuddered, helpless, anguished, as the ardent pressure of his mouth only made the hunger grow.

He felt her tremble and slowly lifted his head.

"Noo...!" She choked, clutching at him, trying to draw his mouth back to her body. "Steve...please...please!"

He drew her face into his throat and held her, his arms punishing, his breath as ragged as her own.

"Please!" she sobbed, clinging.

"Here...!" He fought the buttons of his shirt open and dragged her inside it, pressing her close to him, so that her bare breasts were rubbing against the thick hair on his chest, teasing his tense muscles. "Meg," he breathed tenderly. "Oh, Meg, Meg...!" His hands found their way around her, sweeping down her bare back in long, hungry caresses that made the intimacy even more dangerous, more threatening.

Her mouth pressed soft kisses into his throat, his neck, his collarbone, and she felt the need like a knife.

He turned her head and kissed her again, a long, slow, deep kiss that never seemed to end while around them the night darkened and the wind blew.

Somewhere in the middle of it, she began to cry—great, broken sobs of guilt and grief and unappeased hunger. He held her, cradled her against him, his eyes as anguished as his unsatisfied body. But slowly, finally, the desire in both of them began to relax.

"Don't cry," he whispered, kissing the tears from her eyes. "It was inevitable."

She turned her face so that he could kiss the other side of it, her eyes closed while she savored the rare, exquisite tenderness.

When she felt his lips reluctantly draw away, she opened her eyes and looked into his. They were soft, just for her, just for the moment. Soft and hungry, and somehow violent.

"You're untouched," he said huskily, his face setting into hard, familiar lines. "Even here." His hand smoothed over her bare, swollen breast and as if the feel of it drove him mad, he bent his head and tenderly drew his lips over it, breathing in the scent of her body. "Totally, absolutely untouched."

"I…can't feel like this with any other man," she confessed, shaken to her soul by what they were sharing. "I can't bear another man's eyes to touch me, much less his hands."

His breath drew in raggedly. "Why in God's name did you leave, damn you?"

"I was afraid!"

"Of this?" His mouth opened over her nipple and she cried out at the flash of pleasure it gave her to feel it so intimately.

"I was a virgin," she gasped.

"You still are." He drew her across him, one big hand gathering her hips blatantly into the hard thrust of his, holding her there while he searched her eyes. "And you're still afraid," he said finally, watching the shocked apprehension grow on her face. "Terrified of intimacy with me."

She swallowed, then swallowed again. Her eyes dropped to his bare chest. "Not…of that."

"Then what?"

His body throbbed. She could feel the heat and power of it and she felt faint with the knowledge of how desperately he wanted her. "Steven, my sister died in childbirth."

"Yes, I know. Your father told me. It was such a private thing, I didn't feel it was my place to ask questions. I just know she was twelve years older than you."

She looked up at him. "She was…like me," she whispered slowly. "Thin and slender, not very big in the hips at all. They lived up north. It snowed six feet the winter she was ready to deliver and her husband couldn't get her to a hospital in time. She died. So did the baby." Meg hesitated, nibbling her lower lip. "Childbirth is difficult for the women in my family. My mother had to have a cesarean section when I was born. I was very sheltered and after my sister died, mother made it sound as if pregnancy would be a death sentence for me, too. She made me terrified of getting pregnant," she added miserably, hiding her face from him.

He eased his intimate hold on her, stunned. His hand guided her cheek to his broad, hair-roughened chest and he held her there, letting her feel the heat of his body, the heavy slam of his heart under her ear.

"We never discussed this."

"I was very young, as you said," she replied, closing her eyes. "I couldn't tell you. It was so intimate a thing to say, and I was already overwhelmed by you physically. Every time you touched me, I went light-headed and hot and shaky all over." Her eyes closed. "I still do."

His fingers tangled gently in her hair, comforting now instead of arousing. "I could have reassured you, if you'd only told me."

"Perhaps." She nuzzled her cheek against him. "But I had

terrors of getting pregnant, and you came on very strong that night. The argument...seemed like a reprieve at the time. You told me to get out, and then you took Daphne to a public place so that it would be in all the papers. I told myself that choosing dancing made more sense than choosing you. It made it easier to go away."

He lifted his head, staring out the darkened window. Seconds later, he looked down at her, his eyes lingering on her breasts.

She smiled sadly. "You don't believe me, do you? You're still bitter, Steven."

"You don't think I'm entitled to be?"

She shifted against him, her eyes adoring his hard face, totally at peace with him even in this intimacy now. "I didn't think you cared enough to be hurt."

"I didn't," he agreed readily. "But my pride took a few blows."

"Nicole said you got drunk..."

He smiled cruelly. "Did she add that I was with Daphne at the time?"

She stiffened, hating him.

His warm hand covered her breast blatantly, feeling her heartbeat race even through her anger. He searched her eyes. "I still want you," he said flatly. "More than ever."

She knew it. His face was alive with desire. "It wouldn't be wise," she said quietly. "As you once said, Steven, addictions are best avoided."

"You flatter yourself if you think I'm crazy enough to become addicted to you again," he said with a faintly mocking smile as all the anguish of those four years sat on him.

Meg was arrested by his expression. The mention of the past seemed to have brought all the bitterness back, all the anger. She didn't know what to say. "Steven..."

His hand pressed closer, warm against her bare skin in the faint chill of the car. "Your ballet company needs money. All right, Meg," he said softly. "I'll get you out of the hole."

"You will!" she exclaimed.

"Oh, yes. I'll be your company angel. But there's a price."

His voice was too silky. She felt the apprehension as if it were tangible. "What is the price?" she asked.

"Can't you figure it out?" he asked with faint hauteur in his smile. "Then I'll tell you. Sleep with me. Give me one night, Meg, to get you out of my system. And in return, I'll give you back your precious dancing."

4

Meg spent a long, sleepless night agonizing over Steven's proposal. She couldn't really believe that he'd said such a thing, or that he'd actually expected her to agree. How could his feverish ardor have turned to contempt in so short a time? It must be as she thought: he wanted nothing more than revenge because she'd run out on him. Even her explanation had fallen on deaf ears. Or perhaps he hadn't wanted to believe it. And hadn't he been just as much at fault, after all? He was the one who'd sent her away. He'd told her to get out of his life.

She wished now that she'd reminded him of that fact more forcibly. But his slowly drawled insult had made her forget everything. She'd torn out of his arms, putting her clothes to rights with trembling hands while he laughed harshly at her efforts.

"That was cruel, Steven," she'd said hoarsely, glaring at him when she was finally presentable again.

"Really? In fact, I meant it," he added. "And the offer still stands. Sleep with me and I'll drag your precious company back from the brink. You won't have to worry about pregnancy, either," he added as he started the car. "I'll protect you from it with my last breath. You see, Meg, the last thing in the world I want now is to be tied to you by a child." His eyes had punctuated the insult, going slowly over her body as if he could see under her clothes. "All I want is for this madness to be over, once and for all."

As if it ever would be, she thought suddenly, when he'd left her at her door without a word and driven off. The madness, as he called it, was going to be permanent, because she'd taken the easy way out four years ago. She hadn't confessed her fears and misgivings about intimacy with him, or challenged him about Daphne. She'd been afraid to say what she thought, even more afraid to fight for his love. Instead, she'd listened to others—his father and her own mother, who'd wanted Meg to have a career in ballet and never risk pregnancy at all.

But Steven's motives were even less clear. She'd often thought secretly that Steven was rather cold in any emotional way, that perhaps he'd been relieved when their engagement ended. His very courtship of her had been reluctant, forced, as if it was totally against his better judgment. Meg had thought at the time that love was something he would never understand completely. He had so little of it in his own life. His father had wanted a puppet that he could control. His mother had withdrawn from him when he was still a child, unable to understand his tempestuous nature much less cope with his hardheaded determination in all things.

Steven had grown up a loner. He still was. He might use a woman to ease his masculine hungers, but he avoided emotional closeness. Meg had sensed that, even at the age of eighteen. In a way, it was Steven's very detachment that she'd run from. She had the wisdom to know that her love for him and his desire for her would never make a relationship. And at the back of her mind, always in those days, was her unrealistic fear of childbirth. She wondered now if her mother hadn't deliberately cultivated that fear, to force Meg into line. Her mother had been a major manipulator. Just like Steven's father.

Meg had gone quickly upstairs the night before, calling a cheerful good-night to her brother, who was watching a late movie in the living room. She held up very well until she got into her own room, and then the angry tears washed down from her eyes.

A night of love in return for financing. Did he really think she held herself so cheaply? Well, Steven could hold his breath until she asked him for financial help, she thought furiously! The ballet company would manage somehow. She wouldn't meet his unreasonable terms, not even to save her career.

By the time Meg was up and moving around the next morning, David had already gone to the office. She had a headache and a very sore ankle from just the small amount of walking she'd done the night before. She couldn't quite meet her own eyes in the mirror, though, remembering how easily she'd surrendered to Steven's hot ardor. She had no resistance when she got within a foot of him.

She washed her face, brushed her teeth and ate breakfast. She went to the hospital for her physical therapy and then came back home and did stretches for several minutes. All the while, she thought of Steven and how explosive their passion had been. It didn't help her mood.

David came home looking disturbed.

"Why so glum?" Meg teased gently.

He glanced at her. "What? Oh, there's nothing," he said quickly, and smiled. "If you haven't cooked anything, suppose we go out for a nice steak supper?"

Her eyebrows arched. "Steak?"

"Steak. I feel like chewing something."

"Ouch. Bad day?" she murmured.

"Vicious!" He shrugged. "By the way, Ahmed said that he'd like to join us, if you don't mind."

"Certainly not!" she said, smiling. "I like him."

"So do I. But don't get too attached to him," he cautioned. "There are some things going on that you don't know about, that you're safer not knowing about. But Ahmed isn't quite what he seems."

"Really?" She was intrigued. "Tell me more."

"You'll have to take my word for it," he said. "I'm not risking any more scathing comments from the boss. He was out for blood today. One of the secretaries threw a desk lamp at him and walked out of the building without severance pay!"

Meg's eyebrows arched. "Steven's secretary?"

"As a matter of fact, yes." He chuckled. "Everybody else ran for cover. Not Daphne. I suppose she'd known him for so long that she can handle him."

Meg's heart stopped beating. "Daphne—*the* Daphne he was sleeping with when he and I got engaged?"

David's eyes narrowed. "I don't think they were that intimate, and certainly not after he asked you to marry him. But, yes, they've known each other for years."

"I see."

"She was the reason you argued with him. The reason you left, as I remember."

She took a deep breath. "Part of it," she replied, correcting him. She forced a smile. "Actually she did a good turn. I'd never have had the opportunity to continue my training in New York if I'd married Steven, would I?"

"You haven't let a man near you since you left Wichita," David said sagely. "And don't tell me it's due to lack of time for a social life."

She lifted her chin. "Maybe Steve's an impossible act to follow," she said with an enigmatic smile. "Or maybe he taught me a bitter lesson about male loyalty."

"Steven's not what he seems," he said suddenly. "He's got a soft center, despite all that turmoil he creates. He was deeply hurt when you left. I don't think he ever got over you, Meg."

"His pride didn't, he even admitted it," she agreed. "But he never loved me. If he had, how could he have gone to Daphne?"

"Men do strange things when they feel threatened."

"I never threatened him," she muttered.

"No?" He stuck his hands into his pockets and studied her averted face. "Meg, in all the years we've known the Rykers, Steve never took a woman around for more than two weeks. He avoided any talk of involvement or marriage. Then he took you out one time and started talking about engagement rings."

"I was a novelty." She bit off the words.

"You were, indeed. You melted right through that wall of ice around him and made him laugh, made him young. Meg, if you'd ever really looked at him, you'd have seen how much he changed when he was with you. Steven Ryker would have thrown himself under a bus if you'd asked him to. He would have done anything for you. Anything," he added quietly. "His father didn't want Steven to marry you because he thought Steve was besotted enough to side with you in a proxy fight." He smiled at her shocked expression. "Don't you see that everyone was manipulating you for their own gain? You and Steven never had a chance, Meg. You fell right into line and did exactly what you were meant to do. And the one who really paid the price was poor old Steven, in love for the first time in his life."

"He didn't love me," she choked.

"That's true. He worshiped you. He couldn't take his eyes off you. Everything he did for that one long month you were engaged was designed solely to please you, every thought he had was for your comfort, your happiness." He shook his head. "You were too young to realize it, weren't you?"

She felt as if her legs wouldn't hold her. She sat down, heavily. "He never said a word."

"What could he have said? He isn't the type to beg. You left. He assumed you considered him expendable. He got drunk. Roaring drunk. He stayed that way for three days. Then he went back to work with a vengeance and started making money hand over fist. That's when the women started showing up, one after another. They numbed the ache, but he was still hurting. There was nothing anyone could do for him, except watch him suffer and pretend not to notice that he flinched whenever your name was mentioned."

She covered her face with her hands.

He laid a comforting hand on her shoulder. "Don't torture yourself. He did, finally, get over you, Meg. It took him a year and when he got through it, he was a better man. But he's not the same man. He's lost and gained something in the process. It's hardened him to emotion."

"I was an idiot," she said heavily, pushing back her loosened hair. "I loved him so much, but I was afraid of him. He seemed so distant sometimes, as if he couldn't bear to talk to me about anything personal."

"You were the same way," he prompted.

She smiled wistfully. "Of course I was. I was hopelessly repressed and introverted, and I couldn't believe that a man who was such a man wanted to marry me. I stood in awe of him then.

I still do, a little. But now I understand him so much better... now that it's too late."

"Are you sure that it is?"

She thought about the night before, about his exquisite ardor and then the pain and grief of hearing him proposition her. She nodded slowly. "Yes, David," she said, lifting pain-filled blue eyes to his. "I'm afraid so."

"I'm sorry."

She got to her feet. "Don't they say that things always work out for the best?" She smoothed her skirt. "Where are we going to eat?"

"Castello's. And I'm sorry to have to tell you that so is Steve."

She hated the thought of facing him, but she was no coward. She only shrugged fatalistically. "I'll get dressed, then."

He told her what time they needed to leave and went off to make a last-minute phone call.

Meg went upstairs. "I think I'll wear something red," she murmured angrily to herself. "With a V-neck, cut to the ankles in front, and with slits up both sides..."

She didn't have anything quite that revealing, but the red dress she pulled out of its neat wrapper had spaghetti straps and fringe. It was close-fitting, seductive. She left her blond hair down around her shoulders and used much more makeup than she normally did. She had some jewelry left over from the old days, with diamonds. She got it out of the safe and wore it, too. The song about going out in a blaze of glory revolved in her mind. She was going to give Steven Ryker hell.

As David had said, he was, indeed, in the restaurant. But he wasn't alone. And Meg's poor heart took a dive when she saw who was with him: a slinky, sultry platinum blonde with a smooth tan, wearing a black dress that probably cost twice what Meg's had. It was Daphne, of course, draped against Steve's arm as if she were an expensive piece of lint. Meg forced a brilliant smile as Ahmed rose from the table, in a distinguished dark suit, and smiled with pure appreciation as she and David approached.

"Mademoiselle prompts me to indiscretion," he said, taking her hand and bowing over it before he kissed the knuckles in a very continental way. "I will bite my tongue and subdue the words that tease my mouth."

Meg laughed with delight. "If you intend asking me to join your harem," she returned impishly, "you'll have to wait until I'm too old to dance, I'm afraid."

"I am devastated," he said heavily.

Steven was staring at her, his silver eyes dangerous. "What an interesting choice of color, Meg," he murmured.

She curtsied, grimacing as she made her injured ankle throb with the action. "It's my favorite. Don't you think it suits me?" she asked with a challenge in her eyes.

He averted his gaze as if the words had shamed him. "No, I don't," he said stiffly. "Sit down, David."

David helped Meg into the chair next to Ahmed and greeted Daphne.

"How did you manage this?" David asked the other woman.

"He likes having things thrown at him, don't you, Steven,

darling?" Daphne laughed. "I got rehired at a higher salary. You should try it yourself."

"No, thanks." David sighed. "I'd be frog-marched to the elevator shaft for my pains."

"I don't suppose Meg is the type to throw things, are you, dear?" Daphne asked.

"Shall we find out?" Meg replied, lifting her water glass with a meaningful glance in Daphne's direction.

David put a hand on her wrist, shocked by her reaction.

"Forgive me if I've offended you," Daphne said quickly. She looked more than a little surprised herself. "Heavens, I just open my mouth and words fall out, I suppose," she added with a nervous, apologetic glance toward Steven.

Steven was frowning and his eyes never left Meg's.

"No need to apologize," Meg said stiffly. "I rarely take offense, even when people blatantly insult me."

Steven looked uncomfortable and the atmosphere at the table grew tense.

Ahmed stood up, holding his hand out to Meg. "I would be honored to have you dance with me," he offered.

"I would be honored to accept." Meg avoided Steven's eyes as she stood up and let Ahmed lead her onto the dance floor.

He held her very correctly. She liked the clean scent of him and the handsome face with liquid black eyes that smiled down at her. But there was no spark when he touched her, no throbbing ache to possess and be possessed.

"Thank you," she said quietly. "I think you saved the evening."

"Daphne has no malice in her, despite what you may think," he said gently. "It is quite obvious what Steven feels for you."

Meg flushed, letting her eyes fall to his white shirt. "Is it?"

"This dancing...it hurts you?" he asked suddenly when she was less than graceful and fell heavily against him.

She swallowed. "My ankle is still painful," she said honestly. "And not mending as I had hoped." Her eyes lifted with panic in their depths. "It was a bad sprain..."

"And dancing is your life."

She gnawed on her lower lip, wincing as she moved again with him to the bluesy music. "It has had to be," she said oddly.

"May I cut in?"

The voice was deep and cutting and not the kind to ignore unless a brawl was desirable.

"But of course," Ahmed said, smiling at Steven. *"Merci, mademoiselle,"* he added softly and moved back.

Steven drew Meg to him, much too closely, and riveted her in place with one long, powerful arm as he moved her to the music.

"My ankle hurts," she said icily, "and I don't want to dance with you."

"I know." He tilted her face up to his and studied the dark circles under her eyes, the wan complexion. "I know why you wore the red dress, too. It was to rub my nose in what I said to you last night, wasn't it?"

"Bingo," she said with a cold smile.

He drew in a long breath. His silver eyes slid over the length

of her waving hair, down to her bare shoulders. They fell to
her breasts where the soft V at the neckline revealed their exquisite swell, and his jaw clenched. The arm at her back went
rigid.

"You have the softest skin I've ever touched," he said gruffly.
"Silky and warm and fragrant. I don't need this dress to remind
me that I can't think sanely when you're within reach."

"Then stay out of reach," she shot back. "Why don't you take
Daphne home with you and seduce her? If you didn't on the way
here," she added with hauteur.

She missed a step and he caught her, easily, holding her
upright.

"That ankle is hurting you. You shouldn't be dancing," he said
firmly.

"The therapist said to exercise it," she said through her teeth.
"And she said that it would hurt."

He didn't say what he was thinking. If the ankle was painful
after five long weeks, how would she be able to dance on it?
Would it hold her weight? It certainly didn't seem as if it would.

She saw the expression on his face. "I'll dance again," she told
him. "I will!"

He touched her face with lean, careful fingers, traced her
cheek and her chin and around her full, bow mouth. "For
yourself, Meg, or because it was what your mother always
wanted?"

"It was the only thing I ever did in my life that pleased her,"
she said without thinking.

"Yes. I think perhaps it was." His finger traced her lower lip. Odd how tremulous that finger seemed, especially when it teased between her lips and felt them part, felt her breath catch. "Are you still afraid of making a baby?" he whispered unsteadily.

"Steven!" she exclaimed. She jerked her face back and it flushed red.

"You made me think about what happened that last night we were together before we fought," he said, as if she hadn't reacted to the question at all. "I remember when you started fighting me. I remember what I said to you."

"This isn't necessary...!" she broke in frantically.

"I said that if we went all the way, it wouldn't really matter," he whispered deeply, holding her eyes. "Because I'd love making you pregnant."

She actually shivered and her body trembled as it sought the strength and comfort of his.

He cradled her in his arms, barely moving to the music, his mouth at her ear. "You didn't think I was going to stop. And you were afraid of a baby."

"Yes."

His fingers threaded into her soft, silky hair and he drew her even closer. His legs trembled against her own as the incredible chemistry they shared made him weak. And all at once, instantly, he was fully capable and she could feel it.

"Don't pull away from me," he said roughly. "I know it repulses you, but, my God, it isn't as if I can help it...!"

She stilled instantly. "Oh, no, it isn't that," she whispered, lifting her eyes. "I don't want to hurt you! You used to tell me not to move when it happened, remember?"

He stopped dancing and his eyes searched hers so hungrily that she could hardly bear the intensity of the look they were sharing.

His lips parted as he tried to breathe, enmeshed by his hunger for her, by the beauty of her uplifted face, the temptation of her perfect, innocent body against his. "I remember everything," he said tautly. "You haunt me, Meg. Night after empty night."

She saw the strain in his dark face and felt guilty that she should be the cause of it. Her hand pressed flat against his shirt-front, feeling the strength and heat and under it the feverish throb of his pulse.

"I'm sorry," she said tenderly. "I'm so sorry..."

He fought for control, his eyes lifting finally to stare over her head.

Meg moved away a little, and began talking quite calmly about the state of the world, the weather, dancing lazily while he recovered.

"I have to stop now, Steven," she said finally. "My ankle really hurts."

He stopped dancing. His eyes searched over her face. "I'm sorry about what I said to you last night, when I asked you," he said curtly. "I wanted you to the point of madness." He laughed bitterly. "That, at least, has never changed."

Her eyes adored him. She couldn't help it. He was more

perfect to her than anything in the world, and when he was close to her, she had everything. But what he wanted would destroy her.

"I can't sleep with you and just…just go on with my life," she said softly. "It would be another night, another body, to you. But it would be devastating to me. Not only my first time, but with someone whom I…" She averted her eyes. "Someone for whom I once cared very much."

"Look at me."

She forced her eyes up to his, curious about their sudden intent scrutiny.

"Meg," he said, as the music began again, "it wouldn't be just another night and another body."

"It would be for revenge," she argued. "And you know it, Steven. It isn't about lovemaking, it's about getting even. I walked out of your life and hurt you. Now you want to pay me back, and what better way than to sleep with me and walk away yourself?"

"Do you think I could?" he asked with a bitter laugh.

"Neither of us would really know until it happened." She stared at his chest. "I know you'd try to protect me, but you aren't quite in control when we make love. You certainly weren't last night." She raised her face. "Then what would we do if I really did get pregnant?"

His lips parted. He studied her slowly. "You could marry me," he said softly. "We could raise our child together."

The thought thrilled, uplifted, frightened. "And my career?"

The pleasure washed out of him. His face lost its softness and his eyes grew cold. "That, of course, would be history. And you couldn't stand that. After all, you've worked all your life for it, haven't you?" He let her go. "We'd better go back to the table. We don't want to put that ankle at risk."

They did go back to the table. He took Daphne's hand and kept it in his for the rest of the evening. And every time he looked at Meg, his eyes were hostile and full of bitterness and contempt.

5

David and Meg, who'd taken a cab to the restaurant, rode back to their house with Ahmed in his chauffeured limousine. Steven, Meg noticed, hadn't even offered them a ride; he probably had other plans, ones that included Daphne.

"It's been a great evening," David remarked. "How much longer are you going to stay in Wichita, Ahmed?"

"Until the last of the authorizations are signed," the other man replied. He glanced at Meg with slow, bold appraisal in his liquid black eyes. "Alas, then duty forces me back to my own land. Are you certain that you would not consider coming with me, *ma chou?*" he teased. "You could wear that dress and enchant me as you dance."

Meg forced a smile, but she was having some misgivings about her future. Her ankle was no stronger than when it was first damaged. Her concern grew by the day.

"I'm very flattered," she began.

"We are allowing our women more freedom," he mused. "At least they are no longer required to wear veiling from head to toe and cover their faces in public."

"Are you married?" she asked curiously. "Aren't Moslems allowed four wives?"

The laughter went out of his eyes. "No, I am not married. It is true that a Moslem may have up to four wives, but while I accept many of the teachings of the Prophet, I am not Moslem, *mademoiselle*. I was raised a Christian, which precludes me from polygamy."

"That's the road, just up ahead," David said quickly, gesturing toward their street. "You haven't seen our home, have you, Ahmed?" he added, smiling at the other man.

"No."

"Do come in," Meg asked. "We can offer you coffee. Your chauffeur as well."

"Another time, perhaps," Ahmed said gently, glancing behind them at a dark car in the near distance. "I have an appointment this evening at my hotel."

"Certainly," Meg replied.

"Thanks for the ride. I'll see you tomorrow, then," David said as they pulled up in the driveway.

Ahmed nodded. "Friday will see the conclusion of our business," he remarked. "I should enjoy escorting the two of you and our friend Steven to a performance at the theater. I have obtained tickets in anticipation of your acceptance."

Meg was thrilled. "I'd love to! David...?"

"Certainly," her brother said readily. He smiled. "Thank you."

"I will send the car for you at six, then. We will enjoy a leisurely meal before the curtain rises." He didn't offer to get out of the car, but he smiled and waved at Meg as David closed the door behind her. The limousine sped off, with the dark car close behind it.

"Is he being followed?" she asked David carefully.

"Yes, he is," David said, but he avoided looking at her. "He has his own security people."

"I like him," she said as they walked toward the front door.

David glanced at her. "You've been very quiet since you danced with Steve," he observed. "More trouble?"

She sighed wistfully. "Not really. Steven's only shoving Daphne down my throat. Why should that bother me?"

"Maybe he's trying to make you jealous."

"That will be the day, when Steven Ryker stoops to that sort of tactic."

David started to speak and decided against it. He only smiled as he unlocked the door and let her in.

"Ahmed is very mysterious," she said abruptly. "It's as if he's not really what he seems at all. He's a very gentle man, isn't he?" she added thoughtfully.

He gave her a blank stare. "Ahmed? Uh, well, yes. Certainly. I mean, of course he is." He looked as if he had to bite his tongue. "But, despite the fact that Ahmed is Christian, he's still very much an Arab in his customs and beliefs. And his country is a hotbed of intrigue and danger right now." He studied her closely. "You don't watch much television, do you, Meg? Not the national news programs, I mean."

"They're much too upsetting for me," she confessed. "No, I don't watch the news or read newspapers unless I can't avoid them. I know," she said before he could taunt her about it, "I'm hiding my head in the sand. But honestly, David, what could I do to change any of that? We elect politicians and trust them to have our best interests at heart. It isn't the best system going, but I can hardly rush overseas and tell people to do what I think they should, now can I?"

"It doesn't hurt to stay informed," he said. "Although right now, maybe it's just as well that you aren't," he added under his breath. "See you in the morning."

"Yes." She stared after him, frowning. David could be pretty mysterious himself at times.

David didn't invite Steve to the house that week, because he could see how any mention of the man cut Meg. But although Wichita was a big city, it was still possible to run into people when you traveled in the same social circles.

Meg found it out the hard way when she went to a men's department store that her family had always frequented to buy a birthday present for David. She ran almost literally into Steve there.

If she was shocked and displeased to meet him, the reverse was also true. He looked instantly hostile.

Her eyes slid away from his tall, fit body in the pale tan suit he was wearing. It hurt to look at him too much.

"Shopping for a suit?" he asked sarcastically. "You'll have a hard time finding anything to fit you here."

"I'm shopping for David's birthday next week," she said tightly.

"By an odd coincidence, so am I."

"Doesn't your *secretary,*" she stressed the word, "perform that sort of menial chore for you?"

"I pick out gifts for my friends myself," he said with cold hauteur. "Besides," he added, watching her face, "I have other uses for Daphne. I wouldn't want to tire her too much in the daytime."

Insinuating that he wanted her rested at night. Meg had to fight down anger and distaste. She kept her eyes on the ties. "Certainly not," she said with forced humor.

"My father was right in the first place," he said shortly, angered at her lack of reaction. "She would have made the perfect wife. I don't know why it took me four years to realize it."

Her heart died. *Died!* She swallowed. "Sometimes we don't realize the value of things until it's too late."

His breath caught, not quite audibly. "Don't we?"

She looked up, her eyes full of blue malice. "I didn't realize how much ballet meant to me until I got engaged to you," she said with a cold smile.

His fists clenched. He fought for control and smiled. "As we said once before, we had a lucky escape." He cocked his head and studied her. "How's the financing going for the ballet company?" he added pointedly.

She drew in a sharp breath. "Just fine, thanks," she said venomously. "I won't need any...help."

"Pity," he said, letting his eyes punctuate the word.

"Is it? I'm sure Daphne wouldn't agree!"

"Oh, she doesn't expect me to be faithful at this stage of the game," he replied lazily. "Not until the engagement's official, at least."

Meg felt faint. She knew the color was draining slowly out of her face, but she stood firm and didn't grab for support. "I see."

"I still have your ring," he said conversationally. "Locked up tight in my safe."

She remembered giving it to her mother to hand back to him. The memory was vivid, violent. Daphne. Daphne!

"I kept it to remind me what a fool I was to think I could make a wife of you," he continued. "I won't make the same mistake again. Daphne doesn't want just a career. She wants my babies," he added flatly, cruelly.

She dropped her eyes, exhausted, almost ill with the pain of what he was saying. Her hand trembled as she fingered a silk tie. "Ahmed invited us to dinner and the theater Friday night." Her voice only wobbled a little, thank God.

"I know," he said, and sounded unhappy about it.

She forced her eyes up. "You don't have to be deliberately insulting, do you, Steven?" she asked quietly. "I know you hate me.

There's no need for all this—" She stopped, almost choking on the word that almost escaped.

"Isn't there? But, then, you don't know how I feel, do you, Meg? You never did. You never gave a damn, either." He shoved his hands deep into his pockets and glowered at her. She looked fragile somehow in the pale green knit suit she was wearing. "Ahmed is leaving soon," he told her. "Don't get attached to him."

"He's a friend. That's all."

His silver eyes slid over her bowed head with faint hunger and then moved away quickly. "How are the exercises coming?"

"Fine, thanks."

He hesitated, bristling with bad temper. "When do you leave?" he asked bluntly.

She didn't react. "At the end of the month."

He let out a breath. "Well, thank God for that!"

Her eyes closed briefly. She'd had enough. She pulled the tie she'd been examining off the rack and moved away, refusing to look at him, to speak to him. Her throat felt swollen, raw.

"I'll have this one, please," she told the smiling clerk and produced her credit card. Her voice sounded odd.

Steven was standing just behind her, trying desperately to work up to an apology. It was becoming a habit to savage her. All he could think about was how much he'd loved her, and how easily she'd discarded him. He didn't trust her, but, God, he still wanted her. She colored his dreams. Without her, everything was flat. Even now, looking at her fed his heart, uplifted him.

She was so lovely. Fair and sweet and gentle, and all she wanted was a pair of toe shoes and a stage.

He groaned inwardly. How was he going to survive when she left again? He never should have touched her. Now it was going to be just as bad as before. He was going to watch her walk away a second time and part of him was going to die.

Daphne was coming with him tonight or he didn't think he could survive Meg's company. Thank God for Daphne. She was a friend, and quite content to be that, but she was his coconspirator as well now, part of this dangerous business that revolved around Ahmed. She was privileged to know things that no one else in his organization knew. But meanwhile she was also his camouflage. Daphne had a man of her own, one of the two government agents who were helping keep a careful eye on Ahmed. But fortunately, Meg didn't know that.

Steven was in some danger. Almost as much as Ahmed. He couldn't tell Meg that without having to give some top-secret answers. Daphne knew, of course. She was as protected as he was, as Ahmed was. But despite his bitterness toward Meg, he didn't want her in the line of fire. Loving her was a disease, he sometimes thought, and there was no cure, not even a temporary respite. She was the very blood in his veins. And to her, he was expendable. He was of no importance to her, because all she needed from life was to dance. The knowledge cut deep into his heart. It made him cruel. But hurting her gave him no pleasure. He watched her with possessive eyes, aching to hold her and apologize for his latest cruelty.

Her purchase completed, Meg left the counter and turned away without looking up. Steven, impelled by forces too strong to control, gently took her arm and pulled her with him to a secluded spot behind some suits.

He looked down into her surprised, wounded eyes until his body began to throb. "I keep hurting you, don't I?" he said roughly. "I don't mean to. Honest to God, I don't mean to, Meg!"

"Don't you?" she asked with a sad, weary smile. "It's all right, Steve," she said quietly, averting her eyes. "Heaven knows, you're entitled, after what I did to you!"

She pulled away from him and walked quickly out of the store, the cars and people blurring in front of her eyes.

Steve cursed himself while he watched her until she was completely out of view. He'd never felt quite so bad in his whole life.

Meg spent the rest of the week trying to practice her exercises and not think about Steve and Daphne. David didn't say much, but he spoke to Steve one evening just after she'd met him in the store, and Meg overheard enough to realize that Steve was taking Daphne out for the evening. It made her heart ache.

She telephoned the manager of her ballet company, Tolbert Morse, on Thursday.

"Glad you called," he said. "I think I may be on the way to meeting our bills. Can you be back in New York for rehearsals next week?"

She went rigid. In that length of time, only a miracle would mend her ankle. But she hesitated. She didn't want to admit the slow progress she was making. Deep inside she knew she'd never be able to dance that soon. She couldn't force the words out. Dance was all she had. Steve had made his rejection of Meg very blatant. Any hope in that area was gone forever.

Her dream of a school of ballet for little girls was slowly growing, but it would have to be opened in Wichita. Could she really bear having to see Steven all the time? His friendship with David would mean having him at the house constantly. No. She had to get her ankle well. She had to dance. It was the only escape she had now! Steven's latest cruelty only punctuated the fact that she had no place in his life anymore.

Fighting down panic, she forced herself to laugh. "Can I ever be ready in a week!" she exclaimed. "I'll be there with my toe shoes on!"

"Good girl! I'll tell Henrietta you'll want your old room back. Ankle doing okay?"

"Just fine," she lied.

"Then I'll see you next week."

He hung up. So did Meg. Then she stood looking down at the receiver for a long time before she could bring herself to move. One lie led to another, but how could she lie when she was up on toe shoes trying to interpret ballet?

She pushed the pessimistic thought out of her mind and went back to the practice bar. If she concentrated, there was every hope that she could accomplish what she had to.

David paused in the doorway to watch her Friday afternoon

when he came home from work. He was frowning, and when she stopped to rest, she couldn't help but notice the concern in his eyes, quickly concealed.

"How's it going?" he asked.

She grinned at him, determined not to show her own misgivings. "Slow but steady," she told him.

He pursed his lips. "What does the physical therapist say?"

Her eyes became shuttered and she avoided looking directly at him. "Oh, that it will take time."

"You're supposed to start rehearsing in a month," he persisted. "Will you actually be ready by then?"

"It's in a week, actually," she said tautly, and told him about the telephone call. He protested violently. "David, for heaven's sake, I'll be fine!" she burst out, exasperated to hear her own fears coming from his lips.

He stuck his hands into his pockets with a long sigh. "Okay. I'll stop. Ahmed's going to be here at six."

"Yes, I remember. And you don't have to look so worried. I know that he invited Steve and Daphne, too."

His shoulders rose and fell heavily. He knew what was going on, but he couldn't tell Meg. She looked haunted and he felt terrible. "I'm sorry."

She forced down the memories of her last meeting with Steven, the painful things he'd said. "Why?" she asked with studied nonchalance. She dabbed at her face with the towel around her neck. "I don't mind."

"Right."

She lifted her eyes to his. "What if I did mind, David, what good would it do? I ran, four years ago," she said quietly. "I could have stayed here and faced him, faced her. I let myself be manipulated and I threw it all away, don't you understand? I never realized how much it would hurt him...." She turned, trying to control her tears. "Anyway, he's made his choice now, and I wish him well. I'm sure Daphne will do her best to make him happy. She's cared about him for a long time."

"She's cared about him, yes," he agreed. "But he doesn't love her. He never did. If he had, he'd have married her like a shot."

"Maybe so. But he might have changed his feelings toward her."

He gave her a wry glance. "If you could see the way he treats her at the office, you wouldn't believe that. It's strictly business. Not even a flirtatious glance between them."

"Yes, but you said that it all came to a head when she quit."

He grimaced. "So it did."

Her heart felt as heavy as lead. She turned away toward the staircase. "Anyway, I'm going back to New York soon."

"Sis," he said softly. She paused with her back to him. "Can I help?"

She shook her head. "But, thanks." She choked. "Thanks a lot, David."

"I thought you might get over him, in time."

She studied her hand on the banister. "I've tried, you know," she said a little unsteadily. She drew in a small breath. "I do have my dancing, David. It will compensate."

He watched her go up the staircase with a terrible certainty that ballet wouldn't compensate for a life without Steve. Her very posture was pained. Her ankle wasn't getting any better. She had to know it. But she must know, too, that Steve wasn't going to give in to whatever he felt for her; not when he'd been hurt so badly before. David shook his head and went upstairs to his own room to dress.

The limousine was prompt. Meg didn't have many dressy things, but once she'd bought a special dress for a banquet. She wore it this evening. It was a strappy black crepe cocktail dress with a full skirt and a laced-up bodice. David gave her an odd look when she came downstairs wearing it.

"Ahmed will faint," he remarked.

She laughed, touching the high coiffure that had taken half an hour to put up. Little blond wisps of hair trailed around her elegant long neck. "Not right away, I hope," she murmured. "It isn't really revealing," she added, to placate him. "It just looks like it. It was a big hit when I wore it in New York City."

"This isn't New York City, and Steven's going to go through the roof."

The sound of his name made her heart leap. Her eyes flickered. "Steven can do so with my blessing."

He gave up trying to reason with her. But he did persuade her to add a lacy black mantilla to the outfit by convincing her that Steven might take his rage out on David instead of Meg.

The limousine was very comfortable, but Meg had the oddest

feeling that she was being watched. She glanced out the back window and not one but two cars were following along behind.

"Who's in that second car, I wonder?" she murmured.

"Don't ask." David chuckled. "Maybe it's the mob," he mused, leaning close and speaking in a rough accent.

"You're hopeless, David."

"You're related to me," he replied smugly. "So what does that make you?"

She threw up her hands and laid her head back against the seat.

It was an evening she wasn't looking forward to. All week, she'd dreaded this. But once Ahmed was gone, she wouldn't need to see Steve again socially. She could avoid him until she left to go back to New York. Meanwhile, if the sight of him with Daphne cut her heart out, there was nobody to know it except herself.

6

Steven's reaction to the black dress was almost the same as it had been to the red one she'd worn before, only worse. Meg remembered too late that the dress she'd had on the night she and Steven had parted had been black, too.

After a rather strained but delicious meal, Meg headed for the entrance lobby while the men paid the bill.

An uncomfortable-looking Daphne excused herself. Meg only nodded with forced politeness and stayed where she was. She had no intention of sharing even a huge ladies room with her rival. Unfortunately that left her unexpectedly alone with Steve, when Ahmed and David also excused themselves. Steve was fuming.

"Was that deliberate?" he asked Meg, nodding toward her dress.

She didn't pretend ignorance. She pulled the mantilla closer around her shoulders. "No," she replied after a pause. "Not at all."

He leaned against the wall and stared down at her, oblivious to the comings and goings of other patrons. The buzz of conversation was loud, but neither of them noticed.

"You wore black the night we argued," he said tautly. He caught her gaze and held it hungrily. "You let me undress you and touch you." His face hardened. "My God, you do enjoy torturing me, don't you, Meg?"

"I didn't do it on purpose," she said miserably. "Why do you always think the worst of me?"

"I'm conditioned to it, because I'm usually right," he said through his teeth. He dragged his eyes away, looking toward where the others had disappeared. "Damn them for deserting us!"

His violent anger was telling. She moved closer, unable to resist the power and strength of him. His cologne was the same he'd worn then. She got drunk on the scent as she looked up into silver eyes that began to glitter.

His eyes darkened as she approached, stopping her in her tracks. She hadn't realized quite what she was doing.

"Feeling adventurous?" he asked with a cold smile. "Don't risk it."

She clutched her purse. "I'm not risking anything. I was just getting out of the way of the crowd."

"Really?" He caught her hand in his and jerked. Under the cover of his jacket, he pressed the backs of her fingers deliberately against the hard muscle of his upper thigh, holding it there. "Look at me."

She panicked and pulled back, but he wouldn't let go. His strength was a little frightening. "Steven, please!" she whispered.

"There was a time when you couldn't wait to be alone with me," he said under his breath. "When your hands trembled after you fumbled my shirt open. Does dancing give you that incredible high, Meg?" he asked. "Does it make you sob with the need for a man's body to bury itself deep in yours?"

She moaned at the mental pictures he was producing, shocking herself. She dragged her hand away and all but ran to escape him, blindly finding her way to her brother. She found him in the hall, on his way back to where he'd left her.

"There you are," he said. "Ready to go, sis?"

"Where's Ahmed?" she asked, flustered and unable to hide it.

"He'll be right here."

As he spoke, Ahmed came through another door, looking for a moment as if he were someone Meg had never met. Another man was with him, a smaller and very nervous man with uplifted hands, who was grimacing as Ahmed spoke in a cutting soft tone to him in a language Meg couldn't translate.

The smaller man sounded placating. He made a gesture of subservience and abruptly departed as if his pants were on fire.

Ahmed muttered something under his breath, his black eyes cruel for an instant as he turned to the Americans. He saw the apprehension in Meg's face and the expression abruptly vanished. He was the man she knew again, smiling, charming, unruffled.

He strode to meet her, bending to kiss her knuckles. "Ah, my dancing girl. Are you ready to sample the theater?"

"Yes, indeed," she said, smiling back.

"I will have the driver bring the car around."

"I'll, uh, help you," David said nervously, with an incomprehensible glance over Meg's head at Steven.

"What's going on?" Meg asked curiously.

"A problem with the car," Steven said suavely, smiling down at Daphne as he linked her hand in his arm. "Shall we go, ladies?"

They were on the sidewalk, when the world shifted ten degrees and changed lives. As Steven left the women to follow Ahmed and David across the street to where the limousine had just pulled up, a car shot past them and sounds like firecrackers burst onto the silence of the night.

It seemed to happen in slow motion. The car sped away. Steve fell to the pavement. Ahmed quickly knelt beside him and motioned the others back toward the restaurant.

Daphne screamed. David caught her arm and rushed her toward the building yelling for Meg to follow. But Meg was made of sterner stuff and terror gave her strength she didn't know she had. She ran toward Steve, not away from him, deaf to the warnings, the curses Steve was raining on her as she reached him.

"Get back inside, you little fool!" he raged, his eyes furious. "Meg, for the love of God…!"

She didn't register the terror that mingled with anger in his face. "You've been hit," she sobbed. Her hands touched him, where blood came through his torn jacket sleeve. "Steven!"

"Oh, my God, get her out of here!" he groaned to Ahmed. "Get under cover, both of you! Run!"

But Ahmed wouldn't go and Meg clung. She wouldn't be moved. "No!" she whispered feverishly. "If they come back, they'll have to get both of us...!" she blurted out, shaking with fear for him.

Sirens drowned out any reply he might have made. His stunned eyes held hers while Ahmed got to his feet in one smooth movement, and his gaze searched the area around them. Satisfied that no other would-be assassins were lurking nearby, Ahmed murmured something to Steven and moved away toward two men—a dark one and a fair one—with drawn pistols who made a dive for him, through the crowd that was gathering just as the police and paramedics rushed forward. Meg's heart stopped, but Ahmed apparently knew the men and allowed himself to be surrounded by them and escorted to safety.

Meg sat on the pavement next to Steve, holding his hand, while the paramedics quickly checked his arm and bandaged what turned out to be only a flesh wound. Her white face and huge eyes told him things she never would have. His fingers entwined in hers and he watched her with fascination while stinging medicine and antiseptic was applied to the firm muscle of his upper arm.

"I'm all right," he told her softly, his tone reassuring, comforting, but full of wonder.

"I know." She was fighting tears, not very successfully.

"We'd better get him out of here," the officer in charge said grimly, staring around. "Don't spare the horses. We'll be right behind you with your friends," he told Steve. "Young lady, you can come with me," he added to Meg.

"No." She shook her head adamantly. "Where he goes, I go!"

The policeman smiled faintly and moved away.

"Don't get possessive, Miss Shannon," Steve remarked without smiling. "I don't belong to you."

Meg began to realize just how possessive she was acting and she felt embarrassed and a little guilty. "I'm sorry," she said, falteringly. "I forgot about Daphne…"

His face closed up completely. He averted his eyes. "You were upset. It's all right." He got to his feet a little unsteadily. "Go with the others," he told her. He turned when she hesitated, his eyes flashing. "Will you send Daphne here, please?"

"Of course," she said through numb lips. "Of course, I will."

So much for feeling protective. She'd given herself away and he didn't care. He didn't give a damn. He was still bearing grudges for old wounds. Why hadn't she known that?

He started to speak, but she was already walking away, her carriage proud despite the faint limp. He wondered if his heart might burst at the feelings that exploded into it. He couldn't tell her what was going on; she'd be safer that way.

"Steven wants you to go with him," Meg told Daphne, refusing to meet her shocked eyes. "He's at the ambulance."

"But, shouldn't you…?" Daphne asked uncertainly.

Meg looked at her. "He asked for you," she said unsteadily. "Please go."

Daphne grimaced and went, but there was something new in her face, and it wasn't delight. She passed one of the two men who had guarded Ahmed, the blond one, and smiled at him rather secretively. He gave her a speaking glance before a terse comment from his tall, dark partner captured his attention.

Meg watched curiously until her brother interrupted her thoughts. "Are you all right?" David asked.

"Yes," she said slowly. She moved toward the Arab while his companions were momentarily diverted by policemen. "Ahmed, are you okay?" she asked the tall man gently. "In the confusion, I suppose I acted like an idiot."

"No. Only like a woman deeply in love," he said gently, and he smiled. "I am fine. I seem to invite Allah's protection, do I not? I have not a scratch. But I would not have had my friend Steven shot on my account."

"He'll be fine. Steve's like old leather," David said, chuckling with relief. "They're waiting for us."

"I don't suppose anyone would like to explain what's going on to me?" she asked the men when they were situated in the back of the police car heading toward the hospital.

David thought carefully before he replied. "We're selling some pretty sophisticated hardware to Ahmed's country. He has a hostile neighbor, a little less affluent, and they've made some veiled threats. We've had our security people and some government people keeping an eye on them. Tonight, they came out in the open with a bang. They're making their protests known in a pretty solid way."

"You mean they tried to kill Steve because you bought a plane?" she gasped, turning to Ahmed.

Ahmed grimaced. He exchanged a complicated glance with David and then shrugged. "Ah, that is so. Simplified, of course, but fairly accurate."

"They tried to kill Steven. Oh, my gosh!" she burst out.

"Equally simplified and fairly accurate," David added grimly. It wasn't the truth, but he couldn't tell her what was.

"Steve does have government protection?" she asked.

"Of a certainty." Ahmed gestured over his shoulder, and Meg saw a big black car following them and the police car ahead of them that carried Steven and Daphne.

"Who are they?" she asked nervously.

"CIA," David said. "They had us under surveillance, but nobody really expected this to happen. Now, of course, we'll be on video if we sneeze."

"You're kidding!" Her voice sounded high-pitched and uncertain.

There was a tiny noise and she jumped as "Gesundheit," came in an amused drawl from the police car's radio.

Steven was patched up, given a tetanus shot and released with an uneasy Daphne at his side. Ahmed and David kept Meg too busy talking to suffer too much at the sight.

Then they were all taken to police headquarters where two

tall, tough-looking men—the same two who'd surrounded Ahmed after the shooting—sat down with the group and began to ask questions of everyone except Ahmed. That gentleman had been met by a small group of very respectful Arabs who surrounded him and preceded him into another room. It didn't occur to Meg just then to wonder why, if Steve was the target, these government agents had rushed to protect Ahmed.

As he spoke with his people, Ahmed, again, looked like someone considerably more important than a minor cabinet minister of a Middle Eastern nation. His very bearing changed when he was approached, and he seemed not only more elegant, but almost frighteningly implacable. The liquid black eyes, which for Meg had always been smiling, were now icy cold and threatening. He spoke to the men in short, succinct phrases, which the other Arabs received with grimaces and something oddly like fear.

Meg frowned at the byplay, drawn back into the conversation by the CIA.

"Are you a permanent resident of Wichita?" the blond one asked.

She shook her head. "No. I live and work in New York most of the time. I've had a small injury…"

"Left ankle, torn ligaments, physical therapy and rest for one more week," the big, dark-headed agent finished for her. Her mouth fell open and he leaned forward. "Gesundheit," he said, grinning wickedly.

David laughed. "Meg, I hope you don't have any skeletons in your closet."

Meg suddenly remembered the night in Steve's car and flushed. She didn't dare look at him, but the big, dark agent pursed his lips and deliberately turned his head away. She could have gone through the floor.

There were a few more questions and some instructions, but it was soon over and they were allowed to leave.

Ahmed was in the hall with the other Arabs. The government agents greeted him with quiet respect and a brief conversation ensued. He nodded, said something in Arabic to his companions and moved forward to say goodbye to his friends.

Meg came last. He took her hand in both of his, and the dark authority in his face made her start. This was not the charming, pleasant, lazily friendly man she thought she knew. Ahmed was quite suddenly something out of her experience.

"I hope that the evening has not been too strained for you, *mademoiselle*. I hope to see you again soon, and under kinder circumstances. *Au revoir*."

He kissed her hand, very lightly. With a nod to Steve and David, he strode back toward his men. They surrounded him quickly, flinging hurried, respectful questions after him, and followed him out into the night with the big dark government man a step behind.

Meg had the oddest feeling about Ahmed. She had to bite her tongue to keep the words from tumbling out. But her concern now was only for Steve. Her eyes slid around to where he was standing close to Daphne and the tall blond agent. "They'll catch the men who tried to kill him, won't they?" she asked David worriedly.

"Sure they will. Don't worry, now, it's nothing to do with you." He held up a restraining hand when she opened her mouth to ask some more questions. "Steve was barely scratched, despite the amount of bleeding. He'll be carefully looked after. Everything's fine."

"What is Steve selling to Ahmed?" she asked agitatedly.

"A fighter plane. Very advanced. All the latest technology. The government approves, because we're allies of Ahmed's strategically placed little nation."

"But if they're trying to stop the sale, why shoot at Steve?"

Meg was too quick. "Probably, they were shooting at both of them but Steve got the bullet," he said.

"Oh." She relaxed a little. "But what if they try again?"

"I told you, they're going to be surrounded by government people."

"Won't they try to get Ahmed out of the country now?"

David grimaced. "I don't know. Calm down now, Meg. Try not to worry so much. It's all under control, believe me."

Meg finally gave in. David did look less concerned now, and she had to accept that Steve would be protected from further attacks.

David, meanwhile, was shaking inside. What he and Steven had learned from the CIA agents and Ahmed was enough to terrify anyone. Ahmed couldn't go home just now, and while he was in Wichita, he was in mortal danger. It was far more serious than a protest over an arms sale. A coup was in progress in Ahmed's nation and Ahmed had been targeted by its leaders.

Ahmed's position was top secret, so Meg couldn't be told. Only Daphne knew, because of her engagement to Wayne Hicks, the blond CIA agent. She was an unofficial liaison between the government men and Ahmed. There were secrets within secrets here. It was a tricky situation, made more so by Steven's apparent relationship with Daphne while Meg stood by helplessly and fumed.

Meg glanced at Steven. "Are you going to be all right?" she asked without meeting his eyes.

"I'm indestructible," he said tautly. "I only needed a bandage, believe it or not. I'd better get Daphne home," he added.

"Thanks, Steve," Daphne said gently, smiling up at him.

Meg looked away, so she didn't see Daphne's expression or Steve's. Her heart was breaking. She smiled dully and took David's arm. "In that case, I'll take my brother and go home. Good night, then."

David got them a cab right outside the door. Presumably Daphne was going to drive Steven's Jaguar.

Meg sat quietly in the corner of the cab, still trying to focus on the shocking, violent events of the night. The shots, Steve's wound, Ahmed's incredible transformation from indulgent friendliness to menacing authority, the police, the government men, the hospital…it all merged into a frightening blur. Meg closed her eyes on the memories. Daphne had won and the only course of action Meg had was to concede the field to the other woman once more. If Steve loved her, she'd stay and fight. But he didn't. Hadn't he made it abundantly clear that he preferred Daphne?

Always before, she'd had the sanctuary of her New York apartment to run to. But now, with her ankle in this shape, she knew for certain that it would be a very long time before she was fit enough to dance again. A very, very long time. She had to consider a new career. If she couldn't dance, she had to find a way to support herself. A ballet school was the ideal way. She'd studied ballet all her life. She knew she could teach it. All she required was a small loan, a studio and the will to succeed.

The fly in the ointment was that it would have to be here in Wichita. New York City was full of ballet schools, and rental property cost a fortune. She'd never be able to afford to do it there. Here in Wichita, she was known in local circles, even if the family was no longer wealthy. Her roots went back four generations here. The downside was that she'd have to see Steven occasionally, but perhaps she could harden her heart.

Meanwhile, Steven and David would be fine now, surely, with the CIA watching. And of course, they'd get Ahmed out of the country.

But, would *she* be fine, she wondered? It was like losing Steven all over again. She didn't know how she could bear it.

Meg went to bed and didn't sleep. Steve had taken Daphne home. She was tormented by images of Daphne in Steven's arms, being thrilled and delighted by his kisses. She couldn't bear it.

She couldn't sleep on Friday night, and was listless all day Saturday and Sunday. She worked on her exercises, but her lack of progress just made her more depressed. She went to sleep on Sunday night, but again couldn't rest easily. She got out of bed and decided to go down for a cup of hot chocolate. Maybe it would help her sleep.

She opened her door and heard movement downstairs. Her first thought was that it might be a burglar, but the lights were all on.

She went to the banister and leaned over. David was in the hall putting on a raincoat.

"David?" she called, surprised.

He glanced up at her. He held a briefcase under his arm. "I thought you were asleep."

"I can't sleep."

"I know. Well, I've got to run this stuff over to Ahmed..."

"It's midnight!"

He glowered at her. "Ahmed doesn't recognize little things like the hour of the night. And before you start worrying, I've got an escort waiting outside. Try to get some sleep, will you?"

She sighed. "Okay. Be careful."

"Sure thing."

She wandered back into her bedroom. She heard a door slam twice and David's car pulling away. Odd, two slams, but she was sleepy. Perhaps she'd counted wrong.

She looked at herself in the mirror, in the sexy little lavender night slip that stopped at her upper thighs. She looked very alluring, she decided, with her hair down her back and those spaghetti straps threatening to loosen the low bodice that didn't quite cover the firm swell of her creamy breasts. She sighed.

"Too bad your hair's not platinum," she told her reflection. "And your legs are too long." She made a face at herself before she opened the bedroom door and wandered slowly downstairs, careful not to let her weak ankle make her fall as she negotiated her way down. A cup of hot chocolate might just do the trick.

She yawned as she ambled into the kitchen. But she stopped dead at the sight of the man standing there, staring at her with eyes that didn't quite believe what he was seeing.

"Steven!" she gasped.

He was fully dressed, a light blue sports jacket paired with navy slacks, a white shirt and a blue striped tie. But there was no bulge high up on his left arm, no bandage.

"Why are you here?" she asked bluntly, getting her breath back. She refused to try to cover herself. Let him look, she thought bitterly. "And do try to remember not to sneeze," she added, glancing around paranoidly. "They've probably got video cameras everywhere. Oh, Lord!" she added suddenly, glancing down at her state of undress and remembering that dark-haired agent with the wicked smile.

"There are no hidden cameras here," he returned. "Why would there be?" His silver eyes narrowed. "Which is just as well, because I don't want anyone else to see you like this."

"For your eyes only?" she taunted. "Well, save it all for Daphne, Steve, darling. What do you want here? David just left."

"I know. I'm here to keep an eye on you while he's gone." He shouldered away from the door facing. "You aren't planning to cut your visit short and go back to New York, are you?" he asked bluntly.

She didn't want to answer that. Her ankle was killing her this morning, from the slight exercise it had been put through the night before. She could hardly walk on it. The thought of dancing on it made her nauseous.

"Am I being asked to leave town?" she hedged.

"No. Quite the contrary." He stuck his hands into his pockets and studied her through narrowed eyes. "I think it might be better if you stay in Wichita. But don't go out without David, will you?"

"They shot at you, not me," she reminded him, and had to choke down the fear the words brought back. He could have been killed. She didn't dare think about it too much. "You're really all right, aren't you?" she added reluctantly.

"I'm really all right." He saw the concern she couldn't hide, but he knew better than to read too much into it. She'd loved him once, or thought she had, before she decided that dancing was of prime importance. He stared at her with growing need. Dressed that way, she aroused him almost beyond bearing. He didn't know if he could keep his hunger for her under control. That gown...!

She stared down at her bare feet. "I'm glad you weren't hurt."

He didn't reply. When she looked up again, it was to find his silver eyes riveted to her breasts, to the pink swell of them over her bodice. The look was intimate. Hungry. She could almost see his heartbeat increasing.

"Don't, Steve," she said quietly.

"If not me, who, then?" he asked roughly, moving slowly toward her. "You won't give yourself to anyone else. You're twenty-three and still a virgin."

She gnawed her lower lip. "I like it that way," she said unsteadily, because he was close now, towering over her. She could feel the heat of his body, smell the spicy cologne he wore. It was a fragrance that she'd always connected with him. It aroused her.

"The hell you do. You waited for me. You're still waiting." His silver eyes dropped to her bodice and found the evidence of her arousal. "You can't even hide it," he taunted huskily. "All I have to do is look at you, or stand close to you, and your body begins to swell with wanting me."

She swallowed. "Don't humiliate me!" she whispered tightly.

"That isn't what I have in mind. Not at all." His hands came out of his pockets. They moved slowly to the smooth curve of her shoulders and caressed away the tiny spaghetti straps. His breath was at her temple, on her nose, her mouth. She ached for him in every cell of her body.

"Steve." She choked. "Steve, what about Daphne…?"

"Daphne who?" he breathed, and his mouth settled on hers as his hands moved abruptly, sending the gown careening recklessly down her body to land in a silken lavender pool at her feet.

7

Right and wrong no longer existed separately in Steve's tormented mind. Meg wanted him and he wanted her. All the pain and anguish of the past four years fused in that one thought as he felt her mouth soften and open under his. He kissed her until she went limp in his arms, until his own body went rigid with insistent desire. And only then did he lift his head to look at what his hands had uncovered.

Meg felt the impact of Steven's eyes on her bare breasts like a hot caress on her skin. She stood before him in only a pair of lacy, high-cut pink briefs, insecure in her nudity. But when her hands lifted automatically, he caught her wrists and drew her hands to his chest. His steely eyes held hers while he pressed them there.

"Don't hide from me," he said quietly. His eyes fell to her body and sketched its pink and mauve contours with slow, exquisite appreciation. "You're more beautiful than a Boticelli nude, Mary Margaret."

"You're forgetting Daphne." She choked out the words, beyond protest. "She has a hold on you."

He was still staring at her, unblinking. "You might say that."

"Steve…"

"Don't talk, Meg," he replied, his voice deep and soft, almost lazy as his dark head started to bend toward her. "Talking doesn't accomplish a damned thing."

"Steven, you mustn't…!"

"Oh, but I must," he breathed as his mouth opened just above her taut nipple. "I must…!"

She felt the soft tracing of his tongue just before the faint suction that took her breast right into the dark warmth of his mouth.

Steve heard her gasp, felt her whole body go rigid in his grasp. But he didn't stop. He nuzzled her gently and increased the warm pressure. A little sound passed her lips and then she began to push toward him, not away from him. He groaned against her as his hands slid up the silky softness of her back and drew her into the aroused curve of his body.

Meg had stopped thinking altogether. The insistent hunger of his mouth made her body throb in the most incredible way. She cradled his dark head against her, leaning back in his embrace. She felt as if she were floating, drifting.

Steve was kneeling, easing her down to the floor, his mouth against her. He pulled her over him, parting her smooth legs so that they were hip to hip. His mouth moved to her other breast, then to her throat and finally up to her parted lips. He kissed her with slow, aching passion, all the while exploring her body with deft, sure hands. He whispered things she couldn't even hear for the roar in her ears. And then he shifted her, just a little, and she felt the aroused thrust of him as his body began to rock sensually against hers.

She gasped and stiffened, because even their most intimate time hadn't been quite this intimate.

He lifted his head. His silver eyes were misty with desire as he searched hers. He moved, deliberately, so that she felt him intimately, and a wave of pleasure rippled up her body. She couldn't hide the shocked delight in her eyes. He smiled, slowly, and moved again. This time her hands gripped his shoulders and she relaxed, shyly bringing him into even greater intimacy with her.

His lean hand slid up her thigh, tracing its inner curve. She saw his mouth just before it settled on hers again. He touched her as he never had. Waves of pleasure jolted her. She tried to protest, but it was far too late. She began to whimper.

His tongue tangled with hers, thrust deep into her mouth. She felt tears in her eyes as he held her in thrall. Her body arched helplessly toward him. She felt his mouth sliding down to her breasts, possessing her. He stroked her until she was weeping with helpless desire, her voice breaking as she whispered, pleaded, begged.

The husky pleas, combined with the sensual movement of her

body over his, removed him sufficiently from reality so that it was impossible for him to pull back in time. He kissed her. His mouth bit into hers and she felt him move, felt the soft tearing of her briefs, felt the air on her body. She heard the rasp of a zipper, the metallic sound of a belt.

He pulled her up so that she was sitting with her legs on either side of him. She heard his breathing, rough and unsteady at her ear, as his lean hands suddenly gripped her bare thighs deliberately and he lifted her.

"Easy," he whispered as he brought her to him and slowly pulled her down.

She had a second to wonder about the faint threat of his hold on her, and then his mouth opened on hers and she felt the first insistent thrust of him against the veil of her innocence.

Her eyes flew open. She cried out at the flash of hot pain. He held her still, breathing roughly. His face was rigid, his teeth clenched, his breathing audible through his nose. He looked into her wide, frightened eyes and held them as he pulled her slowly down on him again.

"Don't be afraid, Meg," he whispered deeply. "It's only going to hurt for a few seconds."

"But...Steve..." She gasped, trying to find the words to protest what was happening.

"Let me love you," he said unsteadily. His hands tugged her over him and he shivered. His face was tormented, his eyes like silver fires. "God, baby...let me. Let me!" He ground out the words.

She knew that it would be impossible for him to stop. She loved him. That was all that really mattered now. She gave in, yielding to the pain, her hands taut on his shoulders. Her hold on him tightened and she flinched.

"Just a...little further. Oh, Meg," he growled, shivering as he completed the motion and felt her all around him. His eyes closed and he shivered. Then they opened again and searched hers as he repeated the slow, deliberate movement of his hips until his possession of her was complete and the lines of strain left her face. Then he rested, his body intimately joined to hers, and gently pushed her disheveled hair back from her face.

She swallowed. There was awe in her eyes now, along with lingering pain and doubt and shock.

"I've waited so long, Meg," he said unsteadily. "I've waited all my life for this. For you."

Her fingers trembled on his shirtfront. "Steve, you're...part of me," she burst out.

Color burned along his high cheekbones. "Yes." He moved, as if to emphasize it, and she blushed. "Unfasten my shirt, Meg. Let me feel your breasts against my skin while we love."

While we love. She must be insane, she thought. But she was too involved to stop, to pull back. She was in thrall to him. Her hands fumbled with his tie, his jacket, his shirt. She fumbled, but finally she stripped it all off him.

Her hands speared through the thick mat of hair that covered him from collarbone to below his lean waist. She looked down and stared helplessly, her body trembling. His powerful hands lifted her up just a little, smiling even through his need at the expression on her face.

"Steve…"

He tilted her face and brought his mouth down on her lips with exquisite tenderness as he began to guide her hips again. This time there was no pain at all. There was a faint pleasure that began to grow, to swell, to encompass her. She gasped and her nails bit into his shoulders.

"Like this?" he whispered, and moved again.

She sobbed into his shoulder, her mouth open against his neck, clinging to him as he increased the rhythm and pressure of his body. His hand clenched in the hair at her nape and he caught his breath, shivering.

"Relax, now," he said, sliding a hand under her thigh to pull her to him roughly. "Yes…!"

His image began to blur in her open, startled eyes as the pleasure became suddenly violent, insistent. She felt herself tense as he lifted to her as they knelt so intimately together, shivering with every movement, reaching for something she couldn't quite grasp. Her strength gave out, but his was unfailing, endless.

"Help me," she whispered brokenly.

"Tell me how it feels, Meg," he whispered back, his voice rough, deep as he pushed up insistently. "Tell me!"

"It's so sweet…I can't…bear…it!" She wept.

"Neither can I." His hands tightened on her thighs almost to bruising pain and he lost control. "Meg…. Meg….!"

She felt him go rigid just before her mind was submerged in

a heated rush of pleasure. It was a kind of pain, she thought blindly. A kind of sweet, unbearable pain that hit her like a lightning bolt, lifting her in his arms, making her cry out with the anguish it kindled. She didn't know if she could bear it and stay alive.

Steven's heart was beating. She felt the heavy, hard beat against her breasts, felt the blood pulsating through him as he eased her down on her back, still a part of him. He relaxed, his arms catching the bulk of his weight while he struggled to breathe normally. The intimacy of their position was beyond her wildest dreams. She closed her eyes, experiencing it through every cell of her body.

He could hardly believe what he'd done. The rush of pleasure had almost knocked him out. He'd been so desperate for her that he hadn't even removed all his clothing. He'd fought them both out of their garments and taken her sitting up on the carpet, when her first time should have been in a bed with their wedding night before them and everything legal and neatly tied up. And worst of all, he hadn't had the foresight to use any sort of protection. He groaned aloud as sanity came back in a cold rush. "Oh, hell!" He ground out the words.

He levered himself away from her and got to his feet a little shakily. He zipped his trousers with a vicious motion of his hands before he fumbled a cigarette out of the pocket of his discarded shirt and lit it. He put on his shirt. He didn't look at Meg, who finally managed with trembling hands to slide her gown back on. The briefs were beyond wearing at all.

Steve smoked half the cigarette before he crushed it out in an ashtray on the table, one that David kept for him. He buttoned his shirt and replaced his tie and jacket before he spoke.

By then, Meg was sitting on the very edge of the sofa, feeling uncomfortable and very ashamed.

He stood over her, searching for the right words. Impossible, really. There weren't any for what he'd done.

"You'll be sore for a while," he said stiffly. "I'm sorry I couldn't spare you the pain."

She wrapped her arms around herself and shivered.

He knelt just in front of her, his hand on the sofa beside her as he searched her wan, drawn face.

"Meg," he said roughly, "it's all right. You don't have anything to be ashamed of."

"Don't I?" Tears rolled down her cheeks.

"Oh, baby," he groaned. He pulled her down into his arms and sat on the carpet, cradling her against him. His lips found her throat and pressed there gently. "Meg, don't cry."

"I'm easy, I'm cheap...!"

"You are not." He lifted his head and held her eyes. "We made love to each other. Is that so terrible? If I hadn't gone crazy and chased you away, it would have happened four years ago, and you know it!"

She couldn't really argue with that. He was telling the truth. "Will you tell Daphne?" she asked.

"No, I won't tell Daphne," he replied quietly. "It's none of her business. It's no one's, except ours."

She still felt miserable, but some of the pain eased away as he smoothed her against him. Her eyes closed and she wished that she never had to move away again. He was warm and strong and it felt right to be lying with him this way. What had happened felt right.

His lean hand smoothed over her flat belly. He drew back a little and stared down at it, his face troubled.

She knew what he was thinking. It had just occurred to her, too.

"You didn't use anything," she whispered.

"I know. Damn me for a fool, I was too far gone to care." He lifted his eyes to hers and grimaced. "I'm sorry. It was irresponsible. Unforgivable."

Her blue eyes sketched his dark face, down to his stubborn chin and the breadth of his shoulders.

"What are you thinking?" he asked curiously.

"You were an only child," she said. "Did your father have any sisters?"

He shook his head. His brows curved together and then a smile tugged at his firm mouth as he searched her eyes. "Boys run in my family, Meg. Is that what you wanted to know?"

She nodded, smiling shyly.

His big hand pressed slowly against her belly. "A baby would cost you your career," he said slowly.

She looked up at him. "You don't think my ankle won't?"

The expression drained out of his face, leaving it blank. "What do you mean?"

She threw caution to the wind. It was time for honesty. Total honesty, despite the cost. She'd truly burned all her bridges.

"It hurts just from walking. It's swollen. It's been weeks, and it's no better." She traced a pearly button on his shirt with her fingernail as she forced herself to face the fear she'd been avoiding. "Rehearsals begin at the end of next week, but it might as well be yesterday. Steve, I won't be able to dance. Not for a long time. Maybe not ever."

He didn't move. His eyes searched her face, but he didn't speak, either.

She looked up at him miserably. "What will happen to you and Daphne if I get pregnant? It would ruin everything for you." She sighed wearily, closing her eyes as she laid her cheek on his chest. "Oh, Steve, why is life so complicated?"

"It isn't, usually."

"It is right now." She bit her lower lip. "Would you...want a baby?"

His body began to throb. Light burst inside him. A child. A little boy, perhaps, since they ran in his family. A bond with Meg that nothing could break. The thought delighted him.

But he didn't answer immediately, and Meg thought the worst. She had to fight tears. "I see," she said brokenly. "I guess you'd want me to go to a clinic and—"

"No!"

"You wouldn't?"

"Of course I wouldn't!" he said curtly. He held her face up to his. "Don't you even think about it! I swear to God, Meg, if you do anything…!"

"But, I wouldn't!" she said quickly. "That's what I was going to tell you. I couldn't!"

He relaxed. His hand moved to her cheek and brushed back the disheveled hair around its flushed contours. "Okay. Make sure you don't. People who don't want babies should think before they make them."

"Like we just did," she agreed with a flicker of her dry humor.

He lifted an eyebrow. "Right."

She relaxed a little more. He did look marginally less rigid and austere. "I could have said something."

"Of course. Exactly when did you think of saying something?"

She flushed and dropped her eyes.

"That's when I thought of saying something. It was a bit late, of course." He frowned slightly and his silver eyes twinkled. "It was very intense, wasn't it? Even for you."

"I'd wanted you for a long time," she confessed quietly.

"And I, you." He drew in a long, slow breath. "Well, it's done. Now we have to live with it. I'll get your ring out of the safe and bring it over. We are now officially reengaged."

"But Steve, what about Daphne?" she exclaimed.

"If you mention Daphne one more time today, I'll——!" he muttered. He let her go and got to his feet, pulling her up beside him. "She'll understand."

"You haven't asked if I want to be engaged again," she protested, trying to keep some control over her own destiny.

He pulled her to him and his hand curved around her flat stomach. "If you've got a baby in here, you don't have much choice. My mother would bring the shotgun all the way from West Palm Beach and point it at both of us before she'd see her first grandchild born out of wedlock."

She smiled, picturing his mother staggering under the weight of one of Steven's hunting rifles. "I guess she would at that." She glanced at him wryly. "And I'd already be sitting on your doorstep wearing a sign—*and* maternity clothes—so that everyone would know who got me pregnant in the first place."

He felt the world spin around him. He mustn't read too much into that beaming smile on her face, he told himself. After all, with her ankle in this condition, she had no career left. He was still second best in her life. At least she would want a child, if they'd made one.

She looked up and encountered the cold anger in his face and knew instantly that despite his hunger for her, all the bitterness was still there.

He shrugged. Bending, he pushed back her tousled hair. "I want you. You want me. Whatever else there is, we'll have that." He sighed gently. "Besides, if the attraction we feel is still strong enough four years after the fact to send us making love on the carpet, it isn't likely to weaken, is it?"

"For heaven's sake, Steve!" she exclaimed, outraged.

"Meg, you're repressed." He shook his head. "What am I going to do with you?"

"You might stop embarrassing me," she muttered.

His eyebrow jerked as he stared at her. "My beautiful Mary Margaret," he said softly. "When I wake up in the morning, I'll be sure that I was only dreaming again."

"Did you dream of me?" she asked involuntarily.

"Oh, yes. For most of my life, I think." He searched her soft eyes. "'There be none of Beauty's daughters with a magic like thee…'" he quoted tenderly, and watched the heat rise in her cheeks. "Do you like Lord Byron, Meg?"

"You never read poetry to me," she said with a sad little smile.

"I wanted to. But you were very young," he recalled, his face going hard. "And I was afraid to trust my heart too far." He laughed suddenly as all the bitterness came sweeping back. "Good thing I didn't. You walked out on me."

"You made me," she shot right back. "You know you did." The anger eased as she saw the pained look on his face. "You haven't had a lot of love, Steven," she said. "I don't think you trusted anyone enough to let them close to you—not Daphne, and certainly not me. You like my body, but you don't want my heart."

He was shocked. He stared at her, searching for words. He couldn't even manage an answer.

"I'd love you, if you'd let me," she said gently, her blue eyes smiling at him.

His jaw clenched. "You already did, on the floor," he said coldly. All sorts of impossible things were forming in his mind. He felt vulnerable and he didn't like it. He glared at her. "You didn't even try to stop me. Since you can't dance anymore, what a hell of a meal ticket I'll make!"

She stared at him and suddenly saw right through the angry words. She knew with a flash of intuition that he was still fighting her. He cared. Perhaps he didn't know it. Perhaps he'd even convinced himself that he really loved Daphne. But he didn't. Even though she was innocent, Meg knew that men didn't lose control as Steve had tonight unless there were some powerful emotions underlying the desire. He was fighting her. It had been that all along, his need to keep emotional entanglements at bay. He was afraid to risk his heart on her. Why hadn't she seen that years ago?

"No comeback?" he taunted furiously.

She smiled again, feeling faintly mischievous. "Are you going to bring my ring back tonight?"

He hesitated. "Meg…"

"I know. It's way after midnight and David will be home soon, I suppose," she added. "But you could come to supper tomorrow night. And bring my ring back," she emphasized. "I hope you haven't lost it."

He glared at her. "No, I haven't lost it. I can't bring it tomorrow night. I have a dinner meeting with Ahmed. Daphne's coming along," he reminded her.

She felt a little uncertain of her ground, but something kept her going, prodded her on.

She moved toward him, watching his expressions change, watching his eyes glitter. She caught him by the lapels and went on tiptoe, softly brushing her body against his as she reached up and drew her mouth tantalizingly over his parted lips. She could feel his heartbeat slamming at his ribs, hear his breathing. He was acting. It was a sham. She bit his lower lip, gently, and let go of him, moving away.

"What was that all about?" he asked gruffly.

"Didn't you like it?" she asked softly.

His jaw clenched. "I have to go."

"To dinner, perhaps. But not to Daphne's bed. Not now."

"What makes you so sure that I won't?" he demanded with a mocking smile.

She searched his eyes. "Because it would be sacrilege to do with anyone else what we just did with each other."

He would have denied it. He wanted to. But he couldn't force the words out. He turned and went to the door, pausing just to make sure the lock was on before he glanced back.

"Buy a wedding gown," he said curtly. "And if you try to run away from me this time, I'll follow you straight to hell if I have to!"

He closed the door behind him, and Meg stared at it with a jumble of emotions, the foremost of which was utter joy.

Steve was feeling less than pleased. He had Meg, but it was a hollow victory. Despite the exquisite pleasure she'd given him, he was no closer to capturing her heart. He wanted it more than he'd ever realized.

She cared about him. She must, to give herself so generously. For Meg, physical need alone would never have caused such a sacrifice. But he had to remember that her career was no longer a point of contention between them. Her career was history.

Even if she cared about him, ballet would have come first if it had been an option. He knew it. And that was what made him so bitter.

8

Later that same night, after a refreshing shower, Meg went to bed, feeling tired. But she barely slept at all, wondering at the way things had changed in her life.

David gave her curious looks at the breakfast table. "You look like you haven't slept at all," he remarked.

"I haven't," she confessed, smiling at him. "Steven and I got engaged again last night."

He caught his breath. The delight in his eyes said everything. "So he finally gave in."

"Not noticeably," she murmured dryly.

"He's taken the first step," he replied. "You can't expect a fine fighting fish to just swallow a hook, you know."

"This fighting fish is a piranha. He's very bitter, David," she said quietly. She sipped coffee, her brows knitted. "He's never really forgiven me for leaving—even though he drove me away."

He smiled at her, his eyes kind and full of warmth. "I gather that he'll be over tonight?"

"Probably not. I doubt if Daphne can spare him," she muttered. "He's having dinner with her."

He grimaced at the expression on her face. He knew what was going on, and that Steve couldn't tell her. Neither could he.

"Things aren't always what they seem," he began.

"It doesn't matter, you know," she replied with resignation. "I love him. I never stopped. The past four years have been so empty, David. I'm tired of running from it. At least he still wants me, you know. I may not win entirely, but I'll give Daphne a run for her money," she added with a tiny smile.

"That's the spirit. You might consider, too, that if he didn't care, why would he want to marry you?"

She couldn't tell him that. She changed the subject and led him on a discussion of local politics.

But she did go around in a daze for the rest of the day. She wouldn't have believed what had happened if it hadn't been for the potent evidence of it in her untried body. Her memories were sweet. She couldn't even be bothered to worry about Daphne anymore. She did worry about Steven. If a crazed terrorist was after him, how would the authorities be able to stop him? And what about Ahmed?

The questions worried her, so she found solace in her exercises. Even so, she only did them halfheartedly. Ballet had been her life for years, but now she thought about loving Steven and having a baby of her own. Suddenly her fear of childbirth seemed to diminish, and her disappointment over her injury faded. Ballet was a hobby. It was nothing more than a hobby. She was daydreaming now, of little baby clothes and bassinets and toys scattered around a room that contained Steven and herself as well as a miniature version of one of them. Anything seemed possible; life was sweet.

Steven tossed and turned until dawn and went into the office in a cold, red-eyed daze. His life had shifted without warning. He'd made love to Meg and nothing would ever be the same again. If he was besotted with her before, it was nothing to what he was now that he'd known her intimately. He wasn't certain that he could even work.

Daphne brought in the mail. She saw his worried expression and paused in front of the desk.

"Something's wrong, isn't it?" she asked with the ease of friendship. "Can I help?"

"Sure," he agreed, leaning back in his big desk chair. "Tell me how to explain to Meg, to whom I've just become reengaged, why I'm going out with you tonight."

She whistled. "That's a good one."

"Isn't it?"

"Can't you get permission to tell her the truth?"

He shook his head. "Your own fiancé told me not to tell. He thinks too many people are in the know already." He closed his eyes with a long sigh. His body was pleasantly tired and still faintly throbbing from its exquisite knowledge of Meg.

"Isn't she going back to New York temporarily?" Daphne asked.

"I'm afraid to let her," he said wearily. "At least here she can be protected along with David. But I can't tell her what's going on. I'm going to have to ask her to trust me, when I never trusted her."

"If she loves you enough, she will," Daphne said with certainty. "And anyway, surely it will all be over soon."

"God, I hope so!"

"How's the arm?"

"Is wasn't exactly a major wound," he mused, chuckling. "The bullet broke a small vein. I've got a bandage over it. Funny, I didn't even notice—" He broke off, feeling uncomfortable as he remembered the night before, when he and Meg had both forgotten it. He changed the subject, quickly. "Have we heard from Ahmed today?"

She grimaced. "Indeed we have. He came in surrounded by bodyguards and government agents, and eventually chewed up one of the girls in the typing pool, who stopped bawling long enough to take a leaf out of my very own book. She threw a paperweight at him on his way out."

"What?"

"Calm down, it was a very small paperweight—not in the same league as the lamp I threw at you—and she missed on purpose, too," Daphne said quickly, with a grin. "He was surprised, to say the least. In his country, women don't react like that."

"I don't guess they do. Certainly not with Ahmed!"

"But, then, Brianna our typist didn't know who he was," Daphne reminded him. "And she still doesn't. She told me that if he sets foot in the building again, she's quitting," she added. "She is a very angry young lady, indeed."

"I need to have a word with your fiancé," Steve said. "Just to see what else needs doing so we can wind up this mess."

"Ahmed's under twenty-four-hour guard. He's used to it, of course. I understand he had a slight altercation with his body-guard when they didn't see the assassins coming last night."

"I noticed the bruises," Steven mentioned.

"I'm sorry about Meg," Daphne said, grimacing. "I seem to keep complicating things for her."

"Not your fault this time," he said. "Or last time, either. It was my pride that sent her running. I hope I'll have better luck now."

"So do I," Daphne told him sincerely. "We're good friends, Steve. We always have been. I'm so happy. I hope you're going to be, too, you and Meg."

He only nodded. "We'd better get to work."

"Yes, sir," she said with a grin. "I'll send Wayne in."

Daphne's fiancé was blond and blue-eyed, a screaming contrast to his partner, who was tall and very dark and had a sense of humor that had already sent Steven up the wall.

The dark one looked around very carefully, even peering under Steve's desk.

"Looking for bugs?" Steve asked with a twinkle in his eyes.

"No," he replied. "Paperweights and blue-eyed brunettes." He grinned. "She's a dish."

"Yes, she is, but you're on duty," Wayne told his partner.

"So I am." He straightened, wiped the smile off his face and stared grimly at Steven. "Sir, have you noticed any bombs or enemy missiles in your office—oof!"

Wayne calmly removed his elbow from his friend's ribs. "I'm going to feed you to a shark on our next assignment."

The taller man lifted both bushy eyebrows. "Copycat. James Bond did that to an enemy agent in one of his films."

"Are you sure you're suited to this line of work, Lang?" Wayne asked somberly.

"Plenty of people with badges have a sense of humor." Lang glared at his friend. "Plenty more don't, of course."

"To the matter at hand," Wayne interrupted, glancing at Steve. "We need your itinerary for the rest of the week, right down to the minute. And if you plan any more impromptu evening outings…"

"Not me," Steven said with a slow grin, indicating his arm. "I've gone right off night life without adequate protection."

"Fair enough. We're now in the process of bugging everything you own, from cars to houses to aircraft, as well as Mr. Shannon's home," Wayne continued, noticing Steve's faint color with absent curiosity. "We would have done it sooner, but until this morning we hadn't quite decided about how much surveillance was required. It would be pretty stupid to overlook protection for your chief executive, Mr. Shannon, and his sister, especially since they were seen in the company of Ahmed. These people will use whatever bargaining tools they can get, and Ahmed's fondness for Miss Shannon was pretty obvious."

Steve didn't like remembering that. He was jealous of Ahmed now—jealous of any man who looked at Meg.

"Isn't it dangerous politically to let Ahmed stay here, in the States?" Steve asked suddenly.

"Certainly," Lang told him. "Suicidal, in fact." He grinned and his dark eyes twinkled. "But we're responsible for him. So if we send him home and somebody blows him away, guess who gets the blame?"

"We're in between a rock and a hard place," Wayne agreed. "That's why we're going to keep Ahmed here and see if we can draw the other agents out into the open again."

"They were in the open last night."

"Ah," Lang replied, "but it was just a routine surveillance until then. We didn't have any advanced warning of an assassination try until the coup attempt was made in Ahmed's home country. And by then the terrorists were already in position here and making their move. Now that we know what's afoot, we're ready, too."

"We're on it. We'll handle this. How about Miss Shannon?" Wayne asked Steven. "Can you get her out of town?"

"I can," Steven agreed. "But what if they find out that she and I are engaged again and make a grab for her, where she's totally unprotected?"

The smile vanished from Lang's face. "You're engaged again?"

Steven nodded.

Lang exchanged a long glance with Wayne. "That changes things. We'd better keep her in town. But she can't know why," he emphasized.

Steven just nodded, because Wayne had already told him that. He could break their confidence, of course, but now that the house and his car and God knew what else was bugged, he couldn't tell Meg anyplace that they wouldn't overhear. He was going to have to watch what he said altogether. And the complication was that he not only couldn't tell Meg that, but he wouldn't be able to touch her without being overheard. He could have groaned out loud.

Meg was home alone that afternoon. David was still at work.

Steven drove up to the Shannon house just a few minutes after quitting time, casually dressed in jeans and a knit shirt, topped off with a suede jacket.

He smiled at Meg when she opened the door, approving the pretty blue sundress that complemented her fairness. She'd left her hair down, and he ached to get his hands in its silky length.

"Give me your hand," he said without preamble.

She lifted the left one, and he slid the sapphire and diamond engagement ring he'd given her four years ago smoothly onto her ring finger. It was a perfect fit.

He lifted the hand to his lips and kissed it very gently.

"Oh, Steve," she whispered, reaching up to him.

He caught her wrists and stepped back, painfully aware of surveillance techniques that could pick up heavy breathing a mile away. He laughed a little shortly, trying to ignore Meg's shocked, embarrassed expression.

"How about some coffee?" he asked.

She faltered a little. "Of course," she said. "I'll, uh, I'll just make some." She was near tears. They'd made love, they'd just gotten reengaged, and suddenly Steven couldn't bear her to touch him!

He followed her into the kitchen, grimacing at her expression. He couldn't tell her everything, but he had to tell her this, at least.

As she turned on the faucet to fill the drip coffee maker, Steve reached over her shoulder and took the coffeepot away, leaving the water running just briefly.

He bent to kiss her, whispering under his breath, "We're on Candid Camera."

She let him kiss her, but her wide eyes stayed open. He drew back, shutting off the faucet.

She was suddenly very alert. She looked around the room. "Achoo?" she whispered.

"Gesundheit!" came the deep, chuckled reply.

Meg went every shade of scarlet under the sun as she looked at Steven. She gasped in horror.

"It's all right," he said quickly. "They've only just done it!"

She chewed the ends of her fingers as the flat statement finally began to make sense and she relaxed. "Oh, thank goodness!"

The back door opened and the big, dark agent entered, a finger to his lips.

He whipped out a pad and pencil and wrote something on it, showing it to Meg and Steve. He'd written: *Our team wasn't the only one wrangling bugs around here this afternoon. Watch what you say.*

Do they have cameras? Steve scribbled on the paper.

The agent shook his head, grinning. He made a sign with two forked fingers like someone poking eyes out.

Steve gave him a thumbs-up sign. The agent put away his pad and pencil and looked at the coffeepot longingly.

Meg held up five fingers. He grinned and started back out. Then he glanced at the two of them and made a kissing motion followed by a firm shaking of his head. Meg stuck her tongue out at him. He smothered a laugh as he let himself back out the door.

Meg busied herself with the coffeepot, worried about living in a goldfish bowl. It would be like this from now on, she was sure, until they caught the people who were responsible for the attack at the restaurant.

"Cream?" Steven asked when she poured coffee into two cups.

"I'll get it."

She handed it to him, carrying a cup of black coffee to the back door. A huge hand came out and accepted it. She peered around the door, eyebrows raised. The agent made a sign with his thumb and forefinger and eased back around the side of the house with his cup.

Meg closed the door gently and followed Steve back into the living room.

"I can't stay long. I have a date," he told Meg.

She glared at him. "Of course. With Daphne."

"And Ahmed," he replied. "At the Sheraton. More business discussions."

It didn't occur to her right then why Steve had given away his movements, when he knew the house was bugged. "I don't suppose I could come along?" she asked.

"No."

"I like Ahmed. He likes me, too."

"Of course he likes you. You're blond."

She glared at him.

"And pretty."

The glare softened.

"And very, very sweet."

She smiled.

He sipped his coffee. "Where are we going to live when we're married?"

"I like Alaska…"

He glowered at her. "In Wichita, Meg. I don't work in Alaska."

"What's wrong with your house?" she asked.

"It doesn't have much of a yard," he replied. "We'll need a place for a swing set and some outdoor playthings for the kids."

She flushed, averting her eyes. "So we will."

He stared at her until she lifted her face, and he smiled. He slid his arm over the back of the couch and his eyes narrowed. His head made a coaxing motion.

She put her coffee cup down, her blood throbbing in her veins, and went across to join him on the sofa.

He put his thumb over her mouth and pulled her down into his arms. As his hand lifted, his lips parted on her mouth, and he kissed her with long, slow passion. His hand found her breast, teasing the nipple to hardness while he kissed her as if he could never get enough.

When he lifted his head, her eyes were misty and dazed, her body draped over his lap.

He looked at her for a long, long time.

"I have to go," he said quietly.

She started to protest, but she knew that it would do no good at all.

"Will I see you tomorrow?" she asked miserably as he helped her up.

"Probably." He stood close to her, his eyes troubled. "Lock the doors. David will be home soon."

"My brother is a poor substitute for my fiancé," she muttered.

"It won't always be like this," he said solemnly. His silver eyes searched hers for a long time. "I promise you it won't."

She nodded. "Do be careful. The way you drive…" She stopped when he frowned. "Well, I'd like to think you could get all the way home in one piece."

He lifted an eyebrow. "Do you worry about me?"

"All the time," she said honestly, her blue eyes wide and soft.

His heart raced as he looked down at her. If she was putting on an act, it was a good one.

Gently he brought her against him and bent to brush his open mouth softly over her own. She moved closer. His arms enfolded her, cherished her. She wrapped herself around him and gave way to the need to be held.

But things got out of hand almost immediately. He caught her hips and pushed her away, his face set in deep, harsh lines as he fought to control his passion for her.

"Go back inside," he said huskily. "I'll phone you in the morning."

"Why did you bother to get engaged to me when you plan to spend your nights with another woman?" she asked miserably.

"You know why," he said, his voice deep, his eyes glittering. "Don't you?"

Because they'd stepped over the line and she might be pregnant. How could she have forgotten? She moved back from him, averting her eyes.

"Yes," she replied, freezing up. She'd tried to forget, but he wasn't going to let her. She was weaving daydreams. The reality was that he'd lost his head and now he was going to do the honorable thing. "Of course I know why, Steven. Silly of me to forget, wasn't it?"

He scowled and his face tautened. She had the wrong end of the stick again. But he couldn't, didn't dare, say anything. "David should be here any minute," he added. "Don't go outside, and lock the door after me."

"I'll do that."

He glanced around. Nothing and nobody was in sight, but he was certain that one of the agents guarding Meg was nearby. He'd arranged that before he left the office.

"I'll phone you tomorrow. Maybe we can go out."

"What a thrill," she said.

He glared at her. "Keep it up."

"I'm trying."

He made an exasperated sound, stuck his hands into his pockets and moved toward his Jaguar.

After he drove away, Meg closed the door and locked it, and went back into the living room.

David came home long enough to change and went right back out again, apologizing to Meg. He had to go along with Steve and Daphne to hobnob with Ahmed.

"Is everybody going except me?" Meg groaned, exasperated.

David grinned at her. "Probably. Have a nice evening, now."

She glared at him. He left and she busied herself watering her house plants. The house was unusually quiet, and she kept imagining noises. They made her uneasy, especially under the circumstances. She heard movement in the living room and slowly stuck her head around the door to see what it was, her heart pounding madly.

But it was only the big dark agent standing there, grinning at her. He put a finger to his lips, pushed a button on some small electronic device in his hand, and chuckled as it emitted a jarring noise.

"There'll be plenty of headaches tonight," he murmured dryly.

"What did you do?" she asked, and then clapped a hand over her mouth.

"It's okay. I jammed them." He studied her through narrowed eyes. "I need to talk to you."

"What about?" she asked, and waited almost without breathing for the answer.

He was serious then, the twinkle gone from his dark eyes. He towered over her, almost as tall as Steve and just about as intimidating. He pushed the button on the jamming device with a calculating look on his face, shutting off the interference.

"I'm going to get you out of here, right now. Tonight. I want you to come with me, no arguments."

She hesitated. "Shouldn't we call Steve or your partner?"

"No one is to know. Not even my partner."

She didn't like the sound of that. She liked this man, but she didn't completely trust him.

"Why isn't your partner to know?" she asked curiously.

He muttered something under his breath. Then he calmly pulled out his automatic pistol and leveled it at her stomach. He seemed to raise his voice a little. "Because he would try to stop me, of course," he replied. "I plan to turn you over to Ahmed's buddies outside. You'll be a hell of a bargaining tool for them."

"You can't do this!" she exclaimed, thinking of ways to escape, but unable to come up with anything. There was an automatic pistol pointed at her stomach. She'd heard it said that even a karate black belt would hesitate to fight off an armed man.

"But I can," he assured her. "In fact, I'm doing it. Let's go."

9

Meg felt her breath catch in her chest as she stared down numbly at the muzzle of the pistol. Dozens of wild thoughts passed through her mind, none of which lingered long enough to register except one: she was never going to see Steve again.

Her blue eyes lifted to Lang's dark ones. He didn't look as if he meant to kill her.

He jerked his head toward the front door and indicated that he wanted her to go out it. "I said let's go," he said. "Now."

She hesitated. "Can't we…?"

He took her arm firmly and propelled her forward. She felt the presence of the gun, even if she didn't feel it stuck in her back. She noticed that he looked around from side to side as if he was expecting company.

Perhaps the enemy agents would shoot him. But that wasn't likely. If they'd overheard what he said, and that jammer had seemed to be turned off at the last, they'd be waiting out here for him to turn her over to them. Would they pay him? Of course they would. They'd keep her hostage and use her to trade to Steve for Ahmed. She felt sick.

"Hey!" he called as they got to the front porch. "Let's make a deal, boys. I'm cutting myself in on the action!"

"You turncoat," Meg cried furiously.

"Stop struggling," he said calmly. "How about it!"

"We have already heard you," came a distinctly accented reply. "How much do you want for the woman?"

Lang turned toward the voice. "Let me come over there and we'll talk about it. No shooting."

"Very well!"

A shadowy figure appeared. Lang measured the distance from where the car was to where the man was and began to walk down the middle of it with Meg.

"Keep your nerve," he said unexpectedly. "For God's sake, don't go to pieces now."

"I'm not the screaming type," she muttered. "But I am not going to let you give me to those people without a fight!"

"Good. Uh, don't start fighting until I tell you, okay? I breathe better without extra holes in my chest." He lifted his head and marched her quickly forward, beginning to veer almost imperceptibly when the car was in running distance.

"Wait! Stop there!" the voice called.

Lang broke into a run, dragging Meg with him. The sudden movement startled the two men who were in view now. Guns were raised and Lang groaned.

"Stop!" the accented voice warned harshly. "Do not attempt to enter the car!"

Lang stopped at his dark blue car with the hand holding the pistol on the door handle and lifted his head. The wind whipped his dark hair around his face. "Why not?" he called back. "It's a great night for a ride!"

"What are you doing?!"

"I thought it was obvious," he replied. "I'm leaving."

"You agreed to bargain! Let the girl go and you may go free!"

"Make me."

He pushed Meg into his car and locked the door from the passenger side. He jumped in on the other side and started the car. After a glance in the rearview mirror, he dropped it in gear, and shot off as two men came into view. Shots were fired into the air, but he didn't even slow down.

Meg felt sick. She huddled against her door, wondering frantically if it would kill her to force the handle and jump out at the speed they were going. Lang's actions were more puzzling by the minute. Was he holding out for a better price?

"Don't be a fool," Lang said curtly. He didn't look at her, but he obviously knew what she was considering. "You'd be killed by inches."

"Why?" She groaned. "Why?"

"You'll find out. Be a good girl and sit still. You won't come to any harm. I promise."

"Steve will kill you," she said icily.

His eyebrow jerked. "Probably," he murmured. "He'll have to

wait in line. It was all I could think of on the spur-of-the-moment." He glanced in the rearview mirror and mumbled something about a force the size of NATO coming up behind, in a jumble of international agents.

"They're chasing you?" She smiled gleefully. "I hope they shoot your tires out and kidnap you and sell you into slavery!"

He chuckled with pure delight, glancing at her. "Are you sure you want to be engaged to Ryker? I'm two years younger than he is and I've got an aunt who'd pamper you like a baby."

"She'll be very ashamed of you when you end up in prison, you traitor!" she accused.

He shook his head. "Oh, well. Duck, honey."

"Wha…?"

He pushed her down and dodged as a bullet came careening through the windshield, leaving shattered glass all over the front seat, including Meg's lap.

"Oh, my God!" she screamed.

"Keep your head," he said curtly. "Don't panic."

Another bullet whizzed past. She kept her head down, mentally consigning him to the nether reaches.

"Exciting, isn't it?" he shouted above the gunfire and the roar of the engine. His dark eyes glittered as he weaved along the highway just ahead of his pursuers. "God, I love being a secret agent!"

She stared at him from her hiding place on the floorboard as if he were a madman.

He was singing the theme song from an old spy TV show,

zigzagging the car on the deserted highway as more bullets whizzed past.

"Hold on, now, here we go!"

He hit the wheel hard. Tires spun on the pavement, squealing like banshees, and they were suddenly going in the opposite direction across the median. Blue lights flashed and sirens sounded.

"The police!" she gasped. "Oh, boy! I hope they fill you full of lead! I hope they mount your head on a shortwave antenna and throw the rest of you to the buzzards! I hope...!"

He grabbed for the mike on his two-way radio. "Did you get the signal? Here they are, boys. Go get 'em!" he said into it.

He stopped the car and as Meg peered over the broken dash, three assorted colors and divisions of police car went flying across the median and after the horrified occupants of the two cars that had been in hot pursuit of Meg and Lang.

"Now, admit it," he said, breathing heavily as he turned to her, grinning. "Wasn't this more exciting than watching some stupid game show on TV? The thrills, the chills, the excitement!"

She felt sick all over. She started to speak and suddenly wrenched the door handle. He pushed the unlock button on the driver's armrest just in the nick of time. Meg lost everything she'd eaten earlier in the day.

Lang passed her a handkerchief and managed to look slightly repentant when she was leaning back against the seat of the police car that had picked them up when one carful of enemy agents was in custody.

"They ought to put you in solitary and throw away the key," the young police lieutenant told Lang when Meg had finished sipping the thermos cup of strong black coffee he'd fetched for her. "You poor kid," he told Meg.

"I told you, it was all I could think of," Land replied, lounging nonchalantly against the rear fender of the police car. "I over- heard them talking. They were going to snatch her. So I jammed their signal into the house to get their attention, then let them hear me selling her down the river. I beeped you guys once we were in the car to let you know something was going down. I didn't have time to do any more than that. They were headed toward the house when I decided to get her out."

"You didn't have to hold a gun on her!" the policeman raged.

"Sure I did," he replied. "She's a fighter. She was going to argue or maybe start a brawl with me. But when I pointed the pistol at her, she went with me without a single argument. And because they thought I was going to hand her over to them, they didn't shoot at me until it was too late."

"I still say…"

With a long-suffering sigh, Lang pulled out his automatic and slapped it into the policeman's palm.

The officer stared at him, puzzled.

"Well, look at it," Lang muttered.

The policeman turned it over and sighed, shaking his head.

Lang held his hand out. When the weapon was returned to

it, he pulled the missing clip out of his pocket, slammed it into the handle slot and cocked it, before putting on the safety. Then he slid it back into his underarm holster and snapped it in place.

"It wasn't loaded?" Meg asked, aghast.

"That's right," Lang told her. He glowered at her. "And you thought I was selling you out. She called me everything but a worm," he told the policeman. "A traitor, a turncoat. She said she hoped they hung my head on a radio antenna!"

The policeman was trying not to laugh.

"I didn't know you were trying to protect me," Meg said self-consciously.

"Next time, I'll let them have you," he said irately. "They can throw you into somebody's harem and I hope they dress you in see-through plastic wrap!"

The policeman couldn't hold it back any longer. He left, quickly, chuckling helplessly.

"I like that," Meg said haughtily. "At least I'd look better in it than you would!"

"I have legs that make women swoon," he informed her. "*Playgirl begs* me for photo sessions."

"With or without your gun?" she countered.

He grinned. "Jealous because you don't have one? Pistol envy?"

She burst out laughing. Lang was incorrigible. "All right, I apologize for thinking you sold me out," she told him. "But you were pretty convincing. I had no idea you had on a mask, figuratively speaking."

"You'd be amazed at how much company I have," he said dryly. He glanced up as a car approached. "Oh, boy."

She looked where he was staring. It was a big black limousine. Her heart leaped when it stopped and a white-faced, shaken Steven jumped out, making a beeline toward Meg.

He didn't break stride except to throw a heated punch at Lang, which the younger man deflected.

"She's okay," Lang said, moving back. "I'll explain when you cool off."

"You'd better do your explaining from someplace where I can't reach you," Steve replied, and he looked murderous.

"I told you!" Wayne raged, moving into view behind Steve. "You idiot, I told you not to do things on your own!"

"If I hadn't they'd have carried her off!" Lang shot back, exasperated. "What was I supposed to do, call for reinforcements from the trunk of their damned car on the way to the river?"

"They wouldn't throw you in any river, you'd pollute it and kill the fish!"

Lang's voice became heated as the two men moved out of earshot. Steven paused just in front of Meg and looked down at her from a strained face.

"Are you all right?" he asked tersely.

"Yes, thanks to Lang," she replied. "Although I wasn't exactly thanking him at the time," she added, nodding toward the remains of the car Lang had rescued her in.

Steve didn't look at it very long. It made him sick. He reached for Meg and pulled her hungrily into his arms. He held her bruisingly close, rocking her, while his mind ran rampant over all the horrific possibilities that had kept him raging all the way to the scene after Wayne had gotten the news from the city police about the chase.

"I guess your evening with Daphne was spoiled?" she asked a little unsteadily.

"If anything had happened to you, I don't know what I'd have done," he groaned.

She eased her arms under his jacket and around him, holding on. It was so sweet to stand close to him this way while around them blue and red lights still flashed and voices murmured in the distance.

"You'd better get her home, sir," the police officer said gently. "Everything's all right, now."

"I'll do that. Thanks."

He led her back to the limousine. "What about Lang?" she asked Steve. "And didn't his friend...Wayne...ride with you?"

"They can go with the police or hitchhike," Steve said. "Especially Lang!"

"What about Daphne...?"

"I'm taking you home, Meg," he said. "Nobody else matters right now."

"Is David there?"

He nodded. "He doesn't know about any of this. I didn't want to worry him."

She crawled into his lap when the chauffeur started the car, to Steve's amazement.

"Your seat belt," he began.

"I've had my close call for tonight," she told his chest. "Let me stay."

His arms curved around her, pulling her closer. They rode home like that, without a word, cradled together.

David turned white when he learned what had happened. "But how did they know?" he groaned.

"The house is bugged," Meg said, sitting down heavily on the couch. "Lang had some sort of jamming device..."

"He blew up the bugs," David explained. "Scrambled their circuits. One of the agents explained that device to me, but I hadn't seen one until I got home. When I saw it lying here, and you were gone, I knew something had happened. But I couldn't find out anything."

"Sorry," Steven said. "I took off out the door the minute I heard what had happened, with Wayne two steps behind me. I didn't want to worry you." He grimaced. "I have to phone Daphne and tell her where we are."

Meg didn't look at him as he lifted the receiver on the telephone and dialed.

"I'll go up and change my things," she told David. She had pieces of glass on her skirt and in her hair. "It's been a pretty rough night."

"I can imagine. You're limping!"

"I always limp," she said dully. "It's worse because I've walked on it." She laughed mirthlessly. "I don't think it's going to get any better, David. Not ever."

He watched her go with quiet concern. Steve hung up the phone after he'd explained things to Daphne and turned to David.

"This whole thing is getting out of hand," he said tersely. "I can't take much more of it. She looks like a ghost, and that damned fool agent could have killed her driving like that!"

"What if he hadn't gotten her out of the house, Steve?" David asked, trying to reason with his friend. "What then?"

It didn't bear thinking about. Steve stuck his hands into his pockets. "My God."

"How about some coffee?" David asked. "I was about to make a pot."

"I could drink one. They'll have Ahmed under guard like Fort Knox by now. I'll go up and see about Meg. She was sick."

"That doesn't surprise me. Her ankle is bothering her, too." He turned to Steve. "She's not going to be able to dance. You know that, don't you?"

Steve nodded. "Yes, I know it. Why else do you think she's willing to marry me?" he added cynically. "We both know that if she really had a choice, her damned career would win hands down."

"Try to remember that neither your father nor our mother wanted Meg to marry you."

"I know that."

"And Meg was very young. Afraid, too." He studied Steve. "Has she explained why?"

Steve looked hunted. "She gave me some song and dance about being afraid of pregnancy."

"She wasn't afraid of it, she was terrified. Steve," he added quietly, "she was with our sister when she died in childbirth. She was visiting during that snowstorm that locked them in. She watched it happen and couldn't do a thing to help."

Steven turned around, his face contorted. "Meg was there? She never said anything about that!"

"She won't talk about it still. It affected her badly. All this happened while you were away at college. Meg was only ten years old. It was, is, a painful subject. It was never discussed."

"I see." Poor Meg. No wonder she'd been afraid. He hadn't known, her father had told him, but at the time he had not felt comfortable asking questions. He felt guilty. He wondered if she was still that afraid, and hiding it.

"Go on up and get Meg. I'll fix that coffee," David said, clapping his friend on the shoulder.

Meg was just climbing out of the shower when Steve opened the bathroom door and walked in.

She gasped, clutching the towel to her.

"You blush nicely," he mused, smiling gently. "But I know what you look like, Meg. We made love."

"I know, but..."

He took the towel from her hands and looked down at her, his silver eyes kindling with delight. "Pretty little thing," he mused. "I could get drunk on you."

"David is just downstairs," she reminded him, grabbing at her towel. "And spies have bugged the whole house. They're probably watching us right now!"

"They wouldn't bug the bathroom," he murmured dryly.

"Oh, wouldn't they?"

He moved toward her, pulling her into his arms. "No," he whispered, bending. "Is this better? I'll hide you, Meg, from any eyes except my own."

She felt his mouth nibble softly at her lips, teasing them into parting.

"You taste of mint," he whispered.

"Spearmint toothpaste," she managed to say.

"Open your mouth," he whispered back. "I like to touch it, inside."

She shivered a little, but she obeyed him. His hands smoothed over her firm breasts, savoring their silky warmth as he toyed with her mouth until she felt her body go taut with desire.

"I want you," he breathed into her mouth. His hands lifted her hips and pressed them to his. "We could lie down on the carpet in here and make love."

She felt his lips move down her throat until his mouth hungrily kissed her breasts.

"David—" she choked "—is downstairs."

"And we're engaged," he whispered. "It's all right if we make love. Even some of the Puritans did when they were engaged."

"Steve," she moaned.

He kissed her slowly, hungrily, moving his mouth over hers until she was mindless with pleasure.

"On second thought," he said unsteadily, lifting her gently into his arms, "the carpet really won't do this time, Meg. I want you on cool, clean sheets."

She looked up into his eyes, her arms linked around his neck. Her blond hair was pinned up. Wisps of it teased her flushed cheeks. His gaze went all over her, lingering on her breasts.

"You want me, don't you?" he asked, his voice deep and soft in the stillness of the room.

"I never stopped," she replied unsteadily. "But, Daphne...!"

"I don't sleep with Daphne," he said as his mouth eased down on hers.

Maybe that was why he wanted Meg, she thought miserably. But none of it made sense, much less his hunger for her. He lost control when he touched her, and she was powerless to stop him.

"Steve, I can't," she groaned as he leaned over her with dark intent.

"Why not?"

"David's just downstairs!" she exclaimed.

He was trying to remember that. But looking at Meg's beautiful nude body made it really difficult. She shamed the most prized sculptures in the world.

"Why did you never tell me that you were with your sister when she died?" he asked softly.

She stiffened. Her face drew up and the memories were there, in her wide, hurt eyes.

He smiled wryly and pulled the cover over her. He sat down beside her, fighting to control his passion. She'd had enough excitement for one night and she was right. This wasn't the time.

"Didn't you think I'd understand?" he persisted.

"You wanted me very much," she began slowly. "But you were

so distant from me emotionally, Steve. The one time we came close to being intimate, you acted as if precautions didn't matter at all. And I was young, and shy of you, and very embarrassed about things like sex. I couldn't find the right way to tell you, so I froze up instead. And you blew up and told me to get out of your life."

"I'd waited a month to touch you like that," he reminded her. "I went overboard, I know. But you obsessed me." He smiled with self-contempt. "You still do, haven't you noticed? I touch you and I lose control. That hasn't changed."

"You don't like losing control."

He shook his head. "Not even with you, little one."

She reached up and touched his chin, his mouth. "I lose control when you touch me," she reminded him.

"You can afford to now. Your dancing won't come between us anymore."

"Don't sound like that. Don't be so cynical, Steve," she pleaded, her wide eyes searching his. "You're coming up with all sorts of reasons why I want to marry you, but none of them has anything to do with the real one."

"And what is the real one? My money? My body?" he added with a cold smile.

"You can't believe that I might really care about you, can you?" she asked sadly. "It's too much emotion."

"The only emotion that interests me is the emotion I feel when I've got you under me."

She colored. "That's sex."

"That's what we've got," he agreed. "That's all we've got, when you remove all the frills and excuses. And it will probably be enough, Meg. You can find a way to fill your time here in Wichita and spend my money, and I'll come home every night panting to get into bed with you. What else do we need?"

He sounded so bitter. She didn't know how to reach him. He was avoiding the issue because he couldn't find a way to face it.

"You said you wanted a child," she reminded him.

"I meant it." He frowned slightly, remembering what David had told him. "Did you mean it, Meg?"

"Oh, yes," she said gently. She smiled. "I like children."

"I've never had much to do with them," he confessed. "But I suppose people learn to be parents." He slowly pulled the cover away from her body and looked down at her with curious, quiet eyes. "I didn't think about anything that first time. Certainly not about making you pregnant." He touched her stomach hesitantly, tracing a pattern on it while she lay breathlessly looking up at him. "Meg, how would it be if we made love," he said slowly, meeting her eyes, "and we both thought about making a baby together while we did it?"

She felt her heartbeat racing. She stared at him with vulnerable eyes, her feelings so apparent that she could see his heartbeat increase.

"That would be…very exciting," she whispered huskily. "Wouldn't it?"

He drew her hand slowly to his body and let her feel the sudden, violent effect of the words. His breath stilled in his throat.

"Damn your brother," he said unsteadily. "I want to strip off my clothes and pull you under me, right here, right now!"

She reached up, tugging his face down. He kissed her with slow anguish, a rough moan echoing into her mouth. His hand explored her, touched and tested her body until he made it tremble. She whimpered and he clenched his teeth while he tried to fight it.

"We can't." She wept.

"I know. Oh, God, I know!" He brought her up to him and held her roughly, crushing her against him so that the silky fabric of his suit made a faint abrasion against her softness. "Meg, I need you so!"

"I need you, too," she murmured, shaken by the violence of her hunger for him. "So much!"

"Do you want to risk it?" he whispered at her ear. "It would have to be quick, Meg. No long loving, no tenderness." Then he groaned and cursed under his breath as he realized what he was offering her. "No!" he said violently. "Oh, God, no, not like that. Not ever again!"

He forced himself to let go of her. His grip on her arms was bruising as he lifted away from her and then suddenly let her go and turned away. He was shaking, Meg saw, astonished.

"I'm going to get out of here and let you dress," he said with his back to her. "I'm sorry, Meg." He turned around, slowly, and looked down at her. "I want lovemaking," he said quietly, "not raw sex. And we need to think about this. If you're not already pregnant, we need to think very carefully about making you that way."

She smiled gently. He sounded different. He even looked different. "I don't need to think about it," she said softly. "But if you do, you can have all the time in the world."

Color ran along his cheekbones. He looked at her with eyes that made a meal of her. Finally he closed them, shivering, and turned away from her.

"I'll see you downstairs," he said in a faintly choked tone. He went out without looking back and closed the door firmly.

Meg saw something in his face before he left the room. It was enough to erase every terror the night had held and give her the first real hope she'd had of a happy future with him.

10

But if Meg had expected that look in Steve's eyes to change anything, she was mistaken. He'd had time to get himself together again, and he was distant while he drank coffee with Meg and David downstairs. She walked him to the door when he insisted scant minutes later that he had to leave. David discreetly took the coffee things into the kitchen, to give them a little privacy.

"When this is over," he told Meg, "you're going to marry me, as quickly as I can arrange a ceremony."

"All right, Steven," she replied.

He toyed with a strand of her blond hair, not meeting her eyes. "Daphne isn't who you think," he said. "I can't say more than that. But a lot of people aren't what you think they are." He lifted his eyes to hers. "I'll tell you all of it, as soon as I can."

It was an erasing of doubts and fears. A masquerade, and almost time to whip off the masks. She searched his silver eyes quietly. "I care for you very much," she said simply. "I'm tired of fighting it, Steven. I'll be happy with what you can give me."

His jaw clenched. "I don't deserve that."

She smiled impishly. "Probably not, but it's true, just the same." She moved closer and reached up to kiss him very tenderly. "I'm sorry David wouldn't go away so that we could make love," she whispered. "Because I want to, very, very much."

"So do I, little one," he said tautly. "It gets harder and harder to stay away from you."

"But not hard enough to make you give up Daphne?" she probed delicately, and watched him close up.

"Give it time."

She shrugged. "What else can I do?" she asked miserably. She sighed and leaned closer, so that his mouth was against her forehead. "I love you," she said.

He held her with mixed emotions. She didn't quite trust him, but he hoped she was telling the truth about her feelings. He was in too deep to back out now. "I'll see you tomorrow. Lang had better be on his way to the moon," he added irritably.

"Don't hurt him," she said softly. "He really did save me."

"I know what he did," he muttered, and it was in his eyes when he lifted his head. "Maybe they'll give him to Ahmed as a going-away gift."

"Ahmed isn't going away, is he? I thought he was based in Washington, D.C."

Steve started to speak, but decided against telling her what he'd been about to say. "You'll understand everything in a day or two. Just a few loose ends to wrap up, now that Lang's precipitated things. Don't worry. You're all right now."

"Whenever I'm with you, I'm all right."

"Are you?" he asked dryly. "I wonder."

She drew back and smiled up at him. "Good night, Steven."

He stuck his hands into his pockets with a long sigh. "Under different circumstances, it would have been a hell of a night," he remarked. He studied her long and hard. "You're lovely, Meg, and much more than just physically pretty. I don't know why I ever let you go."

"You didn't feel safe with me. You still don't, do you?"

"You were a career ballerina," he reminded her.

"I was an idiot," she replied. "I didn't know you at all, Steven. I was young and silly and I never looked below the surface to see what things and people really were. You were afraid of involvement. Maybe I was, too. I ran for safety."

"You weren't the only one." His eyes narrowed. "But I get homicidal when you're threatened," he said quietly. "And you get hysterical when I am," he added. "Don't you think it's a little late for either of us to worry about getting involved now?"

She smiled ruefully. "We're involved already."

"To the back teeth," he agreed. He drew in a long breath. "In more ways than one," he added with a quick glance at her belly.

She laughed. "I was so afraid of it four years ago," she said softly. "And now, I go to bed and dream about it."

His hands clenched in his pockets. He searched her eyes closely. "It would really mean the loss of any hope of a career, even if your ankle heals finally," he said. "How could you take a child with you to New York while you rehearse and dance? How could you hope to raise it by long distance?"

"I thought I might teach ballet, here in Wichita," she began slowly. "It's something I know very well, and there are two other retired ballerinas in town who worked with me when I was younger. I could get a loan from the bank and find a vacant studio."

Lights blazed in his eyes. "Meg!" he groaned softly. He bent and kissed her, his mouth slow and tender.

She was stunned. Why, he didn't mind! When he drew back, the radiance in his face stopped her heart.

"I could help you look for a studio," he said, his voice deep and hesitant. "As for the financing, I could stake you at a lower interest than you could get from the bank. The rest of it would be your project."

"Oh, Steven!"

He began to smile. He lifted her by the waist and held her close. "Wouldn't you pine for the Broadway stage?"

"Not if I can work at something I love and still live with you," she said simply. "I never dreamed you'd accept it."

His eyes blazed into hers. "Didn't you?"

Her arms looped around his neck and she put her mouth softly over his, kissing him with growing hunger.

He tried to draw back and her arms contracted.

"Kiss me," she whispered huskily, and opened her mouth.

He made a sound that echoed in the quiet hall and she felt his tongue probing quickly, deeply, into the darkest reaches of her mouth while her body throbbed with sudden passion.

There was a ringing sound somewhere in the background that Steve and Meg were much too involved to hear.

A minute later there was a discreet cough behind them. Steve drew back and looked blindly over Meg's shoulder, his mouth swollen, his tall body faintly tremulous.

"That was Lang," David said with barely contained amusement. "He said to tell you that there's a surveillance camera in the hall and the other agents are discussing film rights."

Steve dropped Meg to her feet. He glared around at the ceiling. "Damn you, Lang!"

Meg leaned against Steve, laughing. "He's incorrigible. One day we'll hear that someone has suspended him over a pond of piranhas at the end of a burning rope."

"Please, give them some more ideas," Steve pleaded, glancing up again.

"Do you really think there are any they haven't already entertained? They're highly trained after all, right, Lang?" Meg called with a wicked grin.

Steve muttered something, dropped a quick kiss on Meg's lips and left the house.

The office was buzzing with excitement the next morning, all about the wild chase and the capture of enemy agents. Daphne had told half the people in the building, apparently, because Steve got wry grins everywhere he went.

Ahmed came in late in the morning, surrounded by his body-guards. He looked a little pale and drawn, but he was smiling, at least.

Daphne started to say something to him, abruptly thought better of it and left him in Steve's office. The door closed softly behind her.

"Meg is all right?" Ahmed asked quietly.

"She's fine. And none the wiser for it," Steve replied heavily. He leaned back in his desk chair and propped his immaculate black boots up on the desk. "But I'm going to have a lot to say to Lang's superiors about the way he protected her. With any luck, they'll send him to Alaska to bug polar bears."

Ahmed smiled slowly. "I understand there was something of a stir among the surveillance people last evening. Something about man-eating fish and burning hemp…"

"Never mind," Steve said quickly. "What's the latest about the coup in your country?"

Ahmed sat down in the leather chair across from the desk and crossed one elegant leg over the other. His bearing was regal, like the tilt of his proud head and the arrogant sparkle in his black eyes.

"Ah, my friend, that is a story indeed," he said pleasantly. "To shorten it somewhat, the assassins captured last night by your government's agents were the weak link in a chain. We will learn much from them." Ahmed looked very hard when his eyes met Steve's.

Steve felt chills go down his spine. Ahmed had been his friend for a long time, but there were depths to the man that made him uneasy. He might not be a Moslem, but Ahmed was every inch an Arab. His thirst for vengeance knew no bounds when it was aroused.

"When do you leave for home?"

Ahmed spread his hands. "Today, if it can be arranged. The sooner the better, you understand." His black eyes narrowed. "I would not willingly have put you and Meg and David at risk. I hope you know this, and understand that it was not my doing."

"Of course I do."

"Meg...you have not told her?" he added carefully.

"I thought it best not to," Steve said. "The less she knows the safer she is. For now, at least."

Ahmed smiled. "I agree. She is unique, our Meg. If she did not belong to you, my friend, I could lose my heart very easily to that one."

"You're invited to the wedding," Steve replied.

"You honor me, and I would enjoy the occasion. But the risk of returning to your country so soon after this unfortunate attempt at an overthrow is too great."

"I understand."

"I wish you well, Steve. Thank you for all that you have done for my people—and for myself. I look forward to future projects such as this one. With your help, my country will move into the twentieth century and lessen the chance of invasion from outside forces."

"Watch your back, will you?" Steve asked. "Even with the culprits in custody, you can't be too careful."

"I realize this." Ahmed got to his feet, resplendent in his gray business suit. He smiled at Steve as they shook hands. "Take care of yourself, as well, and give my best to your brother and the so beautiful Meg."

"She'll be sorry that she didn't have the opportunity to say goodbye to you," Steve told him.

"We will meet again, my friend," he said with certainty.

Steven walked him to the outer office, where a slender, dark-haired girl was glaring at the Arab from behind a propped-up shorthand tablet with information that she was copying into the computer. She quickly averted her eyes.

Daphne motioned to Steve and pointed at the telephone.

"I'll have to go. Have a safe trip. I'll be in touch when we get a little further along in the assembly."

"Yes."

Steve shook hands again and went back into his office to take the telephone call.

Daphne hesitated, hoping to provide a buffer between the angry look in Ahmed's eyes and the intent look in Brianna's, but Steve hung up the telephone and buzzed her. She grimaced as she finally went to see what he wanted.

Ahmed stood over the young woman, his liquid black eyes narrowed as he glared at her. "You have had too little discipline," he said flatly. "You have no breeding and no manners and you also have the disposition of a harpy eagle."

She glared back at him. "Weren't you just leaving, sir?" she asked pointedly.

"Indeed I was. It will be pleasant to get back to my own country where women know their place!"

She got out of her chair and walked around the desk. Her pretty figure was draped in a silky dark blue suit and white blouse that emphasized her creamy complexion and huge blue eyes. She got down on her knees and began to salaam him, to the howling amusement of the other women in the typing pool.

"How dare you!" Ahmed demanded scathingly.

Brianna looked up at him with limpid eyes. "But, sir, isn't this the kind of subservience you demand from your country-women?" she asked pleasantly. "I would hate to offend you any more than I already have. Oh, look at that, a nasty bug has landed on your perfectly polished shoe! Allow me to save you, sir!"

She grabbed a heavy magazine from the rack beside her desk and slammed it down on his shoe with all her might.

He raged in Arabic and two other unintelligible languages, his face ruddy with bad temper, his eyes snapping with it.

Daphne came running. "Brianna, no!" she cried hoarsely.

Ahmed was all but vibrating. He didn't back down an inch. Daphne motioned furiously behind her until Brianna finally got the hint and took off, making a dash for the ladies' rest room.

"In my country..." he began, his finger pointing toward Brianna's retreating figure.

"Yes, I know, but she's insignificant," Daphne reminded him. "A mere fly speck in the fabric of your life. Honestly she is."

"She behaves like a savage!" he raged.

Daphne bit her tongue almost through. She smiled tightly. "You'll miss your flight."

He breathed deliberately until some of the high color left his cheekbones, until he was able to unclench the taut fists at his side. He looked down at Daphne angrily. "She will be punished." It was a statement, not a question.

"Oh, yes, of course, she will," Daphne swore, with her fingers tightly crossed behind her back. "You can count on that, sir."

Ahmed began to relax a little. He pursed his lips. "A month in solitary confinement. Bread and water only. Yes. That would take some of the spirit out of her." His dark eyes narrowed thoughtfully. "It would be a tragedy, however, to break such a beautiful wild spirit. Do you not think so?"

"Indeed," Daphne agreed quickly.

He nodded, as if savoring the thought. "Your country has such odd people in it, *mademoiselle*," he said absently. "Secret agents with quirks, secretaries with uncontrollable tempers…"

"It's a very interesting country."

He shrugged. "Puzzling," he corrected. He glanced at her. "This one," he nodded toward the door where Brianna had gone. "She is married?"

"No," Daphne said. "She has a young brother in a coma. He's in a nursing home. She has no family."

His dark brows drew together. "No one at all?"

She shook her head. "Just Tad," she replied.

"How old is this…Tad?"

"Ten," Daphne said sadly. "There was an automobile accident, you see. Their parents were killed and Tad was terribly injured. They don't think he'll ever recover, but Brianna goes every day to sit by his bed and talk to him. She won't give up on him."

His face changed. "A woman of compassion and loyalty and spirit. A pearl of great price indeed."

Daphne heard the buzzer and went to answer it, leaving Ahmed to rejoin Steve.

Steve put the Arab on a plane—a chartered plane owned by Ahmed's government—later that morning, with Daphne and two taciturn American agents at his side.

"Have a safe trip," Steve said.

"How can I help it?" Ahmed muttered, glancing at the number of armed guards in his country's uniform gathered at the walkway to the plane. "Many thanks for your help," he added to the agents, and Daphne, who was standing close to the tall blond agent.

"It was our pleasure. Anytime," Wayne replied.

Lang grinned at him. "Just give us a day's notice and we'll cover you like tar paper, sir," he replied.

Steve glared at him. "And watch your every move on hidden cameras," he added icily.

"What can I tell you?" Lang sighed, lifting his hands and letting them fall. "I *am* a spy, after all. I get paid to spy on people. It's what I do." He looked somber as he faced Ahmed. "You'd just be amazed at the things you see on a hidden camera, sir. Like last night, for instance…"

Steve moved toward him threateningly.

Lang grinned. "Actually," he clarified, "I meant this rich guy we were watching who likes to play video games and when he wins, he takes off all his clothes and pours Jell-O over himself."

"So help me!" Steve began.

Lang threw up both hands. "I'll reform. I really will. I'm going to ask that little brunette out and see if she'd like to take me on," he added. "She's dishy, isn't she? I hear she likes to throw things at foreign men. Good thing I'm domestic."

Ahmed looked at Lang with kindling anger, and Steve saw problems ahead. "Better get aboard," Steve told the Arab. "Keep in touch."

Ahmed seemed to realize where he was and to whom he was speaking. He shrugged, as if he'd experienced a minor temporary aberration. "Of course. *Au revoir,* my friend."

He waved and turned to go into the plane, with his entourage at a respectful distance, watching his back.

"Regal, isn't he?" Lang said with reluctant admiration. "I'm sorry to see him go." He grinned at Steve. "Now that this is all over, are you sure you're going to marry that girl of yours? I do like her temper."

"So do I," Steve replied. "Yes, I'm going to marry her. And the next time you point a camera in my general direction, it had better have a lens cap on."

"Yes, sir," Lang said, chuckling. "You'll be glad to know that as of now you are officially unobserved. But if you'd like the results of our straw poll last night, we think you'd give Valentino a run for his money." He threw up a hand and walked away.

Wayne followed him a minute later, leaving a sighing Daphne behind with Steve.

"Are you really going to marry Wayne?" Steve asked as they walked back toward the airport entrance.

"The minute we can arrange a ceremony. How about you and Meg?"

"I've got a lot of explaining to do," he replied dryly. "But I think she'll understand. I hope she will, at least."

"She's a sweet woman, Steve. You're very lucky."

"Don't I know it," he mused.

He left Daphne at the office and gave himself the rest of the day off. First on the agenda was to tell Meg the truth.

She was sprawled on the couch going over projection figures the bank had given her when she went to inquire about starting up her own business. Steve came in the old way, through the back door without knocking, and stood over her with relief written all over him.

"It's over," he told her. "Ahmed's on a plane home and the secret agents have gone to root out enemy spies somewhere else. We're free."

She put down her figures and smiled up at him. "So?"

"So," he replied, dropping down beside her, "now that it's over and we're unbugged, I can tell you that Daphne is engaged to that blond agent who hangs out with Lang."

"What?"

"She was the unofficial liaison between us. She had to go where we did."

"But you said...!"

"I wasn't allowed to tell you what was going on," he told her. "Now that Ahmed's out of danger, there's no more risk."

She frowned. "I thought they were after you."

"Only as a way to get to Ahmed." He got up and poured brandy into a snifter and handed it to her.

"Do I need a drink?" she asked.

"You may."

"Why?"

He smiled down at her. "Ahmed isn't a cabinet minister. He's the sovereign of his country. To put it more succinctly...he's a king."

11

Meg took a good swallow of the brandy and coughed a little. "That explains a lot," she told him finally. "He did have a more regal bearing than you'd expect in a political flunky. He's out of danger, then?"

"Yes. The overthrow attempt didn't go down. The agency thought he was safer here until it was dealt with. Ahmed's government is friendly to ours and we're fortunate to have access to his strategic location when there are problems in the Middle East. The government is anxious to accommodate him. That's why they supported the company when we decided to sell him our newest jet fighter. It's also why he got top priority protection here when his life was in danger."

"I still can't quite believe it."

"You have to keep his identity to yourself, however," he told her warningly. "Because he'll be back to have another look at his purchase when we've got it closer to completion. His life may depend on secrecy. Even in this country, there are nationals from his kingdom with grudges."

"Poor Ahmed." She frowned. "He must not enjoy being guarded all the time." Another thought came to her. "He's a king, which means that he has to marry a princess or something, doesn't it? He can't just marry for love, can he?"

"I don't know," he said. His silver eyes searched hers. "I'm glad that I got to choose my own wife," he added huskily. "Now that I've waited four years for her, I don't intend waiting any longer."

"You sound very impulsive."

"I'll show you impulsive." He pulled her to her feet and bundled her out the door. Several hours later, the blood tests were complete, the paperwork was underway and the wedding was scheduled for the end of the week.

"You aren't slipping through my fingers again," he chuckled when they walked arm in arm into his own house. "My mother will be delighted. We'll have to phone her tonight. By the way," he added, "I've found three possibilities for your studio. I thought you might like to go and look them over tomorrow."

"I'd love to!" She reached up and hugged him warmly, feeling as if she'd just come home. She closed her eyes with a sigh as they stood together in the deserted house. Steve's housekeeper had long since left a note about cold cuts and gone home. "Am I staying for supper?" Meg murmured.

He turned her to him. "You're staying for good," he said quietly. "Tonight and every night for the rest of your life."

She hesitated. "But, David will expect me…"

He bent and began to kiss her, softly at first, and then with building intensity so that, after a few minutes, she didn't remember her brother's name. But they agreed that one lapse before marriage was enough. And while Meg slept in his arms that night, sleeping was all they did together. They had the rest of their lives for intimacy, he reminded her.

Early the next morning, Steve took Meg around to the studio prospects he'd found for her. She settled on one in a good location with ample parking, not too many blocks from his office.

"Now," she said, smiling as she looked around, "all I have to do is convince the bank that I'm a good credit risk."

He glowered at her. "I've already told you that I'll stake you."

"I know, and I appreciate it," she said, reaching up to kiss him as they stood in the spacious emptiness of the former warehouse. "But this is something I need to do on my own." She hesitated. "Do you understand?"

"Oh, yes," he said with a slow smile. "You sound just like me at your age."

She laughed. "Do I, really?"

He stuck his hands into his pockets and looked around. "You'll need a lot of paint."

"That, and a little equipment, and some employees who'll be willing to work for nothing until I establish a clientele," she added. "Not to mention an advertising budget." She clenched her teeth. Was she biting off more than she could chew?

"Start with just yourself," he advised. "Less overhead. See if you can time-share with someone who needs a studio at night. Perhaps a karate master. Put up some posters around town in key business windows, such as day-care centers." He grinned at her astonishment. "Didn't I ever tell you that I'm more an idea man than an executive? Who do you think calls the shots on our advertising campaign and trims off fat from work stations?"

"You're amazing!" she exclaimed.

"I'm cheap," he corrected. "I know how to do a lot for a little."

"How about printing?"

"We use a large concern a block away from here. Since they deal in big jobs, they don't cost as much as a small printer would."

She was grinning from ear to ear. She could see it all taking shape. "The only thing is, how will I teach when I can barely walk?" she asked, hesitating.

"Listen, honey, by the time you get your financing, your carpentry done and your advertising out, that ankle will be up to a lot more than you think."

"Truly?"

He smiled at her worried expression. "Really and truly. Now let's get to it. We've got a wedding to go to."

She wondered if she could hold any more happiness. It seemed impossible.

They were married at a small justice of the peace's office, with David and Daphne and Wayne for witnesses. Brianna waited outside with a camera to take pictures.

"I forgot to hire a photographer!" Steve groaned when they exited the office. He was wearing a blue business suit, and a beaming Meg was in a street-length white suit with a hat and veil, carrying a bouquet of lily of the valley.

"That's all right," Brianna told him. "I used to help our dad in the darkroom. He said I was a natural." She said it a little sadly, because she missed her parents, but not in any self-pitying way. "Stand together and smile, now."

They started to, just as a huge black limousine roared up and a tall, dark man leaped from the back seat.

"Am I in time?" Lang asked hurriedly, righting his tie and smoothing back his unruly hair. "I just flew in from Langley, Virginia, for the occasion!"

"Lang!" Meg exclaimed, breaking into a smile.

"The very same, partner," he chuckled. "How about a big kiss?"

Steve stepped closer to his new wife, with a protective arm around her. "Try it," he said.

Lang lifted both eyebrows. "You want me to kiss you, too? *Yeeech!*"

"I do not!" Steve roared.

"That's a fine way to treat a man who flew hundreds of miles to be at your wedding. My gosh, I even brought a present!"

Steve cocked his head and stared at Lang. "A present? What kind of a present?"

"Something you'll both treasure."

He reached into his coat pocket and took out a packet of photographs.

Steve took the photographs and held them as gingerly as if they'd been live snakes. He opened the envelope and peeked in. But the risqué photos he expected weren't there. Instead, they were photos of Meg, from all sorts of camera angles; Meg smiling, Meg laughing, Meg looking reflective.

"Well, what are they?" Meg asked. "Let me see!"

Steve closed up the package and glanced at Lang with a wry smile. "Thanks."

Lang shrugged. "It was the least I could do." He hesitated. "Uh, there's this, too."

He handed Steve a videotape and followed it with a wicked grin. "From the hall camera...?"

Steve eyed him with growing suspicion. "Just how many copies of this did you make?"

"Only one," Lang swore, hand on his heart. "That one. And there are no negatives."

"Lang, you're a good man," Meg told him with conviction.

"Of course I am." He turned to Brianna, still grinning. "Well, hello, hello. How about lunch? I'll take you to this great little seafood joint down the street and buy you a shrimp!"

"A shrimp?" Brianna asked, hesitating.

Lang pulled out the change in his pocket and counted it. "Two shrimps!" he announced.

Brianna smiled, her blue eyes twinkling. "I'd love to," she said. "I really would. But there's someone I have to go and see. Perhaps some other time."

Lang managed to look fatally wounded. "I see. It's because I can only afford two shrimps, isn't it? Suppose," he added, leaning down toward her with a twinkle in his eyes, "I offered to wash plates after and bought you a whole platter of shrimp?" He wiggled his eyebrows.

She laughed. "It wouldn't do any good. But I do appreciate the sentiment." He was very nice, she thought, a little sad under that clownish exterior, too. But she had so many problems, and her stubborn mind would keep winging back to a tall man with a mustache.... It wouldn't be fair to lead Lang on when she had nothing to offer him.

"Ah, well," Lang murmured. "Just my luck to be so handsome and debonair that I intimidate women."

"That's true," Meg told him. "You're just devastating, Lang. But someday, some nice girl will carry you off to her castle and feed you rum cakes and ice cream."

"Sadist," he grumbled. "Go ahead, torment me!"

"We have to go," Steve said. "Thank you all for coming. We both appreciate it."

"Don't mention it," David chuckled, bending to kiss his sister. "Where are you going on your honeymoon?"

"Nowhere," Meg said. "We're going to wall ourselves up in Steven's house and stay there until the food all goes moldy in the refrigerator. And after that," she said smugly, "I've got a business to get underway!"

"Now see what you've done," David groaned. "My own sister, a career woman!"

"I always say," Steve mused, smiling down at his wife, "if you can't beat 'em, join 'em."

"That's just what I say," Meg replied. She took his hand in hers, feeling very newly married and adoringly glancing at the wedding ring on her left hand.

When they got home, Steve lifted her gently in his arms and started up the staircase to the master bedroom. She was a little nervous, and so was he. But when he kissed her, the faint embarrassment was gone forever.

His open mouth probed hers, the intimacy of the kiss making her weak with desire. He was moving, walking, and all the time, his mouth was on hers, gentling her, seducing her.

She didn't come out of the fog of pleasure until he laid her gently on the bed and undressed her. Then he started taking off his own clothes. The sight of that big, hair-roughened body coming slowly into view froze her in a half-reclining position on the bed. He was the most incredibly sexy man she'd ever seen. Their first time, she hadn't been able to look at him because there had been such urgency. But now there was all the time in the world, and her eyes fed on him.

He smiled gently as he sat down beside her, his eyes turbulent and full of desire as he leaned over her. "I know," he said softly. "It wasn't like this before. But we have plenty of time to learn about each other now, Meg. A lifetime."

He bent slowly and put his mouth gently to hers. In the long, lazy moments that followed, he taught her how, watching the expressions chase across her shocked face as he made her touch him. He smiled with taut indulgence until she'd completed the task he set for her, and then he held her hands to him and talked to her, coaxed her into relaxing, into accepting the reality of him.

"It isn't so frightening now that you know what to expect, is it?" he asked, his voice deep and tender as he began to gently ease her out of the last flimsy garments that separated skin from skin.

When he had, he rose and looked at her, his body visibly trembling as he studied the rounded, exquisite flush of her perfect body, her silky skin.

His hand went out and tenderly traced her firm breasts, enjoying their immediate response to his touch, her trembling, her audible pleasure.

"You're beautiful, Meg," he whispered when his exploring hand trespassed in a new way. Despite their former intimacy, the touch shocked her. She caught his wrist and gasped. "No, little one," he coaxed, bending to kiss her wide eyes shut. "Don't be embarrassed or afraid of this. It's part of the way we're going to make love to each other. Relax, Meg. Try to put away all those inhibitions, will you? You're my wife. We're married. And believe me, this is perfectly permissible now."

"I know," she whispered back. "I'll try."

His mouth brushed over her eyes, her cheeks, down her face to her throat, her collarbone, onto the silken softness of her breasts while he discovered her.

His mouth on her breasts made her shiver. The faint suction he made was as exciting as the way he began to touch her, making little waves of pleasure ripple up her spine. She forgot to be nervous and her body responded to him, lifting to meet his touch. Her eyes opened, because she wanted to see if it was affecting him, too.

It was. His face was taut. His eyes were narrow and glittery as he looked down at her, and she could feel the tension in his powerful body as it curved against hers on the cool sheets.

He nodded. His eyes searched hers and his touch became softer, slower, more thorough. She made a quick, shocked sound, and his hand snaked under her neck to grasp a handful of hair at her nape and arch her face up so that he could see every soft, flushed inch of it.

"You…mustn't…watch!" she gasped as a hot, red mist wavered her surprised eyes.

"I'm going to," he replied. "Oh, yes, Meg, I'm going to watch you. I'm going to take you right up to the moon. This is going to be our first real night of love. Here and now, Meg. Now, now, now…"

The deep, slow chant was like waves breaking, the same waves that were slamming with pleasure into her body. She held on for dear life and her voice sobbed, caught, as the pleasure grew with each touch, each hot whisper.

He was moving. He was over her, against her. The pleasure was like an avalanche, gaining, gaining, rolling down, pressing down on her, pressing against her, pressing…into…her!

She felt the fierce throb of it, felt the slow invasion, felt the tension suddenly snap into a stinging, white-hot pleasure so unbearably sweet that it made her cry out.

His hands were on her wrists, pinning her, his body above her, demanding, pushing, invading. She heard his harsh breath, his sudden exclamation, the hoarse cry of pleasure that knotted him above her. As he shouted his fulfillment, she fell helplessly from the height to which he'd taken her, fell into a thousand diamond-splintered fragments, each more incredibly hot and sweet than the one before…

He cried out with the pleasure of it, his eyes wide open, his face taut with the strain. "Oh, God…!"

He sank over her, helpless in that last shudder, and she cradled him, one with him, part of him, in a unity that was even greater than the first one they'd ever shared.

She touched his face hesitantly. "Oh, Steven," she whispered, the joy of belonging to him in her eyes, her voice, her face.

He smiled through the most delicious exhaustion he'd ever felt, trying to catch is breath. "Oh, Meg," he replied, laughing softly.

She flushed, burying her face in his throat. "It wasn't…quite like that before."

"You were a virgin before," he whispered, smiling. He rolled over onto his back, bringing her along with him so that she could pillow her cheek on his broad, damp chest. "Are you all right?"

"I'm happy," she replied. "And a little tired."

"I wonder why."

She laughed at the droll tone and burrowed closer. "I love you so much, Steven," she said huskily. "More than my life."

"Do you?" His arms tightened. "I love you, too, my darling." He stroked her hair gently, feeling for the moment as if he had the world in his arms. "I should never have let you go. But I felt something for you so strong that it unnerved me." His arms grew suddenly bruising. "Meg, I couldn't bear to lose you," he said roughly, letting all the secret fears loose. "I couldn't go on living. It was hell without you, those four years. I did wild things trying to fill up the emptiness you left in me, but nothing worked." He drew in a long breath, while she listened with rapt fascination. "I...couldn't let you go again, no matter what I had to do to keep you."

"Oh, Steve, you won't have to!" She kissed him softly, brushed his closed eyes with her lips, clinging fiercely to him as she felt the depth of his love for her and was humbled by it. "I'll never want to go, don't you see? I didn't think you loved me four years ago. I ran because I didn't think I could hold you. I was so young, and I had an irrational fear of intimacy because my sister died having a baby. But I'm not that frightened girl anymore. I'll stay with you, and I'll fight any other woman to the edge of death to keep you!" she whispered fiercely, clinging to him.

He laughed softly. They were so much alike. "Yes, I feel the same way." He touched her forehead with his lips, relaxing a little as he realized that she felt exactly as he did. "Ironic, isn't it? We were desperately in love and afraid to believe that something so overwhelming could last. But it did. It has."

"Yes. I never thought I'd be enough for you," she whispered.

"Idiot. No one else would ever be enough."

She lifted her eyes to his and smiled. "Are we safe, now?"

"Yes. Oh, yes."

She flattened her hand over his chest. "And you won't grind your teeth in the night thinking that I'm plotting ways to run?"

He shook his head. "You're going to be a responsible business-woman. How can you run from utility bills and state taxes?"

She smiled at the jibe. "Good point."

He closed his eyes, drinking in her nearness, her warm softness. "I never dreamed of so much happiness."

"Neither did I. I can hardly believe we're really married." Her breath released in a soft sigh. "I really did love dancing, Steven. But dancing was only a poor second in my life. You came first even then. You always will."

He felt a surge of love for her that bordered on madness. He rolled her over onto her back and bent to kiss her with aching tenderness.

"I'd die for you," he said unsteadily. His eyes blazed with what he felt, all of it in his eyes, his face. "I hated the world because you wanted to be a ballerina more than you wanted me!"

"I lied," she whispered. "I never wanted anything more than I wanted you."

His eyes closed on a wave of emotion and she reached up, kissing him softly, comfortingly. Tears filled her eyes, because she understood then for the first time his fear of losing her. It humbled her, made her shake all over. She was frightened at the responsibility of being loved like that.

"I won't ever let you down again," she whispered. "Not ever!

I won't leave you, not even if you throw me out. This is forever, Steven."

He believed her. He had to. If this wasn't love, it didn't exist. He gave in at last and put aside his fears. "As if I could throw you out, when I finally know what you really feel." He kissed her again, hungrily, and as the fires kindled in her eyes he began to smile wickedly. "Perhaps I'm dreaming again…"

She smiled under his hard mouth. "Do you think so? Let's see."

She pulled him down to her. Long, sweet minutes later, he was convinced. Although, as he told her afterward, from his point of view, life was going to be the sweetest kind of dream for the rest of their lives together; a sentiment that Meg wholeheartedly shared.

Meg opened her ballet school, and it became well-known and respected, drawing many young prospective ballerinas. Her ankle healed; not enough to allow her to dance again, but well enough to allow her to teach. She was happy with Steven and fulfilled in her work. She had it all, she marveled.

The performing ballet slippers of flawless pink satin and pink ribbons rested in an acrylic case on the grand piano in the living room. But in due time, they came out again, to be fastened with the slender, trembling hands of Steven and Meg's firstborn, who danced one day with the American Ballet Company in New York—as a prima ballerina.

* * * * *

SECRET AGENT MAN

1

Lang Patton felt absolutely undressed without his credentials and the small automatic weapon he'd grown used to carrying on assignment. It had been his own choice to leave the CIA and take a job with a private security company in San Antonio. He was hoping that he wasn't going to regret it.

He walked into the San Antonio airport—weary from the delayed Washington, D.C., flight—with a carryon bag and looked around for his brother Bob.

He was tall and big, dark-eyed and dark-haired, with a broad, sexy face. His brother was an older version of him, but much slighter in build. Bob approached him with a grin, a young boy of six held firmly by the hand.

"Hi," Bob greeted him. "I hope you just got here. I had to bring Mikey with me."

The towheaded boy grinned up at him. He had a front tooth

missing. "Hi, Uncle Lang, been shooting any bad guys?" he asked loudly, causing a security man who was talking to a woman at the information counter to turn his head with a suspicious scowl.

"Not lately, Mikey," Lang replied. He shook his brother's hand and bent to lift Mikey up onto his shoulder. "How's it going, pardner?" he asked the boy.

"Just fine! The dentist says I'm going to get a new tooth, but the Tooth Fairy left me a whole dollar for my old one!"

"Just between us, the Tooth Fairy's going bust," Bob said in a lowered voice.

"Can I see your gun, Uncle Lang, huh?" Mikey persisted.

The security guard lifted both eyebrows. Lang could have groaned out loud as the man approached. He'd been through the routine so often that he just put Mikey down and opened his jacket without being asked to.

The security man cocked his head. "Nice shirt, or are you showing off your muscles?"

"I'm showing you that I don't have a gun," Lang muttered.

"Oh, that. No, I wasn't looking for a gun. You're Lang Patton?"

Lang blinked. "Yes."

"Nobody else here fits the description," the man added sheepishly. "Well, there's a Mrs. Patton on the phone who asks that you stop by the auto parts place and pick her up a new carburetor for a '65 Ford Mustang, please."

"No, he will not," Bob muttered. "I told her she can't do that overhaul, but she won't listen. She's going to prove me wrong or...cowardly woman, to sucker *you* into it," he added indignantly to Lang, who was grinning from ear to ear.

"His wife—my sister-in-law—is a whiz with engines," Lang told the security man. "She can fix anything on wheels. But he—" he jerked his thumb at an outraged Bob "—doesn't think it's ladylike."

"What century is he living in?" the security man asked. "Gee, my wife keeps our washing machine fixed. Saves us a fortune in repair bills. Nothing like a wife who's handy with equipment. You should count your blessings," he added to Bob. "Do you know what a mechanic charges?"

"Yes, I know what a mechanic charges, I'm married to one," Bob said darkly. "She owns her own repair shop, and she doesn't care that I don't like her covered in grease and smelling of burned rubber. All I am these days is a glorified baby-sitter."

Lang knew why Bob was upset. He and his brother had spent their childhood playing second fiddle to their mother's job. "You know Connie loves you," he said, trying to pacify Bob. "Besides, you're a career man yourself, and a terrific surveyor," Lang argued when the security man was called away to a passenger in distress. "Mikey will take after you one day. Won't you, Mikey?" he asked the child.

"Not me. I want to be a grease monkey, just like my mommy!"

Bob threw up his hands and walked away, leaving Lang and Mikey to catch up.

The Pattons lived in Floresville, a pleasant little ride down from San Antonio, past rolling land occupied by grazing cattle and oil pumping stations. This part of Texas was still rural, and Lang remembered happy times as a boy when he and Bob visited their uncle's ranch and got to ride horses with the cowboys. Things at home were less pleasant.

"Time passes so quickly," Lang remarked.

"You have no idea," Bob replied. He glanced at Lang. "I saw Kirry downtown the other day."

Lang's heart jumped. He hadn't expected to hear her name mentioned. In five years, he'd done his best to forget her. The memories were sudden and acute, Kirry with her long wavy blond hair blowing in the breeze, her green eyes wide and bright with laughter and love. There were other memories, not so pleasant, of Kirry crying her eyes out and begging a recalcitrant Lang to listen. But he wouldn't. He'd caught her in a state of undress with his best friend and, in a jealous rage, he'd believed the worst. It had taken six months for him to find out that his good friend had set Kirry up because he wanted her for himself.

"I tried to apologize once," Lang said without elaborating, because Bob knew the whole story.

"She won't talk about you to this day," was the quiet reply. Bob turned into the side street that led to the Patton house. "She's very polite when you're mentioned, but she always changes the subject."

"She went away to college before I left," Lang reminded him.

"Yes, and graduated early, with honors. She's vice president of a top public relations firm in San Antonio. She makes very good money, and she travels a lot."

"Does she still come home?" Lang asked.

Bob shook his head. "She avoids Floresville like the plague. She can afford to since her mother sold the old homestead." His eyes shifted to Lang. "You must have hurt her a lot."

Lang smiled with self-contempt. "You have no idea how much."

"It was right after that when you were accepted for the CIA."

"I'd applied six months before," he reminded Bob. "It wasn't a sudden decision."

"It was one you hadn't shared with any of us."

"I knew you wouldn't like it. But here I am, back home and safe, with some pretty exciting memories," Lang reminisced.

"As alone as when you left." Bob indicated Mikey, who was lying down on the back seat of Bob's Thunderbird, reading a Marvel comic book. "If you'd gotten married, you could have had one of those by now."

Lang looked at Mikey and his eyes darkened. "I don't have your courage," he said curtly.

Bob glanced at him. "And you said I shouldn't let the past ruin my life."

Lang shrugged. "It tends to intrude. Less since I've been away."

"But you still haven't coped with it, Lang, you're getting older. You'll want a wife and a family one day."

Lang couldn't argue with wanting a wife. It was the thought of a child that made him hesitate. "My last case reminded me of how short life can be, and how unpredictable," he said absently. "The woman I was helping guard had a kid brother who'd been in a coma for years. He's older than Mikey, but a real nice kid. I got attached to him." He stretched and leaned his head back against the seat. "I did a lot of thinking about where my life was going, and I didn't like what I saw. So when an old friend of mine mentioned this security chief job, I decided to give it a try."

"What old friend?" Bob asked dryly. "Someone female?"

Lang glowered at him. "Yes."

"And still interested in you?"

"Lorna gave me up years ago, before I started going with Kirry. She was only thinking that I might like a change," he said. "It's nothing romantic."

Bob didn't say anything, but his expression did. "Okay, I'll quit prying. Where is it that you're going to work?"

"A corporation called Lancaster, Inc., in San Antonio. It has several holdings, and I'll be responsible for overseeing security in all of them."

Bob made a sound in his throat.

"What was that?" Lang asked curiously.

Bob coughed, choking. "Why, not a thing in this world!" he said. He was grinning. "I hope you like pancakes for dinner, it's all I can cook, and Connie won't be in for hours yet. I usually make her an omelet when she gets here." His hands tightened on the steering wheel. "I hate mechanics!"

"You knew Connie had this talent when you married her ten years ago," Lang reminded him.

"Well, I didn't know she planned to open her own shop, did I? For the past six months, ever since she went into business, I've been living like a single parent! I do everything for Mikey, everything, and she's never home!"

Lang's eyebrows lifted. "Does she have any help?"

"Can't afford any, she says," he muttered darkly, pulling into the driveway of the stately old Victorian house they lived in. Out back was a new metal building, from which loud mechanical noises were emanating.

The elderly lady next door, working in her flowers, gave Bob an overly sweet smile. "How nice to see *you* again, Lang," she said. "I hope you didn't come home for some peace and quiet, because if you did, you'll find more peace and quiet in downtown San Antonio than you'll get here!"

"You're screaming, Martha," Bob said calmly.

"I have to scream to be heard with that racket going on night and day!" the white-haired little lady said. Her face was turning red. "Can't you make her quit at a respectable hour?"

"Be my guest," Bob invited.

"Not me," she mumbled, shifting from one foot to the other. "Tried it once. She flung a wrench at me." She made a sniffling noise and went back to work in her flowers.

Lang was trying hard not to laugh. He took his flight bag, and Mikey, out of the back seat.

"Is that all you have?" Bob asked for the third time since he'd gotten his brother off the plane.

"I don't accumulate things," Lang told him. "It's not sensible when your assignments take you all over the country and around the world."

"I guess so. You don't accumulate people, either, do you?" he added sadly.

He clapped a big hand on his brother's shoulder. "Family's different."

Bob smiled lopsidedly. "Yeah."

"I'll just go out and say hello to Connie."

"Uh, Lang…"

"It's all right, I'm a trained secret agent," Lang reminded him dryly.

"Watch your head. Place is loaded with wrenches…."

Lang banged on the door and waited for the noise to cease and be replaced with loud mutters.

The door was thrown open and a slight woman with brown hair wearing stained blue coveralls and an Atlanta Braves cap peered up at him. "Lang? Lang!"

She hurled herself into his big arms and hugged him warmly. "How are you? When Bob told me you'd given up the Agency to work in San Antonio, I stood up and cheered! Listen, when you get a car, I'll do all your mechnical work free. You can stay with us—"

"No, I can't," he told her. "I have to be in San Antonio, but I can come and visit often, and I will. I'll get a nice big apartment and some toys for Mikey to play with when you bring him up to see me."

She grimaced. "I don't have a lot of time, you know. So many jobs and only me to do them. I can't complain, though, work is booming. We have a new VCR and television set, and Mikey has loads of toys. I even bought Bob a decent four-wheel drive to use in his work." She beamed. "Not bad, huh?"

"Not bad at all," he agreed, wondering if it would be politic to mention that gifts weren't going to replace the time she spent with her family. He and Bob had scars that Connie might not even know about. God knew, Lang had never been able to share his with Kirry, as close as they'd been.

"Well, back to work. Bob's cooking tonight, he'll feed you. I'll see you later, Lang. Did you get me the carburetor?"

He flushed.

She glowered. "Bob, right? He wouldn't let you." She stamped her foot. "I don't know why in heaven's name I had to marry a male chauvinist pig! He looked perfectly sane when I said yes." She turned and went back into the garage, closing the door behind her, still muttering. Lang was certain then that Bob had never shared the past with her.

"Well, did she scream about the carburetor?" Bob asked hopefully as he dished up black-bottomed pancakes in the kitchen.

"Yes."

"Did she tell you how much stuff she's bought us all?" he added. "Nice, isn't it? If we only had her to share it with, it might mean something. Poor old Mikey doesn't even get a bedtime story anymore because she's too tired to read him one. I even do that."

"Have you tried talking to her?" Lang asked.

"Sure. She doesn't listen. She's too busy redesigning engine systems and important stuff like that." He put some pancakes down in front of Mikey, who made a face. "Scrape off the burned part," he instructed his son.

"There's a hamburger from yesterday in the refrigerator. Can't I have that instead?" Mikey asked plaintively.

"Okay. Heat it up in the microwave," Bob grumbled.

"Thanks, Dad! Can I go watch television while I eat?"

"You might as well. Family unity's gone to hell around here."

Mikey whooped and went to retrieve his hamburger from the refrigerator. He heated it up and vanished into his room.

"Poor kid. His cholesterol will be as high as a kite and he'll die of malnutrition."

Lang was staring at the black pancakes. "If he doesn't starve first."

"I can't cook. She didn't marry me for my cooking skills. She should have found somebody who was a gourmet chef in his spare time."

"Why don't you hire a cook?" Lang suggested.

Bob brightened. "Say, that's an idea. We've got plenty of money, so why don't I? I'll start looking tomorrow." He stared at the black pancakes on his own plate and pushed them away. "Tell you what, I'll run down to the corner and get us a couple of Mama Lou's barbecue sandwiches and some fries, how about that?"

Lang grinned. "That's more like it." He paused. "While you're at it, you might tell Connie exactly why you don't like working mothers. If she understood, she might compromise."

"Her? Dream on. And I don't like talking about the past. Go

ahead," he suggested when Lang paused. "Tell me you ever said anything to Kirry."

Lang didn't have a comeback. He shrugged and walked away.

He spent a lazy two days with Bob and Connie and Mikey, trying not to notice the disharmony. If the couple hadn't each been so individually stubborn, things might have worked out better. But neither one was going to give an inch or compromise at all.

Before Lang left for San Antonio to see his new boss the following Monday, Bob had interviewed four women to housekeep and cook for the family. The one he favored was a Mexican-American girl who had beautiful black hair down to her waist and soft brown eyes like velvet. Her voice was seductive and she had a figure that made Lang's pulse run wild. This was going to mean trouble, he thought, but he couldn't interfere. His brother had to lead his own life.

Lancaster, Inc., was owned by a middle-aged man and his wife, a fashion-conscious socialite. Although public shares were issued, it was basically a family-held company, and Lang liked the owners at first sight. They were straightforward about his duties and salary, and they made him feel welcome.

He was introduced to his immediate staff, a veteran ex-cop and a woman who was ex-military, two very capable individuals who had been running the operation since the previous security chief left because he couldn't take the pressure.

"Couldn't stand the sight of blood," Edna Riley said with faint contempt. She looked at Lang curiously. "I hear you were CIA."

He nodded. "That's right."

"And before that?"

"I was a street cop on the San Antonio police force."

Edna grinned. "Well, well."

Tory Madison grinned, too. "Sure, I remember you," he said. "I retired about the same time you joined. But I couldn't stay quit. Inactivity was killing me. I can't keep up with the younger ones, but I know a few things that help keep the greenhorns out of trouble. I'm administrative, but that's okay. I like my job."

Lang smiled at him. "When I've had time to look over the operation, I may have some changes in mind. Nothing drastic," he said when they looked worried, "like sweeping the ranks clean and starting over, so don't worry about that, okay?"

They all relaxed. "Okay."

"But we do need to keep up with new methods in the business," he added. "I'm pretty up-to-date on that since I've just come back from the front."

"We'd love to have coffee with you and hear all about it," Edna murmured, tongue in cheek.

"Everything I know is classified," Lang said. "But I can sure tell you about weapons technology."

"Oh, we learned all about that by watching the latest *Lethal Weapon* movie," Edna informed him.

"Not quite." He glanced at the dilapidated coffee machine. "First thing we're going to do is replace that."

Edna spread-eagled her thin frame in front of it. "Over my dead body!" she exclaimed. "If it goes, I go."

Lang peered down at her. "Makes good coffee, does it?"

"The best," she assured him.

"Prove it," he challenged.

Her dark eyes sparkled. "My pleasure," she said, and proceeded to crank up the veteran machine.

Ten minutes later, Lang had to agree that they couldn't take a chance on a new coffeemaker being up to those standards. His co-workers chuckled, and decided that the new addition might not be such a pain, after all.

The next day, dressed in his best gray suit, red-striped tie and neatly pressed cotton shirt, Lang made a tour of the five companies under the Lancaster, Incorporated umbrella.

The first was Lancaster, Inc., itself, which owned and was located in a huge office complex that served as headquarters for several other San Antonio companies. There were ten security people, five day and five night, who looked after the safety of the various buildings. One did nothing but assure the safety of the parking garage adjacent to it, and inspected the parking permits of the complex's occupants. The others patrolled in cars and on foot, maintaining a high level of security.

He interviewed the personnel and found one particular man not at all to his liking. There was something about the security officer that disturbed him, more so when Lang caught him calling out a very personal remark to one of the women who worked in the building. Perhaps they were friends, because the woman smiled wanly and kept walking. But Lang remembered the incident later, when he was talking to the building's main security officer.

Two of the headquarters' offices located in this complex— one a canning concern and the other a meat packer—had been targeted by protestors from various radical groups, Lang was told by the main security officer, a man younger than Lang. Security was responsible for seeing to it that none of the tenants got hurt. Lang asked casually if the man had any problems with his personnel. There was a pregnant pause, and he told Lang that he'd had a complaint or two about one of the men, but he was keeping a close eye on him. Lang didn't like the sound of that.

Lang's second charge was a department store of vintage age, where two stories of fine clothing were under the care of two day-security people and one night guard. The younger of the three was a little cocky until he learned Lang's background, and then it was amusing to watch him backpedal and try to make amends.

The third of the businesses was a small garment company that manufactured blue jeans. It had only one security guard for day and one for night. Lang liked the night man, who was a veteran of the Drug Enforcement Administration. He'd have to make a point of stopping by one night to talk over old times with him.

The fourth company was a licensed warehouse where imported goods were brought and stored until they cleared customs.

And the fifth company under the umbrella of Lancaster, Inc.'s security network was a new and thriving company called Contacts Unlimited. It boasted six executives and ten employees in the Lancaster, Inc. office complex where Lang had started out investigating his security force that morning.

Lang spoke to the company president, Mack Dunlap, about any complaints he might have with the company's security. It was a follow-up to the talk he'd already had with the complex's main security official, who was under Lang's authority now.

"Not me," Mack, a tall balding man, said brightly. "But one of our vice presidents says that one of the day-security men made a very suggestive remark to her."

Lang's eyes narrowed. "Did he, now?" he asked. "I'd like a word with her. Naturally I'm going to take such complaints very seriously."

Mack's eyebrows went up. "That's new. Old Baxter, who had the job before you, just laughed. He said women should get used to that sort of talk. She had words with him, let me tell you."

"I can't do anything about Baxter, but I can promise you that a new yardstick will be used to measure our security people from now on."

Mack smiled. "Thanks. Uh, right down there, second door to the left. She's in this afternoon."

"I'll only take a minute of her time," Lang said with formal politeness.

He went to the door, not really noticing the nameplate, and knocked.

"Come in," came a poised, quietly feminine voice.

He opened the door and froze in the doorway.

She was dressed in an off-white linen suit with a pea green

blouse that just matched her eyes. Her blond hair was cut short around her face, curling toward high cheekbones and a bow-shaped mouth.

She was looking down at a spreadsheet, her thin eyebrows drawn into a slight frown as she tried to unravel some figures that had her puzzled.

"What can I do for you, Mack?" she asked absently, without looking up.

Lang's hand tightened on the doorknob. All the memories were rushing back at him from out of the past, stinging his heart, his mind, making him hoarse. Bob's grinning face flashed in his mind, and now he knew why his brother had reacted so strongly to news that Lang was going to work for Lancaster, Inc.

"I said..." Kirry looked up, and those green eyes went from shock to fascination to sheer hatred in a split second. She stood up, as slender and pretty as ever, but with a new maturity about her.

"Hello, Kirry," Lang said quietly, forcing himself to smile with careless indifference. "Long time no see."

"What is the CIA doing here?" she wanted to know.

Lang looked around. "What CIA?"

"You!"

"Oh. I'm not CIA. Well, not anymore," he replied. "I just went to work for Lancaster, Inc. I'm their new chief of security." He grinned from ear to ear at her discomfort. "Isn't it a small world!"

K irry sat back down, as gracefully as she could with her
heart breaking inside her body. She forced a smile,
almost as careless as Lang's.

"Yes," she said, "it is a small world. What can I do for you,
Lang?"

"Your boss says you've had some problems with one of our
security people."

"Oh."

He stuck his hands into his pockets. "Well?"

So he hadn't found out where she worked and come just to
see her. It was business. That shouldn't have disappointed her.
After all, it was five years ago when he stormed out of her life.
But it did disappoint her.

He wasn't smoking. In the old days, there had always been a
cigarette dangling from his fingers. She wondered why he'd

given it up. Perhaps they didn't let secret agents smoke or practice any other addictions that might put the job at risk.

"Mr. Erikson seems to find it amusing to make vulgar remarks to me," she said, easing down into her chair with assumed nonchalance.

"Tell Mr. Erikson to cut it out."

"I have. He can't understand why I should find it offensive. I am a woman, after all. Women were created, or so he says, for man's pleasure," she added meaningfully.

He pursed his lips. "I see. How old a man are we discussing?"

"He's somewhere near fifty, I guess."

"He should know better."

"I hope you'll make that clear. I came very close to filing charges against him yesterday."

"For what?"

She didn't like discussing it with Lang. She hesitated.

"We were friends once," he reminded her.

"He was making remarks about the size of my foundation garments and whether or not I wore black ones. Then he proceeded to say," she said, taking a breath, "that he'd buy me one if I'd put it on for him."

Lang didn't like that, and it showed. "I'll have to have a little talk with him. If it happens again, I want to know."

She met his eyes levelly. "If it does, I'll have him prosecuted. Nobody should have to take that kind of abuse just to hold down a job. This is a good job, too. I don't want to lose it."

"You won't." He turned back toward the door, his hand on

the knob, and looked back at her quietly. "How's your mother?" he asked.

"I have no idea," she replied coolly. "The last I heard, she and her fourth husband were living in Denmark."

He averted his eyes and left without a conventional goodbye.

Kirry unclasped her hands and discovered that they were cold and shaking. It had been a long time since she'd let her nerves affect her like this. Even finals every semester at college hadn't rattled her this badly. Of course, Lang was much worse than tests.

She tried to concentrate on her work, but her mind kept returning to the turbulent days before Lang had left town. She made a cursory examination of a new file, but she couldn't keep her mind on it.

She turned her swivel chair around and looked out the window. Lang had just left the building. He was getting into a late-model car with Lancaster, Inc., Security written on the side of it. His dark hair had the sheen of a raven's wing in the sun. She remembered how it had felt to touch it, to let it ripple through her fingers in the darkness of a parked car. So many years ago....

The buzzer distracted her. She picked up the receiver. "Yes?"

"It's me, Kirry. Betty," her friend said, identifying herself. "You really get results, don't you?" She laughed.

"What do you mean?"

"Our friend Erikson just got the boot. He mouthed off at Daddy Lancaster's new security chief about women being fair game for any man. His jaw is still dangling."

Kirry caught her breath. "Lang fired him!"

"Lang?"

"Lang Patton. The new security chief. I...used to know him, when I was younger."

"Ah, so that's how the wind blows."

"You didn't think I was going to take it much longer?" she asked.

"No. And I wasn't, either. All of us were sick of Erikson's in-nuendos. We're going to take you out to lunch. Just think, maybe Mr. Patton will send us somebody young and handsome and single."

"He'll probably send you an ex-marine with a sweet tooth." Kirry chuckled.

"Spoilsport. Listen, Erikson's pretty mad. You should steer clear of this area until he leaves."

"I'm not afraid of him."

"Well, you might be wise to avoid him, just the same. See you later."

Betty hung up and Kirry bit her lower lip. She hadn't wanted to cause trouble. Most men were polite and courteous. But Erickson had been menacing with his remarks and the way he looked at women. Kirry felt unclean when she had to pass him in the hall.

At first she'd thought that perhaps she was overreacting. After all, she'd just come from university, where men and women enjoyed an intellectual kinship that usually precluded sexist remarks on either side. But in the real world there were men still mentally living in an age when women were treated as sexual property. It had come as a shock to Kirry to find herself working in the same close area with a man who felt free to make suggestive remarks to any woman he chose.

Erikson had actually pinched Betty on the buttocks, and when she'd slapped him, he'd laughed and said wasn't that cute. Women always meant yes, even when they said no, he added.

Kirry could have told Lang a lot more than she had, but apparently he'd found out Erikson for himself. She felt both relieved and sick at the firing. Erikson had no family, but he was an older man and he might have a hard time finding another job. For that, she felt guilty. Even knowing that the man had brought it on himself didn't make her feel a lot better.

The phone rang and Kirry picked it up.

"Don't think you're going to get away with it, telling all those lies about me," Erikson's harsh voice informed her. "I'll get you. Count on it."

The receiver went down and Kirry felt a curl of real fear. Surely it was just bad temper. He'd get over it. But in the meantime, she was going to make sure that she never presented him with any opportunities to make his threat known. And perhaps she should mention it to Lang. Just in case.

That evening when she went home, she made sure that she left in broad daylight. There would be no more working late, she told her boss, until the threat was over, and Mack had agreed wholeheartedly.

It was a long walk from the parking lot into her apartment building. She looked around, but she didn't see anything out of the ordinary. She went inside, grateful that there was a security man even here, and quickly went up to her apartment on the second floor.

She'd decorated it with a lot of greenery and simple furniture. It was a lonely apartment, but very pretty, and she had her own little kitchenette. Not only that, there was a balcony. The balcony had been the drawing card when she settled here. It overlooked the Alamo in the distance, and she had a mesquite tree just outside it, with long feathery fronds of greenery trailing to the ground. She loved the tree and the view. She had a lounge chair out there, so she could laze in the spring sunlight.

After she changed into jeans and a loose-knit blouse, she fixed herself a cup of coffee and slid onto the lounger. The sun, late afternoon though it was, felt good on her face.

She remembered another spring afternoon, the day she'd realized that she was falling in love with Lang Patton. She'd been lazing away in the tree in her front yard in Floresville. She'd been just sixteen years old. The Campbell house in those days was just down the street from the Patton home place. Lang was out of school by then and working with the San Antonio police force, but he came home on weekends sometimes to visit his parents and his brother. He'd been going with a model named Lorna McLane, but they'd just broken up. He was alone now when he came home. Kirry was glad. She didn't like the superior way Lorna looked down her nose at people.

Kirry had always known Lang. He'd been like a big brother to her most of her life.

"Get down out of there before you kill yourself," he'd called up to her, grinning as he stood below in a black T-shirt and blue jeans. He was powerfully built and she loved to look at him. It made her tingle all over.

"It isn't against the law to climb trees," she informed him pertly, laughing. "Go arrest somebody else."

"I'm very happy where I am, thanks." He looked for footholds and handholds, and a minute later he was up in the next limb, leaning back against the big oak's trunk. "Here. Have a pear." He produced one from his pocket and retrieved his own from the other.

Lang had noticed her, too, that day. His eyes had been slow and bold on her long, tanned legs and the thrust of her breasts in the front-tied blouse she was wearing with her cutoffs. He hadn't made a move in her direction. But after that day, he'd teased her and their relationship had turned to friendship.

How long ago it seemed that Lang had made time to listen to her problems at school. Her mother was too busy getting married and divorced to pay Kirry much attention, and she had no other relatives. She gravitated toward the Patton place. Lang's mother had been dead for years. Nobody ever talked about her, least of all Lang. When Lang's father died suddenly of a heart attack, Kirry was there with quiet sympathy and compassion. She sat and held Lang's hand all during the funeral. When Bob and Connie's son Mikey had been born, Kirry had gone with

Lang to the christening. And all at once, Lang was everywhere she went....

The ringing of the telephone made her jump. She went to answer it and hesitated uncharacteristically. Surely it wouldn't be Erikson. Would it?

Her heart was pounding as she lifted the receiver.

"Kirry?"

It was Lang. She relaxed, but only a little. "Hi, Lang."

"I thought you should know that I fired Erikson this afternoon," he said quietly. "He was pretty mad. If he gives you any trouble, I want to know about it."

"He called me before he left," she returned. "He said he was going to 'get me.'"

There was a pause. "Did that frighten you?"

She smiled, and twirled the phone cord around her fingers. "A little."

"Really?" There was a smile in his voice. "The girl I used to know would have laid his head open with a baseball bat."

"My mother never cared about me enough to fight my battles. I had to grow up tough."

"I fought some of them for you," he reminded her.

"Oh, yes. You were my friend." The eyes he couldn't see were sad, full of bad memories. "I have to go, Lang."

"Wait."

"We have nothing to say," she replied sadly.

"I'm sorry you wouldn't read the letter I sent you, Kirry," he said after a minute.

"You didn't trust me," she reminded him. "You thought that I was a two-timing playgirl."

"I was crazy with jealousy," he replied. "Didn't you know that I'd cool down and come to my senses eventually?"

She laughed bitterly. "By the time you did, I'd stopped caring. I was dating a new guy at college and enjoying myself," she lied with finesse. Not for worlds would she tell him how it had really been when he refused to listen to her explanations.

Lang froze inside. He'd thought Kirry loved him. If she'd taken up with someone else so quickly, she couldn't have. It was an unexpected blow to his ego. "Then it was just as well that you refused to accept it."

"Was there anything else?" she asked politely.

"Yes. Let me know if you have any more contact with Erikson," he replied. "He's mixed up with a couple of the local outer-fringe elements. I think he's loopy."

"Nice word."

"Do you think so?" he said, grinning. "I'm thinking of buying the rights to it."

"I'll call you if I have any trouble. Thanks for checking, Lang."

"Sure."

She put down the receiver, idly caressing it as she thought about how it had felt to kiss Lang. Pipe dreams, she reminded herself. She couldn't afford to go that route again. It had really broken her up to lose him, especially since her mother had been in the throes of another divorce at the time. Her home life had been virtually nonexistent, and that was one reason she'd gone off to university without a protest. It seemed like a lifetime ago now. She had to make sure that it stayed that way.

Lang settled in at his hotel and went to work. Within a week he had a grasp on the security setup within the Lancaster organization, and he was confident that he could upgrade it to a more efficient level.

Kirry worried him, though. She'd been very cautious in her movements for a few days after Erikson was fired, but she'd suddenly grown careless. Today she was working late, and it was already dark. Lang knew for a fact that her parking lot would be deserted. He decided that in the interest of keeping her safe, he'd better check on her.

Sure enough, the parking lot *was* deserted, except for an older-model blue sedan with a familiar face in it.

Confrontation, Lang had found, was the best way to avoid real trouble. He pulled up beside the blue sedan and got out of his security car. He was wearing an automatic under his arm, a necessity in his new line of work. He hoped he wouldn't have to pull it.

"What are you doing here, Erikson?" Lang asked. "You're on private property."

Erikson, a thin, cold-eyed man, looked vaguely disconcerted by Lang's direct approach. "I'm enjoying the view."

"Enjoy it from another perspective," Lang suggested to him with a dangerous smile. "And in case you have any ideas about retribution, you'd do better to forget them. You may have had a few years experience in the army and as a security guard, but I was CIA for five years. I've forgotten tricks you never even learned."

The implied threat seemed to be enough. Without a reply, Erikson started his car and pulled out of the parking lot, giving Lang a resentful glare on the way.

Lang watched him drive out of sight before he turned and went into the building.

Kirry was at her desk, talking on the phone to someone who was obviously a client.

"You have nothing to worry about!" she was reassuring the party at the end of the line. "Honestly, it's all under control. That's right. We'll take care of everything. All you have to do is just show up, okay? Okay. We'll take good care of you. Yes. Yes. Certainly. Thank *you!* Goodbye."

She hung up with an audible sigh of relief and leaned back in her chair. Her green eyes found Lang in the doorway and she jumped, but not with fear. The impact of his presence had always caused that reaction, although she was usually able to hide it. Tonight, she was tired. Ten things had gone wrong since she walked in the door, and she'd spent the day untying tangles.

"I didn't think anyone was still in the building," she said, sitting up.

"I came by to check the parking lot," he said, shrugging his big shoulders. The soft fabric of his gray-and-tan sport coat moved with the action, and the bulge under his arm was visible.

"You're wearing a gun," she accused involuntarily.

His expression was unfamiliar as he looked at her. "I've worn a gun for a long time. You never used to pay any attention to it."

"That was before you signed on with the Company and went off to see how many bullets you could collect and still live," she said with a sweet smile that didn't reach her eyes.

"Don't tell me you cared, cupcake."

She lowered her eyes. She was wearing a neat gray suit with a pale pink knit blouse, and she looked fragile and very pretty. Lang couldn't drag his eyes away from her.

"I thought I did," she replied. "But you cured me."

He moved forward, cleared a corner of her cluttered desk and perched himself there. The movement pulled his slacks taut across his powerful thighs. Kirry had to fight not to look at them. She'd touched him there, once. She could still remember the impact of it, his hand guiding hers in the heat of passion, his hoarse moan when she began to caress him....

"Why are you still here?" he asked, breaking into her embarrassing thoughts.

"Business," she said, clearing her throat. "I'm a vice president. I'm in charge of arrangements when we have our clients make personal appearances. Sometimes things go wrong, like today."

"And you have to clean them up."

She smiled. "That's right."

"It's dark outside."

"Yes, I know. I have this, though." She produced a key chain with a small container of Mace.

He sighed gently. "Kirry, what if the wind's in the wrong direction when you use it? And do you realize how close you have to be?"

She flushed. "Well, I have this, too." She held up a canned "screamer."

"Great. What if there's nobody within hearing range?"

She began to feel nervous. If there was one thing Lang did know about, it was personal protection. "I don't like guns," she began.

"A gun is the last thing you need. Have you taken any self-defense courses at all?"

"No. I don't have time."

"Make time," he said bluntly.

He looked concerned. That disturbed her. She began to make connections. His presence here, his insistence on protection for her...

"Somebody was in the parking lot," she said astutely, her green eyes narrowed and intent on his hard face. "Erikson?"

He nodded. "I threatened him and ran him out of the parking lot. But I can't run him off a public street, you understand? There's no law against it."

"But that's called stalking," she said uneasily.

"And right now, it isn't against the law," he replied grimly.

She recalled cases she'd seen on television, mostly of angry ex-boyfriends or ex-husbands who stalked and finally killed women. The police could do nothing because a crime had to be committed before the police could act. And by the time that happened, usually it was too late for the victim.

"He wouldn't kill me," she stammered.

"There are other things he could do," Lang said distastefully.

Her lips parted as she let out a quick breath. "I don't believe this," she said. "I was only defending myself against an impossible situation. I never meant…"

"Do you think it would have gotten better if you'd ignored it?" he asked gently. "Men like that don't stop. They get worse. You know that."

She pushed back her wavy blond hair. "I know, but I never expected this." Her wide eyes sought his. "He'll quit, won't he? He'll get tired of it and go away?"

He picked up a paper clip on her desk and twisted it between his long, broad fingers. "I don't think so."

Her hands felt cold. She clasped them together, with a sick feeling in the pit of her stomach making her uncomfortable. "What can I do?"

"I'll try to keep an eye on you as much as I can," he began.

"Lang, that won't do," she said. "You can't watch me all the time. It wouldn't be fair to ask you to. I have to be able to take care of myself." She looked down at her slender body, remembering that Erikson was much taller and outweighed her by about sixty pounds. She smiled ruefully. "I can't believe I'll ever frighten anyone with self-defense, but I guess I'll see if I can find a class to join."

"Most of them are at night," he said. "Very few karate instructors can afford to operate a martial arts studio full-time."

"Surely there are Saturday classes," she said.

"Maybe." He smiled tenderly. "But nobody can teach you self-defense better than I can. And I can keep an eye on you in the process."

She averted her eyes. "That wouldn't be a good idea."

He studied her down-bent head with faint guilt. "We were friends once. More than friends," he reminded her softly. "Can't you pretend that nothing happened between us, just for a few weeks, until we can solve the problem of Erikson?"

Her eyes were wary, distrustful. "I don't know, Lang."

"We're different people," he said, pointedly. "If I'm not, why would I have left the Company?"

She frowned. "I hadn't thought about that. Why did you leave it? Even when you were younger, all you talked about was becoming an agent."

"I got my priorities straight," he returned.

"Did you really?" Her eyes narrowed. "How did you know that Lancaster, Inc., needed a new security chief?"

"A friend told me," he said. He wasn't going to tell her who the friend was. Not yet. She'd never liked Lorna, and the reverse was also true. Lorna didn't have any romantic designs on him, but he didn't want Kirry to know. Not yet.

His dark eyes slid over her face, down to her slender body and back up again. He wanted so badly to ask if there was a man in her life, but that was too much too soon. Besides, he had to be sure about his own feelings before he started trying to coax hers. He couldn't bear to hurt her again.

"I don't know if I'd be any good at martial arts," she began slowly.

She was going to give in. He knew it instinctively, and it delighted him. He smiled at her without mockery or malice. "Let's find out," he suggested.

Her breath sighed out. "All right. I'll have to fit it in with work, though. When?"

"Two nights a week, two hours a night," he said. "And you'll have to practice at home, too."

"This sounds like a lot of work," she mumbled.

"It is. But it's worth it. It could save your life."

"You're really concerned about Erikson, aren't you?" she asked. If Lang was worried, there was a cause for concern.

"Let's say that I'm staying on the right side of caution," he corrected. His big shoulders lifted and fell carelessly, and he smiled at her. "Humor me. For old times' sake."

She frowned and chewed on a fingernail while she pondered the anguish of being so close to Lang when she'd spent years trying to forget him.

"Or am I overlooking the obvious?" he asked suddenly, and his face changed, hardened. "Is there a man in the picture, someone who expects your company in the evenings?"

She wished with all her heart that she could answer him in the affirmative. Ridiculous, to pine for a man all that time, and after he'd treated her so shabbily. But he did look different. He wasn't the same hard-nosed, arrogant man who'd left Floresville to join the Company several years ago. He'd mellowed. The threat was still there, the ruthlessness, but there was a new tenderness, too.

"No, Lang," she said. "There's no one."

His eyelids flickered, but his face gave away nothing. "All right, then. Suppose we go shopping tomorrow when you get off work, and we'll begin tomorrow night?"

She frowned. "Shopping? For what?"

He chuckled. "Wait and see."

3

Kirry groaned as she looked at herself in the mirror. "Lang, it looks like pajamas," she moaned.

Lang opened the door to her bedroom and leaned against the doorjamb, his arms folded, to study her. She was wearing what they'd bought that afternoon; it was a white gi, the traditional karate uniform of white pants and a white top with one side folded over the other. For a beginner, the first gi was secured by a white belt. Colored belts had to be earned with new skills at each level of accomplishment, the highest of which was black.

Kirry looked fragile in the outfit, slender and not at all threatening. Her head was bent, her shoulders slumped, baring her nape where her hair was short in back.

"Let me explain something to you," he said disapprovingly, jerking away from the doorframe to stand just behind her. "The first rule of self-defense is to never look vulnerable. In the wild, an animal will never show illness, right up to the point of death, to prevent being attacked. It isn't much different with people. A potential attacker can spot an easy victim."

"How?" she asked, peering into his eyes in the mirror.

"You carry yourself as if you've already been beaten, didn't you know?" he asked gently. "Your shoulders are thrown forward. You keep your eyes and head down when you walk. You clutch your bag close—not a bad idea, but the way you do it is a dead giveaway."

"What should I do, walk down the street aiming karate chops at every tree I pass?" she asked.

He grinned. "Not a bad idea, if you can learn how to knock one down that way. Otherwise, pass on it. Listen, you have to walk as if you own the world and know full well that you can break every bone in an attacker's body. Sometimes just your posture is enough to ward off trouble. Stand up straight."

She did, giving her slender body an added elegance.

"Now hold your head up. Don't make long eye contact—a man might construe that as an invitation—but don't keep your eyes down as if you're afraid to look at people."

"I am, sometimes," she confessed with a faint smile. "People intimidate me."

"Right. That's why you're in a public relations job."

"I can bluff enough to do my job. It's after work that gives me problems," she said with a sigh, glancing critically at herself in the mirror. "I don't mix well."

"You always were shy, except with people you knew," he

recalled. His eyes dropped to her soft mouth, pink with lipstick, and he remembered it clinging hotly to him, pleading for more than any honorable man could give her. He hadn't wanted to get married, and Kirry was not the sort of girl he felt comfortable seducing outside of marriage. He'd talked about marrying her, and he knew that it was what she wanted, but things hadn't worked out. It had been a sad situation altogether, and he still wasn't proud of his solution. Instead of just telling her he didn't want to get married, he'd made a run for it. And his best friend had unwittingly given him the escape he needed. Kirry had been the one who'd suffered the most.

"Would you mind not looking at me like that?" she asked, lifting her green eyes to his dark ones in the mirror. "This is nice of you, to teach me how to take care of myself, but I'd rather if it wasn't... uncomfortable."

"Sorry," he said abruptly. "Back to what I was telling you," he said, changing the subject. "Walk with a purpose when you go out, as if you know exactly where you're going—even if you're lost. Keep your chin up, look at people, but just enough to let them know you see them. When you're going to your car, always have your keys in your hand, not in your purse. Look in the back seat and all around before you open the door and get in, and then lock it. Don't ever go into a dark parking lot alone at night, or to an automated bank teller. Women have risked that and turned up dead."

She shivered. "You're frightening me."

"I want to," he said. His dark eyes didn't blink. "I want you to understand how drastic the consequences can be."

"Women should be able to go wherever they like...."

"Don't hand me that," he said shortly. "So should men and kids, but they must abide by the same rules. It's that sort of world. Nobody is safe in a city alone after dark—man, woman or child. Men get attacked, too, you know, even if it isn't usually for the same reasons that women do."

"Our culture is sick," she remarked philosophically.

"Whatever. We deal with it as best we can. What I'm going to teach you will keep you alive, at least. Come on. Get your coat."

"But I thought we were going to practice here...." she began.

"Do you really like the idea of being thrown flat on your back on a wood floor?" he asked pleasantly.

She glowered at him. "What do you mean, thrown on my back?"

"Didn't I mention it? In karate, the first thing they teach you is how to fall correctly. You're going to be falling a lot, flat on your back and every other way."

"You're kidding!"

"Think so?" He handed her the lightweight car coat she wore on cool spring nights.

She put it on with a resigned breath. She hoped she could work with broken bones.

Lang had a friend who ran a gym. The man was middle-aged, but very muscular and fit, and he and Lang seemed to know each other from way back.

"Karate, huh?" the man, Tony, mused, studying Kirry. "Is she tough enough?"

Kirry drew herself to her full height and glared at him. "She sure is," she said with a jerk of her head.

He chuckled. "Good. If Lang teaches you, you'll need to be. Most of his students quit after the first night when he was on the police force, teaching it in his spare time."

Tony ambled away and Kirry followed Lang over to a long, thick mat on the floor of the gym near the wall. "I didn't know you taught karate," she remarked.

"You didn't know a lot of things that I did," he replied carelessly. "You know how to stretch, don't you?"

"Yes. I do that every morning."

"Do some stretches while I get into my gi."

He walked away with his black duffel bag, and Kirry settled onto the mat.

While the minutes ticked away, she became slowly aware of curious glances from some of the other occupants of the gym. Most of them were working out on machines. Two young women were lifting weights. Another was doing isometric exercises.

Loud noises from the other end of the gym drew her attention. She noticed several men gathered around a punching bag near where Lang had gone. Someone was doing kicks and spins with incredible speed and grace, which made Kirry dizzy. She paused in her own stretching just to watch him. He went up with a high jump kick and the gym vibrated as his foot connected with the hanging bag. He landed and turned, laughing, and she suddenly recognized him. It was Lang!

She stared at him as he spoke to the men and walked toward her. The gi fit him very nicely, loose though it was, giving an impression of great strength. Her eyes fell to his belt and she wasn't surprised to see that it was black, the hallmark of the highest ranks of skill in the sport.

"We'd better stop right now," she told him breathlessly, "because I'm never going to be able to do what you just did."

He grinned. "Not today, anyway. Limbered up, are we?"

She grimaced. "I guess." She eyed him warily. "Did you mean it, about making me fall?"

He nodded. "Don't worry. There's a right way to do it. You won't get hurt."

That was what he thought. Just being close to him made all her senses stir.

"Ready to get started?" he asked. His eyes fell to her watch. "Take that off," he said. "Never wear jewelry on the mat, it's dangerous."

"Oh. Sorry." She stripped it off and slipped it into the pocket of her coat. There were no rings to worry about. She hadn't worn a ring since Lang had given her a small emerald one for her birthday. She still had it, safe in a drawer, but she never put it on.

She went back to the mat. He taught her how to approach the mat, because there was ritual and reverence even in that. Then he taught her the bow to an opponent. Afterward, he taught her the rigorous disciplined stretches that preceded all karate lessons. She was worn-out from them before he took her back to the mat and showed her how to do left and right side break falls and back break falls. She spent the next hour falling down. Once she missed the mat and landed on her hip on the hard gym floor.

"You said it wouldn't hurt," she muttered, rubbing her behind.

"It doesn't, if you land where you're supposed to," he returned. "Watch where you're going."

"Yes, sir," she murmured with a mischievous glance.

"Fall down."

She groaned. "Which way?"

"Your choice."

"My choice would be a nice hot bath and bed," she told him.

He smiled. "Tired?"

She hesitated, then she nodded.

"Okay, tiger, that's enough for today. Attention." He called her to the beginning stance. "Bow."

She bowed. He left her to change back into his street clothes and she leaned against the wall, feeling pummeled.

They drove home in a contented silence.

"What kind of karate is it?" she asked. "During that last break one of the men mentioned that there are different kinds."

"You're studying tae kwon do," he told her. "It's a Korean form of martial art, one which specializes in kicks."

"Kicks."

"You've got the legs for it, and I don't mean that in an offen-

sive way," he added. "You have long legs, and they're strong
ones. Kicks are potentially much more dangerous than hand
blows."

"I felt the gym shake when you did that jump kick, just after
you put on your gi," she murmured demurely.

He chuckled. "I did nothing but practice when I first joined
the police force. While the other single guys were out chasing
women and drinking beer in their spare time, I was in the gym
learning how to do spin kicks."

"You're...amazing to watch," she said, searching for the right
word to describe the elegant skill of his movements.

He smiled. "Flattery?"

"Not at all!"

"If you work at it, you can do those same moves," he said.
"Plenty of women are black belts. In fact, I worked on a case with
another Company agent who had a higher rank than mine. She
taught me some new moves."

She closed up. "Did she?" she asked, glancing out the window.

He smiled to himself. The woman he'd just mentioned was a
retired army officer of sixty. He wouldn't disillusion Kirry by
passing that little bit of information along.

"Want to stop somewhere for a cup of coffee?" he asked.

"I can't drink it at night," she said apologetically. "I like to be
in bed by ten."

He scowled. "Woman, what kind of life are you living!"

Not much of one, she could have said. "Oh, I stay up if there's
a good movie on," she said defensively.

"You're twenty-two."

"Twenty-three," she corrected.

"Twenty-three, then," he returned. "You're too young to spend that much time alone."

"I didn't say I was always alone," she said stiffly. "I go out on dates!" And she did. The last one had been a newly divorced man who talked about his ex-wife and cried. The one before that was a bachelor of fifty who wanted her to move in with him. She hadn't had a lot of luck in her search for companionship, least of all with Lang, whose memory had stood between her and the most innocent involvement with anyone else.

Lang didn't know the true circumstances, though. He was picturing Kirry in another man's arms, and he didn't like it. His hands tightened on the steering wheel.

"You used to smoke," she remarked.

"Only occasionally," he replied. "It was interfering with my wind when I worked out, so I gave it up."

"Good for you," she murmured.

He pulled into the parking lot of her apartment building. A car pulled in behind them. A blue sedan.

Lang saw it and suddenly spun his own car around and headed straight for it. He didn't look as if he meant to stop, and the one glimpse Kirry got of his face made her cling to the seat for all she was worth.

Apparently the ruthless maneuver got the message across to Erikson in the blue sedan, because he burned rubber getting out of the parking lot and down the street.

"Damn him," Lang said icily when he'd parked the car. "Maybe I should just beat the hell out of him and put him in the hospital for a few weeks. That might get the idea across."

Kirry was unnerved. She looked at Lang warily. "No," she said. "You mustn't do that. He'd have you put in jail."

"He'd have a hard time keeping me there," he returned with a smile. "I have connections."

She twisted her small clutch bag in her hands. "I thought I was doing the right thing, telling you about him...."

"You did," he replied. "The days of men like Erikson are over. It's just going to take a few lawsuits to convince them of it."

"Stalkers kill people," she said, voicing her worst fear.

"Erikson won't kill you," he replied. "And after I've worked out with you for a few weeks, he'll regret it if he comes within striking range."

She smiled. "Think so? What am I going to do, fall on him?"

"You're pretty good at that," he said with an instructor's pride in his student.

"Thanks."

"I'll walk you up, just in case."

He got out of the car, locked it and came around to take her soft hand in his as they went into the building and stood waiting for the elevator.

Kirry should have pulled her hand away, but she couldn't manage. It brought back memories of their first real date. He'd held her hand then, too, and she could still feel the thrill of it.

"It was your first date, and you were so nervous that you were trembling when I took you home that night," he recalled, glancing down at her surprised face. "Am I reading your mind again?" he asked, lifting their clasped hands. "You aren't the only one with memories. They aren't all bad ones, are they?"

She didn't answer him. The elevator door opened and they stepped into the deserted conveyance. Lang pushed the button for her floor.

"We could have walked up, it's just the second floor," she reminded him.

"Stay out of stairwells," he replied seriously.

"Oh. Yes, I see."

"That goes for work as well as home," he added.

The elevator door opened and he walked her down to the end of the deserted corridor, where her apartment was. He noticed that she had her key in her hand when they got there. No fumbling for it in a purse or pocket. He smiled.

"Kirry?" he asked as she unlocked the door.

She hesitated, with her back to him.

"Do you want the conventional end to the evening?" he asked quietly.

Her hand clenched on the doorknob as she remembered how it felt to kiss him. "It wouldn't be wise."

"Probably not." He shoved his hands into his pockets and leaned his shoulder against the wall next to the door. His dark eyes slid over her profile. "What ever happened to Chad?" he asked.

Her eyes shot to his. "Don't you know? He was your best friend."

"Not after he broke us up," he replied tightly. "Or didn't anyone ever tell you that I knocked two of his teeth out?"

"No," she said. She huddled closer into her jacket, chilled by the look on Lang's face. "It was a little late, though, wasn't it?"

"Made me feel better," he said laconically.

His broad chest rose and fell under the soft knit shirt he was wearing. There was a dark shadow under it. He was hairy under his shirt. Kirry had delighted in burying her hands and her mouth in that soft thicket.

The sadness she felt was reflected in the eyes she lifted to his broad face. "You never really knew anything about me," she said suddenly, "except that you liked to kiss me." She smiled gently. "Maybe that's why you wouldn't listen when I told you that Chad had framed me."

He didn't answer her. His eyes fell to her mouth and lingered there until she moved restlessly and her hand turned on the doorknob.

"The first time I kissed you, you gasped under my mouth," he recalled quietly. "It surprised me that you didn't know what a deep kiss felt like."

She felt uncomfortable. Her green eyes glittered at him angrily. "There's no need to rub it in."

"If you hadn't been a virgin, our lives would have been a lot different," he continued. "I wanted you so badly that I couldn't think straight, but you were the original old-fashioned girl. No sex before marriage."

"I'm still the original old-fashioned woman," she told him

proudly. "My body is my business. I can do whatever I want to with it, and that includes being celibate if I feel like it."

"Nights must get real cold in winter," he chided.

Her eyebrows lifted. "I have an electric blanket, dear man, and no health worries. I sleep like a top. How about you?"

He didn't sleep well. He hadn't for years. His memories were of the violent variety and in the past few months, they'd become constant and nightmarish.

"I don't," he replied frankly.

"No wonder," she returned. "All those women!"

"Kirry…"

He couldn't deny it, of course he couldn't. She fought down the jealousy and smiled. "Thanks for the lesson."

He clamped down hard on his temper. "No problem," he replied after a minute. "We'll do it again in three days. Remember those stretches. Practice them."

Her mind darted back to Erikson in the parking lot, and she felt threatened. Her eyes showed it.

"Don't let him see that he's scared you," Lang said curtly. "Don't you dare let him know. Keep your chin up. Look at him, show him you aren't intimidated. Make sure you're with people when you leave the building, here or at work."

"Okay."

He smiled softly. "You're tough. Remember it."

"I'll try. Thanks, Lang."

"I'll be around. Let me know if you need me."

She nodded.

He pushed away from the wall and looked down at her almost hungrily before he turned and walked slowly back toward the elevator.

Kirry wanted to call him back. She knew the sight of that retreating back, because she'd lived with it all these years. It still hurt to watch him go. Nothing had changed at all.

When he got to the elevator and pressed the button he turned and caught her staring at him. He looked back, aching to hold her. He had a feeling that he was going to get postgraduate courses in self-denial before this Erikson business was through.

Kirry lifted her hand in a halfhearted wave and went into her apartment, closing the door and locking it behind her. She had to stop wanting Lang to kiss her. It would be the same old mess again if she encouraged him. This time, she was going to be strong.

That attitude lasted all night long. It got her to work and into the building, despite the sight of that damned blue sedan sitting on the street in front of her apartment building and following her all the way to Lancaster, Inc. She looked straight at Erikson without a smile or a flinch as she went into the building, and it seemed to disconcert him. Lang had been right, she thought as she went into her office. It really was working! She felt better than she had since the ordeal had begun.

Kirry was promoting a public seminar for a local business firm that specialized in interior design. She'd arranged for a special appearance by a famed European designer at one of San

Antonio's biggest malls, and coordinated it with an amateur competition for local citizens who'd done their own decorating. The European designer was to judge the entries and Kirry had bought advertising on local television stations and newspapers, all of which had promised to send reporters to cover the event.

It was time-consuming and maddening to get all the details to fit together, though, and by the time Kirry had them finalized, she was a nervous wreck.

It didn't help that when she went out to her car that infernal blue sedan was sitting there like a land shark, with Erikson in the front seat glaring at her.

Furious, she went back into the building and called the police. She explained the problem to a sympathetic officer on the desk.

"Is his car in the parking lot of your business, Miss Campbell?" he asked politely.

"Well, no. It's on the street across from the parking lot."

"A public street?"

She grimaced. "Yes."

There was a pause. "I don't like saying this, but I have to. There's no law against a man sitting in his car, no matter what threats he might have made. If he hasn't actually assaulted you, or said anything to you, there isn't a single thing we can do."

"But he's stalking me," she groaned.

"The law needs to be changed," he told her. "And it will be. But right now, the law says that we can't touch him. On the other hand, if he makes a single obscene remark to you, or touches you in anyway..."

"He's been a military policeman and a security guard," she said dully. "I expect he knows the law backward and forward."

"Yes, ma'am, I'm sorry, because I imagine you're right. I wish we could do something."

"So do I. Thanks for listening."

She hung up and sat with her head down. She could call Lang, but she knew what he'd do. If Erikson could get Lang arrested, he'd have a clear field. She didn't want that. And he hadn't harmed her, yet. She had to keep her emotions under control. If she panicked and did something stupid, she'd be playing right into his hands.

But what could she do? She grabbed her purse and went back out to the parking lot. He was still there. She didn't look at him this time. She got into her car, locked the doors, started it and pulled out onto the street.

A glance in her rearview mirror told her that he was following her.

Well, she had a surprise in store for him this time. She'd spotted a police car cruising downtown. She deliberately pulled up beside it and watched as Erikson fell back. So he wasn't quite as confident as he made out. That was useful information.

When the police car turned, Kirry turned behind him. She followed him through the downtown area, with Erikson trailing behind. Then, without warning, she swung the wheel and turned down an alley, cut through and came in behind Erikson.

He was looking around for her, but he didn't seem to see her. Good. She had him where she wanted him.

He turned onto a secondary street and Kirry turned the other way. She'd lost him, just temporarily. It was a relief to know that she could do even that.

She went back to her building, parked the car in her spot, and rushed up to her apartment, quickly securing the door. *That's one for me, Erikson,* she thought.

A few minutes later, the telephone rang. She let the answering machine catch it, certain that it was an irate Erikson. But the voice on the other end was Lang's.

"Are you there, Kirry?" he asked.

She picked up the receiver and turned off the machine. "Yes, I am. Hi, Lang," she said.

"What the hell were you trying to do out there, incite him to violence?" he asked angrily. "You can't play games with a madman, Kirry!"

"You saw me!" she exclaimed.

"Of course I saw you," he muttered.

"But I didn't see you!"

"That's the first rule of shadowing someone—don't be seen."

She smiled. "I didn't know you were looking out for me. Thanks, Lang!"

"I won't always be there. I can't always," he said, "so please exercise some common sense and stop trying to outfox Erikson. He's no fool. He'll realize what you did, and it will make him angrier. Don't you understand that his sort can't bear being beaten by a woman? He takes it as a challenge to his manhood!"

"Well, poor him. What about me?" she stormed. "Do I have no rights at all? I hate having him follow me around and stare at me," she added furiously. "I called the police, and they said there wasn't a thing they could do. Not a thing! What if he kills me? Can they do something then?"

"You're getting too uptight, Kirry," he said. "Calm down. Use your mind. If he was going to hurt you, he'd have done it when I fired him. He's only trying to wear you down and freak you out, to make you hurt yourself or make a fool of yourself."

"That isn't what you said..."

"I didn't know," he replied. "Not at first. I'm still not certain enough to risk your life by guessing which way he'll jump. We'll handle it. I won't let him hurt you."

The calm confidence in his voice soothed her badly stretched nerves. "I know that."

"And when I'm through with you, you'll be able to take care of yourself. We'll have another lesson tomorrow night. Okay?"

She sighed. "Okay."

"Get some sleep. I'll be in touch."

He hung up and she smiled, thinking that maybe it would work out all right. She was just jumpy, that was all.

The phone rang, and she laughed as she picked it up.

"Forgot something, did you?" she teased.

"Yeah," a cold, too familiar voice replied. "I forgot to tell you that tricks like you played on me tonight won't work again."

"Leave me alone, Erikson!" she snapped. "You have no right...!"

"You got me fired, you snooty little tramp," he said. "No woman does that to me. I'm through playing games."

"Listen to me, you lunatic…!" she yelled back, but the line was already dead.

She put the receiver down with a slam, her face hot with temper. Damn him! What was she going to do?

4

Kirry had never felt so threatened in her life. She left her apartment the next morning and found Erikson right in the front of the building, sitting in that blue sedan.

With a fury she couldn't contain, she picked up a rock from the landscaped cacti and flung it at the car with all her might. He ducked, shocked, but her pitching arm wasn't what it should have been. The rock fell short. By golly, she promised herself, the next one wouldn't. She picked up three big rocks and ran toward his car.

Before she could get started, he roared off, leaving her standing there, shaking. She fought for control of herself and slowly dropped the rocks, brushing off her hands. The man was crazy, she thought bitterly. Crazy! And she couldn't do a thing to stop him!

She got into her car and locked it and went to work. She knew the blue sedan would be sitting there, on the street, and sure enough, it was. She was shaking as she got out and locked her own car and started toward the building. There were no rocks in the landscaping here, nothing that she could throw at him. He smiled at her from cold eyes as she walked up the sidewalk toward her office building.

"You can't stop me from sitting here, and there aren't any rocks, baby," he called to her.

She stopped, her knees vibrating from fear and temper. She looked straight into his eyes. "If you don't stop now, you'll wish you had," she said quietly.

"Oh, yeah? What you gonna do, big bad girl?" he challenged.

"Wait and see, Mr. Erikson," she said, and smiled as if she had every confidence that he was going to wind up wearing prison blues.

She turned and walked into the building without looking back.

Mack's eyes narrowed as she passed him. "I saw him sitting there when I came in," he said. "I've phoned the new security chief and Mr. Lancaster. They're working on something."

"A bomb?" she asked pleasantly. "Because that's what it may take. He won't stop. The law can't touch him, and he knows it."

"Isn't your mother married to some rich person overseas?" Mack asked.

She didn't like talking about her mother. "She's married to a wealthy English nobleman."

"Well, couldn't he hire you a hit man?" he asked.

She burst out laughing. "Oh, for God's sake, will you stop watching those mob movies?" she mumbled, walking off into her own office.

"It's worth a thought!" he called after her.

She closed the door.

It was a busy day. She didn't go out for lunch, choosing instead to have one of the other women bring it to her. If Erikson wanted to sit out there and bake in his car all day, let him. She was going to try pretending that he was invisible. Perhaps Lang had been right—if Erikson meant to hurt her, he'd have done it by now. She just had to keep her nerve until he got tired of watching her and gave it up.

Lang was waiting for her when she got to her apartment. For once, Erikson hadn't followed her home. But she knew that he was out there somewhere, watching, always watching.

"Get your gi and let's go," Lang said as they reached her apartment. "I'm taking you out to dinner before we go to the gym."

"You don't have to…"

"Just a hamburger, Kirry, not a five-course meal," he said curtly. "There are some things we need to talk about."

"Okay." She got her things from the closet and turned on her answering machine.

He held her bag while she locked up the apartment. He seemed very preoccupied and not a little concerned. He hardly said a word all the way to a nearby hamburger joint, where they nibbled burgers and fries and drank coffee.

"You're worried, aren't you?" she asked.

He nodded. He sipped coffee, and his dark eyes narrowed over the cup as he studied her. "I had a friend of mine do some hard digging into Erikson's past. He was arrested for killing a man while he was an MP. He was acquitted, but people were generally sure that he did it. It was a racially motivated incident."

"Oh, boy," she said heavily.

"It gets worse," he added. "He's covered his tracks pretty good, or he'd never have gotten a job as a security officer. He's been in jail three different times on assault charges that were dropped because the witnesses refused to testify. The victims were women," he added quietly. "Young women. Two of them claimed that he raped them, but they were too afraid of him to go to court."

Kirry felt her face turning white. She wasn't a fearful person as a rule, but this was an extraordinary circumstance. She put down the rest of her half-eaten hamburger and fought to keep what she'd already eaten down.

"Your mother lives in Europe," he said. "I know you two don't get along, but it would benefit you to go over there and visit her for a few weeks until I can get something done about Erikson."

"Run away, you mean?" she asked. "You're the second person today who's mentioned my mother, but Mack asked if her husband couldn't hire a hit man to deal with my problem."

He pursed his lips and his eyes twinkled. "What a magnificent suggestion."

"Stop that. You were a government agent."

"So I was, dash the luck." He leaned back in his chair and searched her face. "You won't go to Europe?"

She shook her head. "I'm not running. He's not going to make a coward out of me, no matter what he's done in the past."

He smiled. "You always did have guts, Kirry," he said, chuckling.

"Too many to suit you right now, huh?" she teased.

He caressed the paper cup that held a mouthful of warm coffee. "If you won't run, how about a compromise?"

"What did you have in mind?"

"Safety in numbers."

"I won't live at the YWCA," she said, outguessing him.

"That wasn't exactly what I had in mind."

She hesitated. She was doing it again; reading his mind. "You want me to move in with you. You're very sweet, Lang, but I couldn't...."

"I don't want to move in with you," he said bluntly. "I've explained the situation to your apartment manager, and he's giving me the apartment next door to you," he said calmly.

"Oh." She felt chastened. He made it very clear that living with her was not something he wanted to do. Maybe it wouldn't have been a good idea, but it hurt a little to think that he wouldn't even consider it.

"If you moved in with me, nobody would care," she said, surprising herself. "People don't sit in judgment over the moral values of their fellow man anymore."

"Want to bet?"

She felt and looked irritated. "All right, then, move in next door. I don't want you in my apartment, anyway. You'd seduce me," she accused, and was amazed that she could joke about it.

"You wish," he countered dryly. "I'm very particular about my body. You might have noticed that I keep it in rare good condition, and I'll tell you flat that it's in great demand by women. I don't share it with everyone who asks."

Her eyebrows lifted and her eyes twinkled. "You don't?"

His broad shoulders lifted and fell. "It's a dangerous practice these days, sleeping around," he reminded her with a quiet smile.

She smiled back. "Yes, I know. That's why I don't do it."

The smile was still there, but there was something somber in his dark eyes. "Ever come close?" he asked very softly.

She hesitated, and then shook her head. "Only with you, that one time," she said involuntarily, and her eyes flickered with painful memories before they fell.

He slid his hands deep into his pockets. He remembered, as she did, the wonder of that night. Nothing in his life before or since had ever equaled it, as relatively innocent an experience as it had been. Because he knew in his heart that he wasn't ready for marriage, he'd been too honorable to seduce a woman as innocent as Kirry, although their intimacy had been devastating just the same.

Then the very next day, Chad had dropped his bombshell and the relationship had shattered forever.

"You sit pretty heavy on my conscience sometimes," he said unexpectedly.

Her eyes lifted to his. "That's a shocker," she murmured. "I thought I was just one in a line."

"Fat chance." His gaze slid over her slowly, boldly. "I suggested that we get engaged, but I didn't really want to get married and you did. That was the real problem. I guess that's why I believed Chad, and not you."

"That's what my mother said."

"Well, she is astute every now and then," he observed.

"It was the only time in our lives that she really tried to act like my mother," she reminisced. "I needed her, and she was there. Even if it was a fairly innocent thing, it hurt once it was over."

"Did you think I got away scot-free?" he asked curiously.

She shrugged. "You wanted out and you got out."

"I didn't want to get married," he repeated. "That didn't mean I wasn't involved emotionally. It hurt me, too."

"That's hard to imagine," she said. "You never took anything seriously, least of all me."

"You'd be surprised." He looked at her intently before continuing. "The apartment I'm getting isn't very large, but I like the view. And it's convenient to yours, if Erikson tries anything."

She didn't like to think about that. Knowing what she'd learned about the man made her very nervous. "Couldn't we manage better if you moved in with me?" she said, thinking out loud. "I have two bedrooms and I can cook."

"I can cook, too," he volunteered, ignoring her offer. "And I don't have a phobia of vacuum cleaners. This last one I bought has lasted a whole month."

"A month!"

"Well, the damned things are like elephants. When you drag them around by the trunk and get them hung on furniture, and jerk real hard…it pulls their little trunks off!"

She laughed. He was as incorrigible as ever. He made her forget Erikson, even if just for a little while.

"Feel like helping me move tonight?"

"If we'll have enough time, I guess so." She had visions of lugging furniture up on the elevator as she toyed with her napkin. "Is there someone who'd mind if you stayed in my apartment?" she prompted, curious about his reasons for refusing.

"A woman, you mean?"

She nodded.

"No," he said gently. "There isn't anyone."

"I see."

"Probably not." He chuckled. "Finished? Let's go fall on a mat for a couple of hours."

"I'm still sore from the last time," she groaned.

"And we haven't even gotten to the bag, yet." He sighed. "You'll have to take more vitamins."

"It sure does look like it," she agreed grimly.

The side and back break falls went on forever, but this night he began to teach her the hand positions as well. The more she learned about economic movement, the more fascinating it became. She could understand how people loved the sport. There were several women in the gym this particular night, being taught a self-defense class by Tony, the man who managed the gym.

"They're doing a lot more than we are," she said pointedly to Lang while she was catching her breath.

"Sure they are. It's a two-week class. He has to get through a lot of material. And it's just basic stuff, like how to bring a high heel down on an instep or put a knee in a man's groin. You're learning a lot more, and it will take longer."

"Oh, I see."

"You're a promising pupil, too," he had to admit. "You're taking to it like a duck to water."

"Why didn't you ever show me any of this years ago, when we were together?" she asked.

He searched her curious eyes. "Because it was hard enough to keep my hands off you. A class like this, with constant touching, would have put me right over the edge."

Her eyebrows arched. "But you never wanted me." She blurted out the words. "Only that once...."

He moved closer, so that his voice wouldn't carry, so close that she could feel the strength and heat of his body. "I wanted you night and day," he said huskily. "You were too innocent to notice."

"I must have been," she agreed. "But it doesn't seem to bother you now."

"I'm older," he replied. "And a good deal more experienced."

Her eyes went cold. "Of course."

He turned away. The jealousy he saw in those green eyes made his body ache. She still felt possessive about him, but that didn't mean she still cared. He had to remember that, and not read too much into her reactions.

"Let's try this again."

He positioned her on the mat and invited her to use one of the hold-breaking positions on him. She went through the motions smoothly, but she couldn't get him onto the mat. He countered every move she made, laughing.

"That's not fair, Lang," she panted, pushing. "You won't co-operate."

"Okay, go ahead. Throw me." He relaxed, standing still.

She put her whole heart into it, stepping in with one leg, tripping with the other, pushing and pulling until she broke his balance and put him down. But she underestimated her own stability, and in the process, she went down heavily on top of him.

"You aren't supposed to fall *with* the victim," he instructed.

She was too winded to move momentarily. One of her legs was between both of his, her breasts flattened on his chest, her hands on either side of his head. It was a surprisingly comfortable position, if she'd been a little less aware of the intimacy of it.

"Could you help me up?" she asked breathlessly.

"Why not? You've certainly helped me up," he said with a blatant sensuality that brought a blush to her face when he shifted and made the point very clear.

"Lang!" she gasped.

He chuckled with pure delight as she scrambled off his body and got to her feet, red faced.

"Well, fortunately for us both, these jackets are loose and hip length," he said as he rose to tower over her.

"You're horrible!" she exclaimed, pushing back strands of damp blond hair from her eyes.

"You might consider it a form of flattery," he remarked. "Actually this condition isn't as easy to create as you might think. Not with other women, at least...."

"I want to go home," she said stiffly.

"Suit yourself, but you're going to miss the best part. I was going to teach you how to deal with a kick."

"You can do that another time," she said, fighting for composure.

"I was only teasing, Kirry," he said gently.

She let out a long sigh. "I'm not laughing," she muttered.

"Get your stuff and we'll drop by my apartment and get my stuff."

She hesitated. "Maybe he'll give it up."

He shook his head, and there was weary wisdom in his eyes. "Not a chance."

Lang's apartment was on the sixth floor of an old downtown hotel, and the decor was Roaring Twenties. It was dark and cramped, and Lang's belongings barely filled one suitcase.

"That's all?" she asked uneasily, lifting her eyes to his when he'd changed in the bedroom and came out with one suitcase and a long suit bag.

"That's it," he agreed. "I travel light."

"But you must have more than that!"

"I do. It's at Bob and Connie's place."

"Oh, of course. I forgot. You wouldn't want to carry heirlooms around the world with you."

"Speaking of heirlooms," he said slowly, "what did you ever do with the emerald I gave you?"

She averted her eyes. "Do you really think I'd keep something that reminded me of you, after the way you dumped me?"

"Yes, I do," he said.

She glared at him. "I meant to throw it away."

"I wouldn't have blamed you," he assured her. He smiled. "But I'm glad you didn't hate me enough to actually do it."

"It's a pretty ring," she commented.

"But you don't wear it."

"It's part of the past. I wanted to start over. I went to university and when I came out, with a major in public relations, I walked right into this job. I've been very lucky."

"You're alone," he remarked.

"I wanted it that way," she said shortly. "When I'm ready, I'll start looking for a husband."

"Have anyone in mind?" he asked carelessly, gathering his stuff.

"Mack," she said triumphantly.

He raised an eyebrow and grinned. "Do tell."

"Mack's settled and financially secure, and good company."

"You'd shrivel up like a prune if he touched you," he scoffed. "I've seen the way you draw your legs up when he comes close."

"You have not!"

"Kirry, you don't know a damned thing about modern surveillance techniques, do you?" he asked dryly. "Maybe that's good. I'd hate to make you inhibited when you dance around your bedroom in the nude."

She gasped audibly and went scarlet. "You Peeping Tom!"

"Accidental, I swear it," he said, holding up a hand. "It was the mirror. I had the camera just a little too far to the left...."

She aimed a blow at him, and he sidestepped just in time.

He laughed delightedly. "I thought you were spectacular," he said deeply. "All pink and mauve and blond. A nymph caught cavorting among the ferns. I didn't sleep all night long."

She glared at him. "I hate you."

"Kirry," he said softly, "I didn't see much that I haven't already seen before. I know, you don't like remembering that, but it's true."

"If I'd known what was going to happen later, that you'd believe those sick lies of Chad's...!"

"You'd never have let me touch you. I know that," he replied, his voice quiet and somber.

She wrapped her coat closer around her gi. "I'm ashamed of that night, anyway."

That stung. "I can't imagine why," he said matter-of-factly. "We were engaged. Most engaged people make love, and it isn't as if we went all the way."

"They make love when they actually plan to get married. That's why you always held back before, wasn't it, because you never had any intention of marrying me?"

"Once or twice, I thought about it," he confessed. "You were hungry for that damned ring, for the proposal. I humored you, because you wanted it that badly. But I knew that I'd be no good as husband material until I got the wanderlust out of me. I tried to tell you that, but you were so young."

"Young and stupid," she agreed. "And desperately in love."

He averted his eyes. "In love, hell," he said curtly. "You wanted to sleep with me."

"Of course I did, but it was much more than that," she argued.

"You were only eighteen," he returned, moving toward the door. "It's ancient history now, anyway, and we have more important things to think about."

"Sure." She opened the door for him, refusing to look up.

He went out, let her move past him and then turned off the lights and locked the door. Later, he'd have a talk with the manager about his brief absence, to make sure the man knew that he was only leaving temporarily. He'd pay the rent up in advance, too, just in case. With any luck, Erikson was going to be a bad memory in the near future.

Kirry held his clothes bag while he unlocked the apartment next to hers and opened the door. It was smaller than hers, but not much. It had a better view than hers did of the Alamo, and it looked as though it had just been decorated. It was done in greens and browns, and somehow it suited Lang.

"Yes, I like this," he remarked as he looked around. He glanced back at her. "We live close enough to share kitchen duty. You could cook one night and I could cook the next."

"That would be nice," she said.

"But you can't sleep over," he added sternly. "No use begging, it won't work. I don't allow women into the bedroom. It's too hard to get them out."

She smiled faintly. "I'll bet it is."

His eyebrow jerked. "Want to find out why?" he asked sensually.

"I have a pretty good idea," she replied, dropping her eyes. "You're a hard act to follow."

He turned back toward her with his hands deep in his pockets. "So are you," he replied honestly.

Her eyes scanned his broad face and she had to bite down hard to keep from begging him to kiss her. That way lay disaster, she reminded herself. She knew better than to encourage Lang.

She turned. "Well, I'll let you get settled. I'm tired and I want to go to bed."

He followed her to the door and opened it for her. "I've already checked out this place," he said. "The bedroom where you sleep is on the other side of the wall of mine. If you rap on the wall, I'll hear you. I don't sleep heavily, ever."

"Thanks. That's nice to know."

"Wear a gown, will you?" he asked on a groan. "I have to keep you under surveillance for your own protection. Don't make it any harder on me than you have to."

She glared at him. "I'll wear body armor, in fact," she said with a curt nod of her head. "Good night, Lang."

"Sleep well."

"I want a nice hot bath and…" She hesitated, her eyes shooting to his.

He sighed with resignation. "Okay, I'll cut the camera off when I hear water running, will that do?"

"You don't need a camera in the bathroom!" she exclaimed.

"That's odd, the last man we protected said the same thing," he told her frankly. "We got some very interesting pictures of him and his lady…."

"How is it that you're still alive?" she asked, exasperated.

"Not for lack of effort by irate taxpayers, that's for sure," he said with twinkling eyes. "Sleep well, little one. I'll be as close as a shout if you need me."

"You'll get a shout if you don't turn those cameras off," she informed him.

"Spoilsport," he muttered.

"I don't watch you take baths," she assured him.

He didn't smile as she expected him to. His dark eyes held hers until she felt her knees buckle. "Want to?" he asked softly.

5

She glowered at him. "Fat chance," she said smartly. He shrugged. "Your loss," he informed her with dancing eyes. "Keep the door locked."

She gave him a speaking look.

"Overkill, huh?" he teased as he went to the door and opened it. "How about riding in with me in the morning?" he suggested. "I can guarantee you won't see your blue sedan buddy while I'm around."

"He might take that as cowardice," she said simply.

"Listen," he replied, leaning back against the door, "you can push your body just so far before it gives out on you. Stress is dangerous. Don't let it get to the point that your nerves are shot. If you go in with me, it will take some of the pressure off. Don't you even realize how tense you are lately?"

She felt the coldness of her own hands with irritation. "Yes,

I know, but I don't want to make him think I'm afraid, even if I am."

He smiled. "He won't. He'll assume that I've taken you over. It's the way that kind of man thinks."

"Well, I guess I could ride with you," she said. "As long as you don't really try to take me over."

His dark eyes narrowed and wandered over her as if they were caressing hands. "Could I, Kirry, if I worked at it?" he asked, and there was something unfamiliar in the glint of his eyes.

"Sorry, I'm immune," she replied pertly.

"To measles, maybe," he agreed. "But not to me. You still blush when I look at you, after all these years."

"Skin hysteria," she countered. "My pores are all allergic to you."

He chuckled. "Remember when we went to the park that time, and wound up with six lost little kids in tow? They wanted to know why you had freckles across your nose and I told them it was because you were allergic to ice cream."

"And they almost cried for me." She smiled back. "Oh, Lang, we had such good times." The expression in her eyes became sad. "You were my best friend."

He winced. "And you were mine. But several years ago, I was a bad marriage risk. You must have known it. There was so much I wanted to do with my life, things I couldn't have done with a family."

"Yes. Like joining the CIA." She dropped her gaze to his broad chest, because she didn't want him to see the remnants of the terror in them. She hadn't known exactly where he was for years, except when Connie and Bob, with whom she was still friends, let slip little bits of information about his work. She'd worried and watched the whole time, afraid that he was going to be killed, that he'd come home in a box. The reality of seeing him again that first day he'd come to work for Lancaster, Inc. had knocked her legs out from under her. She was still reeling from the impact of knowing that he'd given up the old life. And wondering why he had.

"Kirry?" he asked softly, interrupting her memories.

"What?"

He shook his head. "You weren't even listening, were you?" he mused.

"I was thinking about how it was while you were away," she said involuntarily, scanning his eyes. "I read about covert operations in the newspapers and wondered if you were in the middle of them, if you were all right." She laughed. "Silly, wasn't it?"

His face hardened. "That was what I wanted to spare you."

"You wanted to spare me the fear?" Her green eyes wandered over his broad face. "And you thought you had. Of course, I stopped loving you the minute you walked away from me, right?"

He leaned back heavily against the wall. "Right," he said doggedly. "You hated me when I left."

She smiled sadly. "I thought I did," she agreed. "But it wasn't that easy to put you in the past, Lang. It took a long time. There were so many memories. Almost a lifetime of them." She turned away. "I guess it's different for men. It's only physical with you."

"Why do you say that?"

"It's true. Men think with their glands, women with their hearts."

"That's stereotyping," he accused. "Men feel things as deeply as women do."

"You wanted me, but you couldn't bring yourself to do anything about it," she said. "If you'd loved me enough, you couldn't have walked away."

"You let me walk away," he said shortly. "You could have opened that damned letter I sent you!"

"Did it say something besides goodbye?" she asked, her voice harsh. "I thought it was another accusation, that you figured you hadn't said enough about my lack of character and morals."

He stuck his hands into his pockets. "I knew about Chad by then. I'd had time to get my priorities straight."

"I didn't know that," she reminded him. "All I knew was that when you left, you held me in contempt and never wanted to see me again. You said so—explicitly."

His eyes narrowed with painful memory. "I'd never had to handle jealousy before," he said. "It was new to me. Besides that, I felt betrayed. Chad was my best friend."

"Oh, why rehash it?" she muttered, turning away. "You wanted a way out and he gave you one. That's it in a nutshell. I hope you enjoyed your stint with the government, Lang. What I can't understand is why you gave it up and came back."

His dark eyes slid over her hungrily. "Can't you?"

She ignored the caress in his voice. "I'm tired," she said over her shoulder. "I'll see you in the morning."

"That you will." He opened the door. "And you're riding in with me, whether you want to or not." He closed the door on her openmouthed expression.

She picked up a vase and almost—almost—flung it at the closed door. But it would only mean a cleanup that she was too tired to do. Arguing with Lang wasn't going to change anything, and she didn't have enough nerve left to dwell on a dead past.

She started past her answering machine and noticed that it was blinking. She didn't want to listen to the messages, because one of them was probably Erikson. But her job sometimes infringed on her free time, because clients often called at night when they had more time to talk. She couldn't afford to ignore the calls.

Grimacing, she pushed the Replay button.

The first message was from Mack, reminding her that he was bringing in a new client for her to work with the next morning and to be on time. The second was a wrong number.

The third, as she'd feared, was Erikson. "One night, your bodyguard won't be close by, and I'll get you." He purred. "What are you going to do then, Your Highness?"

The line went dead. She took out the tape and replaced it with another one. That nasty little remark might come in handy in court if Erikson made a wrong step. She slipped it into a drawer and went to bed, to toss and turn all night.

* * *

When Lang rang her doorbell the next morning, she was dressed in a neat lavender dress with a patterned scarf. He was wearing a gray sport coat with tan slacks and a red-and-white striped shirt. He looked very nice, but she pretended not to notice.

"Here," she said, handing him the tape from her answering machine. She told him what it was.

He slipped it into his pocket with cold eyes. "He'll overstep one day soon," he promised her. "And when he does, I'll be right there waiting."

"He's sick, isn't he?" she asked.

"Sick, or just plain damned mean," he replied. He waited while she locked her door and escorted her out to his car in the parking lot.

"Wait a minute," he said, holding her back before she could open the door.

He went around and did a quick check of the car, even under the hood. Satisfied, he opened the door and helped her inside.

"What was that all about? You don't think he'd go so far as to blow up your car?" she asked.

He shrugged as he pulled out into traffic. "Caution is worth its weight in gold sometimes, and you never know which way a man like that is going to jump."

"I see."

He glanced at her with a smile. "Don't look so worried. I can defuse a bomb."

"Can you really?"

He nodded. "If it's a simple one. There was this case in Europe, when we were…" He hesitated. "Well, that's classified. But I had to defuse a bomb, just the same."

"Is that something they taught you?" she asked, curious.

He chuckled. "No. It's something I learned the hard way."

Her eyes were saucer-big. "The hard way?"

"Sure, by getting blown up." He glanced at her expression amusedly. "Kirry, it was a joke. I'm kidding!"

She made a futile gesture with her hands. "I never could tell when you were," she said, shaking her head. "I guess I'm hopelessly naive," she muttered, glaring down at the purse in her lap. "At least I can fall down pretty good, though," she added brightly.

"Sure you can. And when I get you through the basics of self-defense, you'll be a holy terror on the street. Grown men will run from you screaming," he promised. "I can't imagine why you haven't done that before. Every woman should know how to take care of herself. They should teach it in school."

"They have enough to do in school without that."

"No kidding, it could be part of gym class in high school, physical education. Mothers could stop worrying so much about their girls if they knew how to foil an attacker." He glanced at her. "That includes an overamorous date."

"I have heard of date rape, thanks," she returned.

He chuckled. "In our case, I was the one with all the worries. You were one eager woman."

"Go ahead, rub it in," she grumbled, shifting away from him.

"How can I help it? You were beautiful, and you wanted me. You could have had anybody."

"Not quite, or you'd never have gotten away," she said, tongue in cheek. It was getting easier to handle the old rejection, now that she and Lang were friends again.

"Think so?" He parked the car just outside her office building, glancing around. "No Erikson," he said, nodding. "Good. Maybe he's terrified and gave it up."

"Right," she said dryly.

"I could get testimonials from people I've protected who'll tell you I'm terrifying," he informed her haughtily. "This last guy, in fact, said that it was a miracle we still had a country with people like me guarding it."

She laughed. "The man whose bathroom you bugged?" she asked.

"They said to watch him all the time," he replied. "So I watched him. *All* the time."

She just shook her head. Then she remembered that he was watching *her* all the time, too. Her eyes spoke for her.

"Not in the bathroom," he said. "Not when the door is opened or closed. Scout's honor."

"You were never a scout," she countered.

"I was until I started my first fire." He sighed, remembering. "Unfortunately it was in the scoutmaster's living room, on his carpet. Never could get him to understand how that accident happened. It was Bob's fault, anyway," he added darkly.

"Bob was the one who gave me the stuff to do it with and showed me how."

"Did Bob like the scoutmaster?"

"Come to think of it, he didn't."

She chuckled. "I see."

They got out of the car and Lang's hand slid into hers as they walked toward the building. He felt her jerk and his fingers contracted. He stopped and looked down at her.

"Too good to hold hands with the hired help, are we?" he murmured dryly.

She felt his big fingers caressing hers and his thumb found its way to her soft palm. It was starting all over again, the magic she'd felt when he came close.

"No," she answered softly, looking straight up into his eyes. "But I don't want to relive the past."

"Not even with a different ending?" he asked softly. "A happy ending this time?"

Her heart skipped. It was just a game, she told herself. Lang was playing and she was letting herself take him seriously.

She began to laugh and tugged at her hand. "Let me go, you tease," she murmured.

He looked stunned. "Kirry, it's not…"

The sudden roar of a car engine caught his attention. He jerked Kirry onto the curb just as an old, dark-colored sports car swept by on the road.

"Lunatic," Lang said angrily, glaring after the car. If it had been a blue sedan, he'd have gone right after it.

"Careless drivers are everywhere," she said, brushing down her skirt. "I'm all right. He missed me by a mile."

"Not quite." He was pale. His eyes went over her like hands. "That was too close."

"At least it wasn't our friend Erikson," she said.

Lang nodded, but he wasn't convinced. He took her arm and escorted her into the building.

Later, he took out his laptop and plugged in with a secret access code. He called up Erikson's name and did some cross-checking. He closed the terminal a few minutes later feeling angry and sick. Erikson had two vehicles. One was an old black sports car.

Kirry had a long day. Part of it was taken up with a staff meeting and the rest would have dragged on endlessly, because she was caught up with all her current projects. Mack had promised her a new client first thing this morning, but the client had a conflict in her schedule, so they'd postponed it until the next day.

Betty stopped by her office that afternoon. "How's the new client?" she asked with a grin.

"I don't know. She didn't show. Mack said we'd try again tomorrow morning," she replied.

"I was going to suggest that we go out to a movie, but I guess that's not a good idea, with Mr. Nasty on the prowl."

"Lang would have a screaming fit," she agreed.

"He's good-looking," Betty ventured. "And there's no competition there."

"None that I can see," Kirry replied. "In the old days, it was a different story. When Lang and I started going together, he'd just broken up with his current heartthrob. She was a dish, too, a model. Lorna McLane."

Betty frowned. "Lorna McLane?"

Kirry stared at her. "What do you know that I don't know, Betty?"

"The name of the client who didn't show up this morning. It's Lorna McLane."

Kirry sat down. "What does she want with us?"

"She's worked her way up the ladder to an executive position at a local model agency that specializes in south Texas location work. Mack says that she wants us to coordinate a fashion show for her, publicity and all."

"Well, we can't afford to turn down something of that magnitude," Kirry said. "Besides, she and Lang were all washed-up before he and I even started dating. Not that it would matter anymore," she added quickly when she noticed Betty watching her. "Lang and I are just friends now. He's our security chief. That's all."

Betty studied her ringless left hand. "Lorna and Mrs. Lancaster are good friends, did you know?"

Kirry's heart stopped. "Good enough that Mrs. Lancaster might have told her about Lang's new job?"

The other woman nodded. "In fact, good enough friends that she told Lang about the job and put in a good word for him with her friend, Mrs. Lancaster."

So that was how he'd managed to get the job. "Nobody ever tells me anything," Kirry muttered darkly, hating the world and fate for playing such a monumental joke on her.

"I'm sure everybody meant to. Listen, just because Lang works here, it doesn't mean that Lorna will be hanging on his sleeve all the time. You can lead a horse to water..."

"Spare me." Kirry sighed and leaned back in her chair. She'd entertained false hopes and now they were being dashed. She felt depressed. Erikson was going to destroy her peace of mind, and here was Lorna to aid and abet him. She remembered the woman all too well; she was tall and slender with very dark eyes and hair. She was beautiful. If she still looked as she had when Lang left her, it wasn't beyond the realm of reason that Lang might be tempted to try his luck again. After all, there was nothing to stop him. Lorna was presumably unmarried, and so was Lang. And Kirry...well, she was right off the menu. She wasn't bad looking, but she couldn't compete with a top model. And while Kirry was old-fashioned, Lorna had never been saddled with cautious habits.

"You can't quit," Betty told her, reading her expression. "For one thing, I'd have nobody to go out to lunch with."

"I won't promise not to," she said stubbornly. She glared out the window. "Did you ever have one of those spells where everything seemed to go wrong in the space of a week?" she asked.

Betty let out a long breath. "I'm going to get you a cup of

coffee," she said, turning around. "It isn't on my job description, but I think I know my way around a coffeepot."

"Betty, why did Lorna pick this agency when there are several in San Antonio? Was it because of Lang, do you think?"

"If I were a betting woman, that would be first on my list," the other woman had to admit. "Still carrying a torch for Lang?"

Kirry glared at her. "I am not. I don't even like Lang."

"And pigs fly," Betty said under her breath as she went out and closed the door behind her.

Lang picked Kirry up late that afternoon, his eyes cautious and wary as he looked around the parking lot.

"I haven't seen a blue sedan all day," Kirry told him as they drove out of the parking lot.

"Or an old black sports car?" he asked.

She frowned. "There *was* a black car." His expression gave him away. He looked resigned. "Don't tell me," she said sardonically. "Erickson has two cars, and one of them is black."

"Bingo."

"This just hasn't been my day."

"Why?"

She looked at him and felt her life going into eclipse. It would be the old story, all over again, Lang walking away from her.

"Did you know that we're getting a new client at the agency?" she asked instead.

"If that expression is anything to go by, it must be someone I know. Do we play twenty questions, or do you just want to spit it out?"

"Lorna McLane is going to let us promote her new modeling extravaganza."

He didn't look at her. She knew. He was sure of it. "Well, good for her."

Kirry didn't move a muscle. She went right on staring through the windshield as if she'd taken root in the seat. "You knew she was here."

He shrugged. "Yes, I knew. How do you think I got this job?" he asked. "She phoned me in D.C., said that it was on offer and suggested that I apply. You might remember that Lorna and I were an item before you and I started going together," he reminded her gently. "But it was never that serious. Then," he added to madden her.

She felt her heart drop. "Have you seen her since you've been back?" she asked, trying to sound casual.

He speared a glance toward her, finding her brooding expression enlightening. "We had lunch today, in fact," he admitted, smiling at the venomous look in Kirry's face at the remark. "She's a little older, but still a knockout. Pretty as a picture, in fact."

Kirry clutched her bag and stared out the side window.

He felt ten feet tall. There was hope. She did still care! "Don't forget. We're having another lesson tonight."

"But I thought we were doing that tomorrow night," she asked abruptly.

"It was. Erikson's making me nervous," he said. "I think a good workout might benefit us both. How about you?"

She couldn't disagree. It would take her mind off at least one of her problems.

"You and Lorna almost got married once, didn't you?" she asked.

"She wanted to be a model and I wanted to be a government agent," he said easily, pulling up to the apartment building they shared. "She made some demands and I made some, then we both decided that a parting of the ways was the best idea." He turned off the engine and looked at her, his dark eyes somber. "I wanted a career more than I wanted anything at that time. I'm not really sorry, in a way. I've done a lot of exciting things, Kirry. I've grown up."

"It shows," she replied. There were lines in his face that had never been there in the old days. He had a new maturity, along with the clowning personality. "But I liked you just the way you were."

"I liked you," he returned, smiling. "You used to be a lot more spirited and full of fun. You've gone quiet on me, Kirry."

"I have a lot of responsibility with this new job," she said evasively. "And Erikson's been on my mind." She didn't add that it was killing her to be around Lang all the time, with the anguish of the past between them.

"He's been on my mind as well. But he'll make a slip, I promise you, and when he does, I'll be standing right next to him."

"Or I will," she said darkly. "Are we ever going to get to do anything besides fall on a mat?" she added plaintively. "I want to learn how to do something!"

"What did you have in mind?" he asked in a deliberately seductive voice, and leaned toward her with mock menace.

"Learning how to break somebody's arm would do nicely," she said, smiling.

He shivered. "As long as it isn't mine!"

"Would I damage my friend?" she chided. "Shame on you!"

They went to the gym, and Lang was aware, as Kirry wasn't, that they were being followed again. He wanted nothing more than to stop the car and get out, and beat the devil out of Erikson. But that would be playing right into the man's hands. He had to play a cool and careful hand here, or he could put Kirry in even more danger.

Meanwhile, it was going to be a very good idea to teach her some damaging moves.

They did the warm-up exercises, and went through the hand positions. Then Lang began to teach her escape maneuvers.

"This is boring," she muttered when he had her break a chokehold for the tenth time.

"Pay attention," he replied tersely. "This isn't a game. Pretend that it's for real, and act accordingly."

She tried to, but her hands were getting tired.

"Okay, honey, if this is the only way I can get through to you..."

His hands tightened, and he moved in with a menacing expression. Kirry panicked, but she kept her nerve. Using the technique he'd taught her, she broke his handhold around her neck, stepped in, broke his balance and pushed him neatly onto the mat.

He rolled as gracefully as a ball, got to his feet in a combat stance and rushed her, his hand rising sharply in a side hand position. He gave a harsh, sharp yell and brought his hand down.

Kirry did what came naturally. She threw her hands over her face and screamed.

There were chuckles from the other side of the gym, from men who'd seen Lang use that shock tactic on young cops he was training, years ago.

Kirry caught her breath and swatted angrily at Lang. "You animal!" she raged. "That wasn't fair!"

"People are born with two natural fears," he informed her. "Fear of sudden, sharp noises and fear of falling. A sharp cry can temporarily paralyze, as you saw. That's one of the methods I like to teach. Sometimes just the yell is enough to buy you some time."

"It's very unpleasant to be on the receiving end of it!"

"I don't doubt it. But getting used to the idea of an attack might save you one day."

She saw his point. She was still getting her breath, and her heartbeat was frantic.

"Had enough?" he taunted, bringing back her fighting spirit.

"Not on your life," she told him shortly. "If you can take it, I can take it. Do your worst!"

He proceeded to, grinning all the way.

6

K irry slumped beside Lang on the mat after an hour of exercises in breaking handholds, balance and repelling attacks. She could barely breathe at all, and every bone in her body felt as if it had taken a beating.

"Giving up?" he teased.

"Only for the moment," she said, panting. Her face was red and her hair was all awry. Lang thought she looked like a charming urchin.

"Remember the day we went swimming in the river?" he reminded with a gentle smile. "You almost drowned because you wouldn't admit that you couldn't last long enough to get across. I had to tow you back."

"I almost made it," she said, recalling the incident.

"And on the way back," he said, lowering his voice as he bent to stare into her eyes, "your top came off."

She felt the impact of his gaze as she'd felt it that day, when she'd experienced her first intimacy. Lang's eyes on her bare breasts had made her blush all over, had made her heart run like a mad thing. He hadn't embarrassed her, or made fun of her plight. He'd lifted her very slowly out of the water and looked at her; just that, then he'd put her back down, found her top and turned his back while she put it on again. It had been so natural and tender that she'd never regretted the experience.

"I remember the look on your face most of all," he continued quietly. "You were shocked and delighted and excited, all at the same time. An artist would have gone nuts trying to capture your expressions."

"It was the first time," she replied simply. "I was all those things. Of course, it wasn't unique for you."

"Wasn't it, Kirry?" He wasn't smiling, and his eyes were dark with secrets.

She averted her face. "Well, it was a long time ago. We're different people now."

He thought of all the places he'd been, all the adventures he'd had. He thought about the close calls and Kirry's laughing eyes, suddenly filled with tears because he wouldn't believe her the one time when it really mattered.

"I failed you," he said aloud.

"You wouldn't have been happy tied to me," she said, looking back at him. "You wanted your freedom too badly. That's why it didn't work out for you with me or Lorna."

His eyes narrowed. "Lorna was different," he said shortly. "She knew from the beginning that I wasn't interested in marriage, and she took me on those terms. But I never laid any conditions on the line with you. I didn't even really rule out marriage at first."

"Until you thought I'd slept with Chad." She finished the thought for him. "And that hurt your pride more than your heart."

"Love comes hard to some men, Kirry." He searched her eyes for a long moment. "And settling down..." His voice trailed off as he remembered, without wanting to, his own childhood.

"I knew you weren't ready." She dredged up a smile. "And despite the fact that you'd proposed, I wouldn't have married you, knowing that you really wanted the Company more than me. It was nice to pretend, though."

"Kirry," he began slowly, "I asked you once how you'd feel about trying again. You never really answered me. I wasn't kidding."

Her heart leaped, but her expression was wary. "I don't know, Lang."

"We could start from where we left off," he told her. "You're a woman now, not a girl just past adolescence. We can have a full relationship, without any of the hang-ups."

"You mean, we could sleep together, don't you?" she asked bluntly.

He stretched out his leg and studied it, not looking at her. "Yes. That's what I mean."

"I thought so." She reached into her bag for her shoes and socks and began putting them on, without answering.

"Well?" he asked shortly.

Her eyebrows lifted. "Well, what?"

"How would you feel about starting over?"

"I don't like glueing broken mirrors back together," she told him. "And you know how I feel about sleeping around already."

"It wouldn't be sleeping around," he said angrily. "You'd only be sleeping with me."

"For how long, Lang?" she asked matter-of-factly, her green eyes boring into his. "Until you had your fill?"

He saw the bitterness in her eyes. "You're twisting my words."

"No, I'm not. You need a woman, and I'm handy," she said, her eyes glittery with anger. "Thanks. Thanks a heck of a lot, Lang. It's so flattering to have a man look at me and see a half-hour's entertainment!"

She got to her feet and so did he, feeling frustrated and angry. She wouldn't let him finish. It seemed as if she didn't want him to make any serious propositions. On the other hand, she didn't want or love him enough to settle for just him, without the promise of permanent ties. That had always been the barrier between them, and it was still firmly in place. Kirry didn't trust him.

"Let me tell you something," she continued hotly, "when I want a man to sleep with, I'll find my own. And it won't be some hotshot with a string of ex-lovers! I wouldn't sleep with you if you had a medical certificate signed by the surgeon general!"

She picked up her bag and walked past him toward the entrance.

"Hold it right there," he said when he caught up with her and blocked her way. His face was livid, but he was in perfect control of his temper. "You go nowhere without me at night, or have you forgotten your 'other' beau?"

She hesitated. Anger suddenly became less important than the fact that Erikson could be out there waiting for her.

"I'm glad you've used your sense," Lang replied curtly. "Wait until I've changed and I'll take you home. After that, except for doing my job, you and I are quits. Happy?"

"Ecstatic," she said with a forced careless smile. "I don't have to have a man in my life. I get along very well on my own."

"So do I," he responded. "But if I get desperate, there's always Lorna. And she was never the old-fashioned type."

With that parting stroke, which went right through her heart, he sauntered off to get changed. Just as she thought, he was going back to Lorna. Well, he needn't think that she was going to stand around bleeding to death emotionally because he couldn't make a commitment.

She stared down at the gi bag with dead eyes. She'd hoped that Lang might be different, but those years abroad hadn't changed his basic attitudes at all. He still didn't need anyone in his life permanently, while Kirry couldn't survive a loose relationship. She was too intense, too possessive to live with the constant knowledge that she was just a pastime. Lang would take her for granted, use her and cast her off like a worn-out shoe. And where would she be then? With her heart broken all over again, that's where.

Lang was back five minutes later. He looked fresh and cool despite the frantic activity of the past hour. Kirry, by comparison, felt sticky and sweaty. She followed him out to the car in silence and climbed in on the passenger side.

With quiet caution, Lang checked the car out before he got in and started it. Even in his present mood, he couldn't let himself forget how unbalanced Erikson was. A man like that was a cunning enemy. It wouldn't do to become lax.

He left Kirry at her door with a good-night that was just barely civil—like hers to him—and went to bed uncommonly early. He hadn't wanted to start a fight with her over the past or the present. He wanted to settle down; it was why he'd come back here in the first place.

But Kirry wouldn't listen. Perhaps she didn't want to. Her career might be all she needed now, and just because she was jealous of Lorna, that didn't ensure that she was in love with him.

He'd exaggerated his relationship with Lorna, just to irritate Kirry. Lorna had been a delightful fling years ago, and she'd no more been serious than Lang had. She was still a pretty woman, and he found her attractive. But Kirry had his heart. The thing was, she didn't want it anymore. Even less did she want him. That was what had angered him so much, when just looking at her made him go rigid with desire.

Well, he wasn't going to worry himself into a fit about it. He'd cross the bridges when he came to them. He rolled over and closed his eyes. What he needed now was sleep. Plenty of sleep.

* * *

For days on end, there was no sign of Erikson at all. It was a shock to Kirry, who looked for him everywhere with nervous apprehension. But as time went by, and there were no more phone calls or surveillance from him, she slowly became complacent. She was happy, too, because she believed that he'd given up. Maybe he'd put it all into perspective and decided that harassing her wasn't worth the possible cost to himself. It even made sense—if he wasn't playing some psychological game with her, that was, lulling her into a false sense of security. She grew cautiously optimistic, though, when nothing happened.

Erikson's absence was the only thing that gave her cause for pleasure, however, because she'd landed Lorna's account. That meant she had to spend considerable amounts of time with Lorna, who was now dating Lang again. And Lorna apparently felt obliged to share every little detail with Kirry.

"I do like the idea of making this ribbon-cutting appearance, dear," Lorna purred as they conferred over a business lunch. "But it mustn't interfere with my private life. They'll simply have to change it to the afternoon. Lang is taking me to the opera."

Kirry didn't betray her feelings by even the batting of an eyelash, but she was certain that the durable plastic smile she reserved for Lorna was going to be on her lips when she was buried.

"I'll see what I can do," she promised the other woman,

mentally anticipating being cussed out royally by the business in question. She would have to do some really fast talking to get them to agree to what Lorna wanted. Even then, they might not cooperate.

"Good. And one more thing, Kirry. Is it absolutely necessary for you to have an apartment next door to Lang's?" she asked with visible irritation. "It seems to inhibit him when we're together."

"He moved next door to me because of the threats an ex-employee here was making," she told Lorna. She didn't mention that Lang made sure she heard him bringing Lorna to his apartment every other night. Or that hearing the two of them laughing next door, after midnight, had left her sleepless for the past four days. "Since the threat no longer seems to exist, I don't see why Lang couldn't move back to his old place." In fact, she'd be delighted if he left. Then she would at least be spared the audible evidence of Lang's pleasure in Lorna's company.

"I knew you'd agree! I told him it wouldn't hurt your feelings if I made the suggestion to you! Men are such cowards about women's emotions, aren't they?"

So she'd been discussing it with Lang, had she? Kirry was as angry as she was hurt. "He might have asked me himself," she said.

"Oh, he couldn't bring himself to do that." Lorna dismissed it. "But when I tell him, he'll be pleased."

"I'm sure he will."

"Now, about the network coverage, do you think you could get CNN to come…?"

By the end of the day, Kirry was totally washed-out. She couldn't remember ever feeling quite so bad.

Lang had stopped by just briefly, a stranger with his cold face and eyes. He hardly spoke to her at all lately unless he had to. He was remote and polite. She knew that he was still keeping her under surveillance for her safety's sake, but there was nothing personal about it, and no warmth in him. Kirry grieved all over again for the past. Why couldn't he have stayed out of her life? she wondered miserably.

He'd stuck his head into her office door just to tell her that she'd be on her own that one afternoon, as he was to meet Lorna at a local restaurant for a quick dinner. He cautioned her about watching out for Erikson, which led to a heated exchange of words. It was a relief when he left. She could function, she told herself, without someone shadowing her. She really felt that way. Until she got to her car.

Erikson was sitting in the front seat. She came to a sudden halt and gaped at him. He was back. She wasn't safe. He hadn't given up. She could have cried. It was going to start all over again, and she felt her stomach tying itself in knots as she wondered how she was going to cope with this.

"Hello, sweet thing," he said with a cold smile. "Did you think I'd forgotten you?"

"Get out of my car!"

"Make me," he challenged.

She knew better than to try that. Erikson was a trained security officer. Her few hold-breaking routines might work on a novice, but he probably had a colored belt, and hers was still white. Knowing when to back off was as important, Lang had once told her, as knowing when to attack. And you never attacked; you waited for the opponent to come at you, which gave you the advantage. All these thoughts worked through her mind while she stared at the man occupying her car. "Okay, Mr. Erikson. I'll let the police extricate you for me."

She turned and went quickly back toward the building, red-faced with temper. As she got to the door, she heard a car door slam. She whirled. Erikson had left her car and was on the way to his. As she watched, he got into it and drove slowly away, tooting the horn as he reached the corner.

For a moment she wavered, wondering if she should call the police anyway. But it would hardly do any good, when he was no longer there.

She walked back to her car and opened the door, just in time to see the grenade on the floorboard. She gasped and started to step back, but it exploded. She covered her eyes instinctively, expecting the concussion to knock her backward, but it was only a gas grenade. There was a loud noise that hurt her ears, then her car filled with noxious fumes and she got out of the way in time to escape everything except a stinging pain in her eyes and throat. The fumes made her cough.

It was the last straw. Damn Erikson! Sobbing with bad temper, she got into the building and called 911. Minutes later, two police officers arrived. Lang was just behind them.

He started toward her, grim-faced, but she resisted the need for comfort. She turned to the first police officer who reached her and told him exactly what had happened.

Lang stood by, his face hard and unreadable, and listened while she talked and then answered questions.

"He's long gone, now," she said miserably. "I didn't think he'd try to hurt me...."

"If he'd wanted to do that, it would have been a hand grenade, not a gas grenade," the young patrolman assured her. "But this qualifies under the terroristic threats and acts law, and we can also get him for breaking and entering."

"If we can get any prints off the car," an older officer amended quietly. He looked at Kirry. "Was he wearing gloves?"

She remembered Erikson's hands on the wheel, and as they flashed into her consciousness, she remembered the black covering on them.

"Yes," she said miserably.

"There goes the case. It's your word against his," the older man said.

"But...!"

"It's the way the law's written," he said irritably. "None of us like it. Do you have any idea how many creeps prey on women and get away with it because we can't do anything to help them? God, I'd give anything for a stalking law with teeth, but we haven't got one yet! You aren't the only victim, although I expect it feels that way right now."

"It does."

"Watch this guy," the older police officer said suddenly. "You shouldn't have been out here alone."

Lang's face went hard and he actually flinched. "No, she shouldn't have," he agreed. "I'm chief of security here, and I thought he'd given it up. My mistake."

"It could have been a fatal one, for her," the older man said brutally.

Lang's eyes were anguished. "Don't you think I know that?" He gritted out the words.

Something in his expression made the other man leave it alone. He apologized once again to Kirry and left with his partner.

"I have to drive it home," Kirry said dully.

"You do not. We'll lock it and leave it. For one thing, it will have to be cleaned before you can drive it again."

"Oh. Yes, I see, I hadn't realized..." She went to lock it, feeling numb from the brain down.

Lang helped her into his car and drove her back to her apartment. "I'm sorry," he said through his teeth.

"It isn't your job to watch just me all the time," she said patiently. "You have lots of people to protect."

"I really thought he was through. It's been almost two weeks since we've even seen him. I acted like a green agent, not like a professional. I heard the call over the city band on my scanner on the way back to the office. I had no idea what I'd find when I got here. I should have known!" His hand hit the steering wheel hard with impotent rage.

His pride was hurt, she decided. He'd fallen down on the job because his mind had been on Lorna. He didn't have to say so, but Kirry knew it. She stared out the window until he parked the car, and then she followed him inside the building and up on the elevator without a word.

She turned to him outside her apartment, feeling haggard and worn-out. "Thanks for bringing me home."

He scowled. "Are you going to be all right?"

"Of course. I'm not bric-a-brac," she chided. "I won't break."

"Keep your doors locked," he said. "And don't stand near any windows."

"You're getting paranoid," she muttered. "He isn't going to come at me with a high-powered rifle."

"I don't know what he's going to do," he said grimly, running a hand through his thick hair. "But we're not going to get careless again. Got that?"

"I wasn't careless. I looked, and I didn't see anybody anywhere in the parking lot," she said angrily. "I didn't see him until I was standing right next to the car. I didn't go close enough to get grabbed."

"What if he'd had a gun, Kirry?" he asked in a haunted tone.

"Oh, for God's sake, he isn't going to shoot me!"

He didn't answer her, or smile. He was seeing her lying facedown on the pavement, her eyes open, her body broken from gunfire. He'd seen other agents go that way. He knew, as Kirry didn't, how unpredictable people like Erikson were.

"I'm all right," she said, driven to reassure him. "Don't go off the deep end, Lang, I'm fine." She hesitated. "And if you want to move out, I've already told Lorna it's all right with me. I'm not afraid...."

He frowned. "What the hell are you talking about?"

"Lorna told me that you were getting tired of having to live next door to me," she said. "She must be insecure, because I get every little detail of what you do with her."

"I didn't say anything to her about moving out of here," he told her angrily. "I wouldn't even consider it until this Erikson situation is resolved, one way or the other."

That made her feel light-headed with joy. Lorna had lied. He didn't want to get rid of her!

"I didn't know that she was having that much contact with you," he said curtly.

"I'm having to handle her account," Kirry told him. "The others jumped out windows and hid in rest rooms until I got saddled with her. She's a perfectionist and she doesn't like me, but we get along. I let her think she's killing me with her tales of doglike devotion from you. Works like a charm."

He didn't like that. "Doglike devotion isn't what she gets from me."

"Oh, I know what she does get from you. She tells me *that,* too," she added, and this time she couldn't keep the sting it caused out of her face.

"There isn't anything to tell," he said through his teeth. "I'm not sleeping with her!"

She shrugged with majestic acting ability. "Don't deprive

yourself on my account," she said carelessly. "I'm certainly not nursing any hopes in that direction. When I marry, and I will someday, my husband is going to be my first lover."

His pride felt as if she'd lanced it. His face felt hot as he glared down at her. "He'll have to be something special, to settle for a virginal wife these days," he said icily, striking out.

"Maybe he'll think he's blessed," she countered, refusing to allow his words to bother her. "It takes an intelligent woman not to risk her health and her future husband's for the sake of not standing out in a crowd."

"You puritan," he accused coldly.

"My morals are my own affair, and none of your business. You're just the security chief for my company!"

His dark eyes slid over hers. "Try again."

"You have no right to... Oh!"

He pulled her close in his arms, and his mouth was hard and hungry over her soft lips. She stiffened and tried to reject him, but his arms only closed more firmly, enveloping her against his big, powerful body while his mouth nudged and coaxed and teased until her lips finally parted.

Even then, he didn't take immediate advantage of it. His open mouth brushed lazily over hers, tormenting it until she moaned and began pushing upward, trying to capture his elusive mouth against her own. It was yesterday, and she was in love and aching for Lang, all over again.

"Tell me what you want," he coaxed. His hands were on her hips, now, pulling and dragging them against the hard male thrust of him, so that she could feel the evidence of his need.

"Lang." She choked out his name.

"Come on," he said, daring her, "tell me what you want me to do, Kirry."

"Not...fair," she stammered.

"Is life?" His hand slid into the thick short hair at her nape and contracted, tilting her face at just the angle he wanted. His eyes were vaguely frightening as they glittered down into hers. "Now," he breathed, lowering his head, "now, open your mouth and taste me inside, and let me taste you. Make me forget..."

She felt his mouth, warm and moist, burrowing slowly into her own. The contact with his body, the strength of his arms, took her own strength away. She yielded, melting into him, unmindful of the past or the future while she savored the intimate touch of his tongue sliding into her mouth.

The erotic symbolism of the caress made her body go taut with sudden desire. She shivered, and he laughed, then deepened the kiss with a slow, teasing rhythm.

Knots coiled in her lower belly. Her legs trembled helplessly and she moaned as the fever burned higher between them.

His other hand dropped to the very base of her spine and began to move her against him. She made a sound that went right up his backbone, and his mouth echoed it in the stillness of the hallway.

Only the steady hum of the elevator broke them apart. He stepped back from her just as an elderly couple got off the conveyance, glanced toward them indulgently and walked hand in hand down the other end of the hall to their own apartment.

Lang felt too drained to move. He heard the door close in the distance and only then did he look at Kirry. She seemed to be as devastated as he. She was leaning back against her own door, and her soft mouth was swollen and red from his kisses.

"I could have you right now," he said. His voice was deep with feeling. "You know it, too."

"Let's not forget Lorna," she said through the maelstrom of emotions that were buffeting her mind.

"Damn Lorna! I want you!"

She had to drag her eyes away from his. "You've overheated, that's all," she said stiffly. "A nice cold shower should fix you right up."

"Lorna wouldn't send me into a shower," he said in a soft, threatening tone.

Her eyes narrowed. "Then why don't you go and see her, dear man?"

Her lack of cooperation made him furious. "Thanks for the suggestion," he said. "I might do that."

He whirled on his heel, in a furious temper, and stalked to the elevator. He jabbed the Down button furiously, and as if the elevator knew his mood, it appeared promptly from the floor above. He got into it without even darting a glance at Kirry.

She could have screamed. She wasn't going to go to bed with him just to keep him away from Lorna, and if he thought she was, he still didn't know her very well.

She unlocked the door and slammed it firmly behind her. How could he! Why had he kissed her in the first place? Now she was going to toss and turn all night, sickened by images of Lorna nude in his big arms in bed. She hated him! How in the world had she ever imagined that she could love someone as cruel as Lang? She was going to have to get herself together. Lang was no longer her concern. The sooner she realized it, the better.

Lang, meanwhile, was driving aimlessly around town, and nowhere near Lorna's apartment. He should never have touched Kirry that way. Now he was going to spend hours remembering her soft warmth in his arms, the hunger in her kisses. She wanted him; she couldn't hide it.

But he'd let her throw him off-balance with those stinging comments she made. She was jealous of Lorna and afraid to trust him. That was the crux of the matter. He'd just have to learn to keep his temper and try harder. But meanwhile, there was Erikson to deal with. The gas grenade had shaken Lang as much as it had Kirry. He had to do something about Erikson while there was still time.

The next morning, Lang was more cautious than ever. He buzzed Kirry's doorbell thirty minutes before she was due at work. She dragged herself out of bed in her short nightie and looked through the peephole before she reluctantly opened the door.

"Don't stare," she told him irritably, her hair tousled from sleep, her green eyes half-closed with it. "I'm not a peep show."

"Darlin', I never said you were," he drawled, smiling at the exquisite tanned length of her legs and the soft thrust of her breasts against the thin fabric. She had a devastating figure. "But in that rig, you could turn a blind man's head."

"I don't want to turn your head. I just want to get dressed and go to work. There's some coffee in the kitchen. You can drink it while I get changed."

"You're sure you wouldn't like to go in like that?" he asked, smiling at the pleasure she gave him in the skimpy outfit.

She put her hands on her rounded hips and glowered at him. "It's only a body. Lorna has one just like it, as I'm sure you found out all over again last night!"

His eyebrows lifted and he smiled. "Jealous?"

"Of Lorna? Hah! Why should I be jealous? I don't want you!"

"You did last night," he reminded her.

"I won't dignify that statement with an answer. And I did not want you!" She whirled and went into the bedroom, pushing the door almost shut. She stripped off the nightie and was standing there in her lacy pink bikini briefs, fuming with bad temper, when the door opened and Lang's eyes froze on her body.

7

Kirry couldn't even breathe. The way Lang was looking at her made her go hot all over.

"Don't panic and start leaping for cover," he said quietly. He put his hands into his pockets and leaned back against the door facing. "I can't help staring—you're unbelievably pretty like that—but I promise I won't touch until you want me to."

She felt hot and cold all over, and there were swellings in her body that were familiar, left from the days when Lang made soft, slow love to her without ever crossing the line.

She should get dressed, she told herself. She was brazen, standing there with her body open to him, letting him look. Oh, but it was sweet to feel his eyes! They made her throb with forbidden pleasures.

He saw the need in her face, in the faint trembling of her legs. With a soft sound in the back of his throat, he jerked away from the door and moved toward her.

Run, her mind said. But her legs wouldn't work. He came closer, filling the room, filling her hungry eyes.

He still didn't touch her. He searched her face in silence. After a minute, a soft smile flamed on his mouth. His hand went to his tie and slowly unfastened it. He tossed it aside. He slid out of his jacket, and it followed the tie into a chair, while Kirry shivered at what she saw in his face.

"I don't...want to...now," she whispered when his hands went to his shirt. But she still wasn't moving.

"Neither do I," he replied quietly. "But some things are fated, I suppose."

His shirt was unbuttoned, removed, baring a broad, bronzed chest thick with black, curling hair. He brought her hands to his belt.

"Take it off," he whispered.

Her hands trembled on the buckle and her wide eyes sought his for reassurance.

"I'll take care of you. We won't take risks," he said, reading the apprehension. He saw her relax, despite the traces of guilt that remained in her soft green eyes. He bent and brushed his mouth over her closing eyelids, hiding the accusation in them. "I'll take a long time," he whispered. "Do you trust me not to hurt you?"

She moved closer, drawn like a magnet to the feel of his hair-roughened chest against her bare breasts. She shivered as the nipples went hard when she pushed into him and let her arms encircle his waist. "I trust you," she stated.

He let out a savage breath. He hadn't dreamed that it would happen like this. Years of wanting her, waiting, hoping... And she was giving in, without a single protest.

The stillness in the bedroom was haunting. Above it, he could hear faint street noises in the distance. Closer, he could hear Kirry's tortured breathing, feel the warmth of it against his chest where her lips touched.

"Will you hate me?" he asked heavily.

She lifted her misty eyes to his. "Will you think I'm cheap?" she asked with equal concern.

He smiled. "You?" he whispered tenderly.

She pressed closer, resting her cheek against his warm chest. She clung, trembling, as the finality of it trespassed into her mind.

His big hands smoothed over her bare back, savoring its silkiness. "There's a condition," he said through a tight throat.

"What?"

"Afterward, you have to put the ring back on."

Her eyes opened. She could see the heavy vibration of his chest. "The ring?"

His mouth brushed hungrily against her hair and his hands pulled her closer. "The engagement ring, Kirry," he whispered, and his mouth quickly worked its way down her flushed face to her mouth. He took it hungrily and felt it open, felt her body quicken even as he heard her helpless moan of pleasure.

He interpreted her response as an agreement, a sacred oath. After that, nothing on earth would have stopped him.

He lifted her, his mouth still covering hers, and carried her to the bed.

She looked up as he laid her gently on the covers. "Are you going to close...close the bedroom door?"

"Who's going to see us, my darling?" he whispered. He slid down beside her, letting his eyes caress the soft thrust of her breasts before his mouth lowered to tease and torment them into rigid peaks.

Kirry couldn't have imagined the pleasure. It was frantic, all-consuming. She let him remove the final barrier and then lay trembling, watching him with hungry eyes while he undressed for her. She'd never seen him totally nude. She looked at him now without embarrassment, glorying in the perfection of his powerful body.

He lowered himself against her, smiling at her expression. "We can't have secrets anymore, can we?" he asked gently. His mouth touched hers, and then roamed over her face while his hands began to learn her with infinite patience and tender caresses. He felt her tremble, heard her soft gasps as he went from one intimacy to another in the rapt silence.

She'd never imagined making love in broad daylight. Now it seemed natural, perfect. She led where he followed, awash in pleasure so intense that she had no control left when he finally paused for a moment to protect her, and then moved down. She felt his body slowly invade hers and she shivered, her hands clutching with anticipation and a little fear.

His mouth was at her ear, his breath hot and quick. His tongue teased inside her ear. His hand slid down her belly and he touched her, laughing with intimate tenderness when she gasped and her hips arched up to accommodate him.

"Lang!" she cried out.

"Yes, isn't it shocking?" he breathed with joyful conspiracy. "Shocking, earthy…" He pushed down and heard the breath leave her body. "And now you know it all, don't you?" he whispered, as he possessed her completely. "You know me. All of me. And I know all…of…you."

His body was moving. She felt him around her, within her, felt a tension that made her reach up to him, move with him, searching for the right pressure, the right rhythm. She swallowed, gasping. She felt the heat and dampness of him with wonder. She heard his rough breath at her ear, felt his control give way at last.

His lean hand gripped her thigh and the rhythm grew ruthless. She was beyond caring about how he held her. It was there, the pleasure was there, and she was… about…to touch it…!

She was sobbing. She heard her own voice with a sense of disassociation, as if she was no longer in her body at all, but sailing around with Lang in a miasma of golden heat and throbbing satisfaction. She cried out something and arched her back to prolong the exquisite sensations that rippled over her in waves of pleasure.

For a few seconds, there was nothing else in the world except Lang, who had become completely part of her.

Far away, she heard ragged breathing and felt a crushing

weight the length of her body. She opened her eyes. The ceiling was there, with the sunlight reflecting on the light fixture. She moved her fingers experimentally and felt the cold silk of Lang's thick hair. She remembered then, and smiled.

He felt the smile against his cheek and lifted his head. His eyes, like hers, were soft in the aftermath of fulfillment. He lifted himself enough to see her face and smiled back.

Her body began to throb all over again. He hadn't moved away and when she shifted one leg, she felt him intimately. His eyes grew misty with the return of desire, like her own.

He moved, too, and watched her lips part.

She reached up, arching her hips so that she caressed him in the most exciting way, and he reacted with incredible ease. His breath caught at the quickening.

"That's impossible," she assured him. "I read it in a book...."

"Written by a virgin, no doubt," he breathed into her open mouth, and began to move again.

"Lang...isn't it risky...?"

He stilled. "Yes." He bit off the word. "My God, yes!" With anguish in his face, he lifted away from her, and fell onto his back. He lay there, his fists clenched, totally vulnerable while he fought to still the demons.

She leaned over him, boldly watching his face while he struggled with the desire he didn't dare satisfy. His eyes held hers while he forced himself to breathe normally until the pain subsided. His gaze slid down to her soft breasts and lingered there. He pulled her closer and kissed them hungrily.

"I want to do it again and again and again," she whispered softly, savoring his mouth on her body.

"So do I. But I don't want to make a baby in the fever of it," he whispered back. He held her close then, while they slowly came down from the heights.

She closed her eyes and went heavy against him, gloriously contented. "Do you really want to marry me?" she asked daringly.

"Yes," he said.

She drew her cheek against his chest, and the clean scent of him came up into her nostrils. "When?"

"We can talk about dates later," he murmured, oddly reluctant to pin it down to a certainty. He smoothed her hair. "We have to get to work."

She lifted herself to look at the clock and groaned. "Oh, my goodness, I'm an hour late!"

"The world won't end," he murmured dryly.

"That's what you think! I have a business meeting in a half hour!"

"Look at me."

She did, and his smile was her undoing. "Don't panic," he said. "I'll get you there in time."

He kissed her gently and put her out of the bed, stretching lazily as he got to his feet. "Come on. We'll have time for a quick shower."

He led her into the bathroom and put her into the shower with him. It took longer than it normally would, because he made her bathe him and that led to exploration and soft kisses that made him grit his teeth.

"I'm not prepared." He chuckled, lifting her out of the spray. He turned the shower off and dried her. "No accidents."

His concern seemed rather beyond what she might have expected. She felt insecure. "I'll see the doctor," she promised, "so that we can make sure nothing happens until we want it to."

He studied her rapt face quietly. "Your career means a lot to you, doesn't it?" he asked solemnly. "For now, at least?"

She read the thoughts in his face. "Yes," she said slowly. She frowned. "You...do eventually want a child?"

He smiled, but it didn't reach his eyes. "Of course I do. Now, let's get to work. Tonight, we'll drive down to Floresville and tell Bob and Connie our good news."

She wanted to pin him down on the subject of a family. Perhaps he was just thinking of her. But there had been something in his eyes when she mentioned children....

He smoothed down the frown. "Stop borrowing trouble and get dressed. Just look what you've made me do," he said, glowering. "I've been seduced, for God's sake!"

Her eyes twinkled. "Why, so you have. Would you like to press charges?"

"I'd like to press something," he murmured, chuckling.

"I did offer," she reminded him.

He bent and kissed her carelessly. "I'll be prepared next time."

"Or I will," she added.

While Lang gathered his own clothes and began to dress, she

moved to her dresser and pulled out a bra and slip and quickly put them on with her back to Lang. Feeling a little shy now, she walked to the closet and took out a green, patterned shirtwaist dress and put it on.

"You look nice in green," he said.

"Thanks." She hesitated, suddenly remembering his abrupt arrival. "Why did you come by this morning?" she asked.

"I'm giving you a ride into work. And I wanted to know if you got any calls last night," he said with a lazy smile.

She smiled back and shook her head. "There was nothing on the answering machine. Nobody bothered me at all. Is this some new tactic he's using?" she asked then. "Is he trying to drive me crazy by waiting several days between incidents?"

"It's a good psychological trick," he agreed. "I wouldn't put it past him. But that gas grenade was dangerous. Sometimes they start fires. If it had been beneath the seat, and it had exploded under you..."

"I get the message," she said uneasily. Her eyes met his in the mirror while she put on makeup and ran a comb through her short hair. "In other words, we're not out of the woods yet."

He nodded.

She put down the brush and searched in another drawer for her panty hose. She put them on while Lang watched with appreciative eyes, then she slipped on her high heels and picked up her purse.

"What about my car?" she asked. "You didn't get it picked up, did you?"

He shook his head. "Sorry. I'll see to it this morning."

She turned and looked at him blatantly. "Did you see Lorna last night?" she asked slowly.

He lifted an amused eyebrow. "If I had, do you think I'd have been so hungry for you?"

She flushed. "Well..."

He drew her against him. "You still don't know much. Some men can go all night. I can't. If I'd been with another woman all night, I wouldn't have been capable this morning. Does that answer the question you can't quite ask me?"

"Yes," she said ruefully. "Sorry, I shouldn't have pried."

He frowned. "Kirry, you trusted me enough to let me make love to you," he reminded her softly. "That gives you every right in the world to know about me. I haven't slept with Lorna, and I won't. I want to marry you."

He said he did. But he wouldn't talk about a date and he didn't want to risk making her pregnant. She almost mentioned that, but what they'd shared was too new and exciting to spoil. She decided to live one day at a time. At least he did want her for keeps this time. She could settle for that. For now.

She reached up and kissed him very softly. Her eyes adored him. She tried not to notice the indecision in his. "Let's go see if we're fired," she teased, and stepped away from him.

"Right."

He drove her to the office in a faintly strained silence. He'd burned his bridges this time. There would be no going back. He'd compromised her, and as old-fashioned as it might seem to another modern man, he felt obliged to do the right thing and marry her. He did care about her, very much. It was just that he was trapped now. It didn't feel as comfortable as he'd thought it would, to be totally committed. And she wanted children.

He loved Mikey, of course, but it would be different when the child was his own, and he became responsible for it and Kirry. She was a working woman. She wanted a career. But she'd slept with him, and now his old footloose days were gone forever, because he hadn't been able to hold back. He'd wanted Kirry to the point of madness. He glanced at her, remembering how it had been, and he couldn't manage to regret that heated loving in her bed. No matter what the cost, it was worth it! He only had to get used to the idea of being committed. That shouldn't be so hard, he told himself firmly. He'd gotten used to being on the road all the time when he joined the Company, he'd gotten used to wearing a gun. He'd even managed to live with worse things. It would grow on him. And as for children, he'd find some way to put her off. With that certainty in mind, he smiled at Kirry and broke into casual conversation.

But she wasn't fooled. She saw the worry on his face, the indecision he couldn't hide. He'd gone over the edge with her and now he was sorry about it, she could tell. He was going to make the best of it, but how was she going to be able to live with a man who was forcing himself to act contented? It was a glimpse of a nightmare.

The one nice thing about the morning was that Erickson was

nowhere in sight, in either of his cars. But she'd been overly relieved one time too many, so she wasn't taking anything for granted. He might be hiding nearby, waiting for her to relax.

Lang stopped the car at her office door and turned to her. "Don't let your guard down," he said gently. "Just because we don't see him doesn't mean that he isn't around."

"I was just thinking the same thing," she replied. Her eyes searched his. "I'm sorry," she said gently.

He frowned. "About what?"

She shrugged a thin shoulder and forced a smile. "You aren't ready," she said. "You thought you were, but you aren't. I was as much to blame as you were for what happened, so you don't need to feel guilty. You don't need to feel obligated to marry me, either. We were careful. There won't be any…consequences."

He stared at her with conflicting emotions. "Are you sure you don't want to marry me, Kirry?" he asked slowly.

The way he phrased it said everything. She didn't dare cry or look regretful. "I enjoyed what we did," she said. "But when the newness wore off, we'd still be stuck with each other. You have your job and I have mine, and marriage isn't the end of the rainbow anymore. Maybe we 'd better think about this before we jump into it."

"That's exactly how I feel," he said, and looked relieved. "But we can still be engaged, while we're thinking about it. Okay?"

Wimp, she told herself. "Okay," she agreed too readily, and then grimaced at her own scramble for crumbs.

"We can drive down and have supper with Connie and Bob. I'll call them."

"I'd enjoy seeing them again."

"I'll pick you up here after work. Be careful."

She nodded, hesitating weakly.

His eyes began to glitter. "Want me to kiss you?" he murmured, teasing.

She started to deny it, but the irony of the situation made her smile. "Yes," she said.

He smiled. "I like that honesty," he said, his voice husky and deep. "I want to kiss you, too."

She moved closer and tilted her face up for him. He framed it in his big hands and bent, drawing his lips softly over her own. But the passion between them was too raw and new to allow for tenderness just yet, and very quickly, he had her close in his arms and was kissing the breath out of her. She moaned, and he came to his senses.

"I can't take much of that," he said with graveyard humor. He took out his handkerchief and removed the smeared lipstick from around her mouth and then his own. "I'll come by and take you out to lunch, if you're free."

"I'm not," she said miserably. "I have to meet some of Lorna's group for a business lunch."

He sighed. "Okay. Another time."

She nodded, reaching for the door.

He stayed her hand. "I haven't given Lorna any messages for you," he said quietly. "If she starts handing out tidbits about me, take them with a grain of salt, will you?"

She smiled over her shoulder. "Okay."

"I'll see you later."

"Sure." She got out and walked into the building, and had to force herself not to look back. She'd made her bed. Now she was going to have to lie in it.

"You're late," Mack grumbled the minute she walked in the door. "Lorna McLane has been on the phone ten times asking where you were. She couldn't seem to locate our security chief, either." He looked at Kirry suspiciously. "Do you know where he is?"

"He was with me," she said, fighting a blush.

Mack hesitated. "Oh."

"You needn't look so shocked. Lang and I are engaged," she added.

His face relaxed into a beaming smile. "Congratulations."

"Those might be a little premature. We're not planning an elopement."

"You never know," he replied. "Lang strikes me as an impulsive man."

"He strikes most people that way. But he's actually very cautious," she said, remembering him with the familiarity of years. "He's very methodical. He always thinks first."

She remembered that when she was alone in her office. Lang was extremely cautious, in fact. He never leaped before he looked, or let his emotions lead him around. So why had he let himself go with her this morning? Despite the fact that he took precautions, it was totally unlike him to leap in without considering the consequences. At the very least, Kirry's feelings for him would lead her to expect commitment from a man who seduced her. He knew that. Had he really lost his head? Or had he changed enough that he might actually want to marry her?

She didn't have time to ponder the question for very long. Lorna McLane called again, and she was fuming.

"Where have you been, Miss Campbell?" she asked in a scathing tone. "I really don't have all day to chase you down. Do you want this account or not?"

Kirry bit her tongue to keep from telling the truth. "Certainly we want it, Miss McLane," she said in a pacifying tone. "I'm sorry, I was unavoidably detained getting to work this morning."

"By Lang?" came the poisonous reply.

Kirry's hand tightened on the receiver. "If you must know, yes," she replied curtly.

"You little tramp," Lorna said huskily.

"Lang and I are engaged to be married, Miss McLane," Kirry informed her. "What we do in our private lives is hardly any of your business!"

There was an indrawn breath and a long pause, with audible breathing. "He wouldn't...he isn't the marrying kind! You're lying!"

"If you think so, you're at liberty to ask him."

"I've called him a number of times, but he's never around. I guess he's been with you."

"I've had some problems here. Lang has been teaching me self-defense," she returned.

"And a few other tricks, I'll bet. He's a wonderful lover, isn't he?" she drawled. "But wait until you get him to the altar before you start looking for congratulations. He was engaged to me, once, too. He doesn't want children, did you know?" she added with a poisonous note in her voice. "He has to be free to walk out if he wants to, so kids are out of the question."

"He wants children. We both do," she said hesitantly.

"Really? Pin him down, dear. I dare you."

"Miss McLane, this is really..."

"I'll expect to see you at lunch," Lorna continued unabashed. "I've asked the Lancasters to join us while we discuss the details of this promotion. I would really prefer to have your colleague, Mack, work on it. I find that women aren't quite as cooperative as men when I make suggestions."

I'm not surprised, Kirry thought, but she didn't dare say it. She was trying to picture Miss McLane wrapped from toes to eyes in green satin and pinned with safety pins. It kept her sane.

"I'm sure I'd have no objections to Mack replacing me," Kirry volunteered, thinking that Mack would kill her for stepping down. He had no affection for Lorna.

"Then, we'll be able to settle this amicably. I'm so glad."

"I'll see you at lunch, then."

"Indeed you will," Lorna purred, and made it sound like a threat.

8

Lorna had a surprise for Kirry at lunch. Not only had she insisted that the Lancasters be in attendance, but Lang was there, too, looking irritable and reluctant.

"I'm sure you won't mind if Lang joins us," Lorna told Kirry privately. "I thought you might like the Lancasters to share in the news of your engagement."

She moved away in a cloud of expensive perfume to greet the dark, elegantly dressed Lancasters before Kirry could reply. "I know that I won't be giving away any terrible secrets if I tell you that Lang and Miss Campbell are to be married," Lorna told the Lancasters, smiling.

Kirry wanted to tell her that feathers were sticking out of her mouth, but she didn't dare. She smiled instead, although she couldn't keep it from looking strained.

"Is this true?" Mrs. Lancaster asked, delighted.

Lang straightened. He glared at Lorna and moved closer to

Kirry, taking her hand in his. "Yes, it is," he said, but he didn't sound like a happy bridegroom.

"Well, we must help with the arrangements for the wedding," Mrs. Lancaster continued, and her husband smiled his agreement. "When is it to be?"

"We haven't set a date," Lang said stiffly.

"Surely you plan to make it soon, Lang, dear?" Lorna mused, leaning back to smile at him with hatred in her eyes.

"There's no rush," he said firmly. "Kirry and I have plenty of time."

Kirry knew that he didn't like to be pushed, but there was more to it than that. He was so obviously reluctant to be pinned down on a date that it was embarrassing.

"That's right," Kirry said quickly, backing him up only because she didn't like Lorna. "We plan on a long engagement."

"I see," Mr. Lancaster replied with narrowed eyes.

"Well, if you're not planning to start a family right away, I suppose there's no hurry about it," Lorna purred. "How many children are you going to have, Lang?" she asked. "Two or three?"

Lang's face went rigid. "We haven't discussed that."

"Surely you want a son?" Lorna persisted.

He glared at her and then deliberately glanced at his watch.

"We'd better get started," Mr. Lancaster said, taking the hint. "We all have duties to perform. Now what is this about switching the service on your account, Miss McLane?" he asked politely.

"It's nothing against Miss Campbell," Lorna assured him, "but

I think Mack would be more… accessible. I've spent the entire morning trying to track down Miss Campbell, who seems to be celebrating her engagement with a little, shall we say, excessive enthusiasm? You know how the job can suffer when people have their heads in the clouds," she added with a silvery little laugh.

Why, you vicious shrew, Kirry was thinking. In one stroke, Lorna had managed to make her look like an incompetent airhead.

"I was late to work, yes," Kirry said angrily. "But it was hardly dereliction of duty…!"

"Miss Campbell," Mr. Lancaster said sharply, and smiled pointedly. "We wouldn't want to alienate Miss McLane, now, would we?"

Kirry flushed. "Excuse me. I'm sorry that I wasn't available this morning, and I can assure you that in the future…"

"In the future, I would prefer to deal with Mack," she said, smiling at her warmly. "He and I will get along very well. And this account is *so* important…." She let her voice trail away.

Kirry was being railroaded, and the Lancasters were taking it all in without question. Mrs. Lancaster's friendship with Lorna obviously inclined her to believe whatever the former model told her. She gave Kirry a speaking glance.

"Indeed the account is important," Mrs. Lancaster said coolly. "I'm sure that Miss Campbell won't mind letting Mack take it over."

The inference was that she'd better *not* mind. Kirry was losing ground and she didn't know how to regain it.

"Of course I don't mind," she said diplomatically. "Miss McLane's satisfaction must be our first priority."

Lorna inclined her head graciously. "I'm delighted that you're willing to cooperate. Heaven forbid that I should cause any trouble. But this promotion must be perfect. And it will lead to others. I have many connections in the fashion industry."

"I'm aware of that, my dear," Mrs. Lancaster said brightly. "Your influence is far-reaching, indeed."

Mr. Lancaster was watching Kirry closely. "You have other accounts to service, I presume?" he asked her curtly. It was the first time he'd taken any real interest in what she did for his company.

"I've been working on a promotional campaign for a new chain of soup and salad bars," Kirry told him. "The first television ad runs tonight, in fact, at eight."

"We'll be sure to watch," he informed her.

Kirry was confident that the campaign would be successful, and she wasn't worried, despite the faint threat in Lancaster's voice. She was obviously on trial now, thanks to Lorna's dirty work, but she wouldn't cower. She held her head up through the rest of the meeting and smiled as if she hadn't a care in the world.

"I hope I'll be invited to the wedding," Lorna told Lang as the meeting broke up. "And the first christening, of course."

Lang didn't smile. "That was a low thing to do," he said quietly. "Whatever vendettas you have against me shouldn't extend to Kirry. She's never done anything to hurt you."

"No?" Lorna's eyes glittered. "She took you away from me, didn't she?"

"No woman can take a man who isn't willing," he informed her. "You and I are water and wax. We're too different to make a pair."

"You wanted me!" she accused.

He nodded. "You were an important part of my life for a while. I hope I was as important to you. But I never told you any lies, or made any promises, and you damned well know it."

She was barely in control of her temper. She glanced at Kirry, talking to Mrs. Lancaster, and took a sharp breath. "She looks slept with," she said bluntly, looking up in time to catch Lang's expression. "So that's it. Poor little compromised virgin. Did you feel obligated to offer her marriage in exchange, Lang?" she asked. "How interesting. Do you know what sort of people the Lancasters are? They're fundamentalists."

"Are you making threats, Lorna?" he asked.

"Why, yes, I am," she said with a smile. "Either you break that engagement or I'll give the Lancasters an earful about her lack of morals. And when I get through, she won't have a job...or a reference. You do know what I mean, don't you, dear?"

She walked away, smiling. Lang stared after her with murderous eyes. He hadn't dreamed that she could be so spiteful. He'd taken her out to make Kirry jealous, but he hadn't done it in any spiteful or obvious way. For all Lorna knew, he was simply renewing an old acquaintance. Only Lorna had taken it seriously, and she wanted to play for keeps. Now Lang was between a rock and a hard place. Either he had to marry Kirry immediately or give her up, because if Lorna carried through with her threat, Kirry would literally be asked to sacrifice her career. Her job meant a lot to her. He knew too well how much careers mattered to some women....

"You're very quiet," Kirry remarked when they were on the way down to Bob and Connie's house in Floresville. "What's wrong?"

He glanced at her and back at the road. "Just thinking. Have you seen anything of Erikson today?"

She shook her head and wrapped her arms tightly around her chest, leaning back in the seat with a shiver. "Could you turn up the heat, Lang?"

"Sure." He frowned. "You aren't catching a cold, are you?"

She shook her head. "I'm just tired and worried. The Lancasters didn't like what Lorna said at lunch, I know they didn't. What if they think I'm too incompetent to keep on?"

"Aren't you good at your job?"

"Well, yes, but so are a lot of other people. I'm original, at least. Which is more than I can say for poor old Mack," she said, grimacing. "He doesn't like Lorna and he hates high fashion. He finds it boring. He's not going to do a job she'll like."

"What did you have in mind?" he asked, smiling.

"A star-studded extravaganza with some socialites helping to model Lorna's clothing line," she said. "They'd not only love the limelight, they'd buy the clothes. It would mean quick sales and

a lot more than just surface promotion. At least one local debutante has a father who owns a network of boutiques internation-
ally. Even Lorna doesn't have connections like that." She
shrugged. "But she's not interested in my ideas. I tried to show
her what I had in mind, and she just ignored me. She wouldn't
even listen."

"Pity she doesn't have any competition," he mused. "You could
put her nose in a sling."

"She does have competition," she remarked. "But they're rep-
resented by another company and as far as I know, they don't
have any promotions planned for the rest of the year."

He gave her a lingering look at a traffic light. "There is such
a thing as taking the bit between the teeth. Why don't you go
to the competition and outline your ideas and offer to take the
thing on as an independent promoter?"

She gasped. "That would be unethical."

"Give your notice at Lancaster. Change jobs. Gamble."

"Lang, I have bills to pay," she exclaimed with a surprised
laugh. "I can't take a chance like that. I'm not a gambler."

"I'm not, either, as a rule. But sometimes you have to take a
chance."

"You don't take chances."

"No? I asked you to marry me."

She averted her eyes and stared out the window with a sinking
heart.

"That was badly put, wasn't it?" he asked quietly. "I'm sorry.
I was trying to cheer you up."

"Lorna saw right through you today," she said. "She pushed you into a corner and as much as made you admit that you didn't want to marry me."

His hand tightened on the steering wheel as he was forced to remember the threat Lorna had made.

"I admitted nothing."

She turned in her seat, adjusting her seat belt, and studied his profile. "You aren't ready," she said simply. "To you, commitment is still the boogeyman. You think of marriage as a sort of prison, with children as the chains that keep people there."

He winced. "Kirry…"

She touched his sleeve, feeling the warm strength of his arm under it. "We can be engaged for a little while, until I make up my mind what I'm going to do—stay with the agency or take that chance and go independent. But I won't take the engagement seriously, and I don't want you to. Your conscience may sting for a while about what we did, but you'll get over it. Nothing happened, Lang. We just made love. People do it all the time. No big deal."

"It was to me," he said shortly, glowering down at her. "And if it was no big deal, why haven't you done it before now with some other man?"

She leaned her head against the seat and looked at him quietly. "You know why. You've always known. It's because I belong to you."

His heart shivered in his chest. He couldn't look at her again. She was tying him in knots, but they were of his own making.

He didn't want her to belong to him. He didn't want to be a prisoner of his conscience or even of love.

She withdrew her hand and looked out the windshield. She'd embarrassed him. At the very least, she'd made him uncomfortable. "Don't torture yourself," she said quietly. "I'm not asking for anything."

"I know that," he said tersely.

She closed her eyes, enjoying the company and the darkness as they sped toward Floresville. If only they could keep driving forever, she thought. It would be lovely not to have to go back to all her problems and the future, when Lang would be out of her life again, and forever this time.

She was dreaming. Lang had made love to her, and they were sprawled under a big oak tree by a beautiful stream in a meadow, holding each other. He was whispering how much he loved her...

"Will you wake up?" he demanded curtly, shaking her. "We're here, and all hell has broken loose from the sound of things!"

She sat up, her dream shattered by his harsh tone. "What?" she asked, confused.

"Listen!"

The car was sitting in the driveway of the old Victorian house where the Pattons lived. A loud voice—Bob's—was disclaiming some accusation that came from Connie. In the background, a soft Spanish voice was trying to assert reason.

"Housekeeper, my blue elbow! You were kissing her!" Connie was raging.

"I was holding her while she cried, because you hurt her feelings!" Bob yelled. All three of them were outlined on the front porch. "You didn't have to accuse her of being a home-wrecker!"

"Well, she is!" Connie said. "She's even taken over Mikey! He wants Teresa to read to him, he wants Teresa to take him to school, he wants Teresa to sit by him when we eat…he's *my* son!"

"He'd never know it, would he, when you've got your nose stuck in engines all day and half the night!"

"Oh!" Connie threw up her hands and started to say something else when she noticed the car in the driveway. She smoothed down her greasy coveralls and glanced from the car to Bob.

"Lang!" his brother exclaimed, grateful for the diversion. "Lang, is that you?"

"Looks like it," Lang said ruefully. He got out and waited for Kirry to join him at the steps. "We just got engaged and thought we'd come and tell you. This doesn't look like the best time for an announcement."

"Engaged?" Connie stumbled. "You and Kirry? Again?"

"We weren't actually engaged then," Lang said irritably. "We were almost engaged."

Connie's face softened. "Well, well. And when are you getting married, soon?"

"I wish everybody would stop asking that!" Lang burst out, running an irritated big hand through his hair.

"We haven't set a date," Kirry said quickly. "It was very

sudden. We haven't really had a lot of time to talk about it, what with our jobs…"

"Well, of course they haven't," Bob told his wife. "Can't you stop throwing questions at them when they've only just gotten here? Teresa, make some coffee and slice some cake, will you?!"

"*Sí,* Señor Bob," Teresa's soft voice came back, followed by the scurrying of feet.

"She's a sweetheart," Bob said with a smile. It faded when he looked at his haggard wife. "She doesn't think so. She doesn't even appreciate all the hard work Teresa does here to save her work."

"I'm sure Connie appreciates it, Bob," Kirry interjected. "Can we go inside? I'm cold."

"It's all but summer," Lang muttered. "How can you have chills?"

"Are you feverish?" Connie felt Kirry's forehead. "Not at all, thank goodness. You know, I had chills when I got pregnant with Mikey…"

"There's no possibility whatsoever that Kirry's pregnant," Lang said shortly.

"Oh, I know that, for heaven's sake," Connie muttered at him. "I was just making a statement."

Lang flushed, but no one noticed except Kirry. She averted her eyes. They'd taken precautions, and it had only been the one time. She couldn't be pregnant. The thing was, precautions did fail one time out of a hundred…. But, no, she wouldn't think about it.

"This is Teresa." Bob introduced the young Mexican-American woman with a smile. His eyes were twinkling as he looked at her. "*Ninita, éste es mi hermano,* Lang."

"*Mucho gusto enconocerlo, señor,*" she said with a smile. She had a lovely round figure and big brown eyes in a frame of long, jet black hair. She was a beauty. No wonder Connie was furious!

"*Y mi,*" Lang replied. "*Se alegro de trabajar aquí, señorita?*" he added.

"*Oh, sí,*" she said without enthusiasm, and she looked worried. "*Éste familia es muy simpático, especialamente el ninito.*"

She liked Mikey. She didn't mention liking Connie, who was glaring at everybody who spoke Spanish, because she didn't.

"Speak English," Connie said harshly.

"She's learning. It takes time." Bob shot back the words. "Stop being so unpleasant!"

Connie put her hands on her hips and glared at him. "I will not. You're imagining yourself in love with her, aren't you?"

Bob flushed. "For heaven's sake…!"

"Admit it, you coward!" Connie goaded him. "Come on, admit it!"

"She's a sweet, kind little thing who likes kids and housework and men!" he said finally, his dark eyes glaring at her. "How do you expect me to feel about her, when my wife looks and smells like a grease pit and never has time for me or her son?"

Connie gasped and suddenly turned and ran for the bedroom, where she slammed the door with a loud sob.

Bob grimaced. "Now I've done it."

Lang and Kirry exchanged looks. "I think we picked a bad night to come," Lang began.

"There aren't any good ones," he muttered. He saw Teresa's huge eyes fill with tears and moved to put an arm around her. *"No sea triste, amada,"* he said softly. *"Todo es bien."*

"Everything is not well," Lang replied darkly. "And she should be sad, since it seems to me that she's about to break up your marriage. You're a married man, Bob. Why don't you act like it? The person who needs comforting is your wife, not your housekeeper."

Bob's face flamed. He took his arm from around Teresa and glowered at Lang. "I don't need you to tell me how to conduct my marriage!"

"No?" Lang looked past him. Connie was coming out of the bedroom with a suitcase in one hand and Mikey by the other.

"Where are we going, Mom?" he asked sleepily.

"To my sister's!" she informed the world. She glared at Bob. "When you come to your senses, if you do, I'll be at Louise's."

"What about your precious business out back?" he asked.

"Put up a Closed sign. You can spell that, can't you?" she asked sweetly. "In the meanwhile, Todd Steele has a vacancy for a mechanic in his garage, and he'll hire me in a minute."

His eyes bulged. "I won't have you working for your ex-sweetheart who just got divorced!" he told her.

"Why not? I'm about to be divorced myself!"

"Connie!" he wailed.

"Mom, why are you yelling at daddy?" Mikey asked, still drowsy and not making much sense of the confrontation.

"Because he's deaf," Connie replied, glaring at her husband. "He doesn't understand simple language like 'fire her!'"

"You can't tell me who to fire in my own house," Bob informed her.

"It used to be my house, too, and Mikey's," Connie returned proudly. "Now it seems to be Teresa's."

Bob seemed to realize all at once what was happening to his life. "She's just the housekeeper," he began.

"That's right," Connie replied. "But you don't treat her like one."

"You don't treat me like a husband," he retorted.

Connie didn't answer him. "Say good-night to everyone, Mikey," she told their son.

"Good night," he said obligingly.

Connie smiled apologetically at Lang and Kirry, ignored the others and stalked out the door with Mikey. Minutes later, her car started up and moved out of the driveway around Lang's.

Bob's eyes narrowed. "Connie isn't my wife, she's the resident mechanic. She has no time for anything except her damned job! Mikey and I were just flotsam, don't you realize that? She doesn't want to be a wife and mother, she wants a career! Okay, I let her have it. But it's not working out."

Kirry stared at Bob with carefully concealed horror. Was she seeing what marriage to Lang would be like, except in reverse? Would he only have time for his job, and his family would be little more than an afterthought?

Lang, too, was having some difficulties with his thoughts. Kirry loved her job, too. She would be like Connie, trying to juggle a job and children, if she had any. It would be a division of loyalties that could be managed, if she loved and was loved enough. But he was seeing in Bob's relationship with Connie all the inherent dangers of marriage. He didn't like what he saw. He'd had cold feet before about marriage. They were ice-cold now.

"See what you're asking for?" Bob asked Lang with a humorless laugh. "She said she wanted a husband and a family, but what she really wanted was a garage. You'd better agree beforehand about what kind of marriage you're going to have," he said bitterly.

"Did you ever tell Connie how you felt?" Kirry asked hesitantly.

"Until I was blue in the face, but it's always been what Connie wants, not what I want." He glanced at Teresa as she came into the room, shy and quiet. "Are you leaving, too?"

Teresa explained in Spanish that she wanted to go to her brother's home in San Antonio. She asked if Lang and Kirry would drop her off.

"Come on, Teresa," Lang said. "You can ride with us."

"Muchas gracias." She walked to Bob and looked up at him with those huge, soft eyes. *"Lo siento. No te puse furioso a mi, por favor,"* she whispered.

Bob's face contorted. "Of course I'm not mad at you," he said softly, and his expression and tone got through even if the words didn't quite register.

She smiled at him. *"Hasta luego. ¿Nos vamos?"*

Lang nodded. "We go. I'll be in touch, Bob."

Bob hesitated. "Don't...blame me too much," he said miserably.

Lang moved forward and hugged him warmly. "You're my brother, you idiot, I only want you to be happy."

9

Lang and Kirry dropped Teresa off at her brother's house on the outskirts of San Antonio. Lang went with her to the door, explaining that his sister-in-law had left the house for the night—without going into any detail about the reason for it—and that it wouldn't be fitting for Teresa to spend the night alone with Bob. The brother was gracious and appreciative, and Lang came back to the car feeling less sad.

"She's got a nice family," he told Kirry.

"Your brother is really smitten with her," Kirry replied. "I'm sorry for Connie, because I don't think Bob is going to be able to resist Teresa."

"Don't be so sure," he said curtly.

"You're worried."

"I believe in marriage. Sometimes people give up too easily on a relationship."

"Sometimes they hang on to one that has no future."

He glanced at her, and his eyes became searching on her face. "Connie shouldn't have married," he said. "She should have opened her own garage and spent years building it up before she settled down."

"Yes."

He sighed heavily. "You don't really want to get married yet, do you?" he asked with his attention on the road ahead. "You want a career, just like Connie."

Her heart leaped. Was that what he thought, that a job meant more to her than making a home for Lang and their children? Or was that what he wanted to think? Was he looking for a way to break the engagement already? It felt like a replay of the past.

She twisted her fingers in her lap and watched them tangle and untangle. "Some women aren't cut out to be mothers, I think," she said. "Connie loves Mikey, but she's never been particularly maternal."

"It's a little late for her to find it out," he said angrily.

"Perhaps she didn't know herself," she said.

He didn't reply. He was taking it hard. Unusually hard.

She glanced at him. "Some men aren't cut out to be fathers, either, I guess."

He stiffened. "Really?"

"You freeze up every time someone mentions a family, Lang, haven't you realized?"

His hands gripped the steering wheel and then relaxed. "Children mean permanent ties."

"I know." She smiled. "You aren't ready, anymore than Connie was."

"Neither are you," he returned angrily. "You want a career."

"Of course I do. Everyone wants to make their mark in the world, but it's possible to combine a career with a family," she said, laughing. "People do it all the time."

"Like Connie has?" he asked angrily.

"Connie is having trouble. She's acting too single-mindedly to juggle a job and a family."

"Juggle them!" he snapped.

Kirry was surprised at the antagonism in his deep voice. She knew that the Patton boys had lost their mother when they were just a little older than Mikey, but Lang never spoke of her. Their father had raised them and he'd died when Kirry and Lang were just noticing each other.

"Lang, you never talk about your mother," she remarked.

"I never will."

She was shocked at the vehemence in the assertion. "Not even to me?"

"What do you want to know about her?" he asked.

She hesitated. "What was she like?"

"She was a career woman," he said with a cold smile, glancing her way. "She was one of those women who should never have married. She didn't have time for Bob and me. She was too busy flying all over the country to sell real estate. And one day she went up in a plane that was due for an overhaul, but she couldn't wait because she might miss a sale. The plane went down and we buried her in pieces."

Her breath caught in her throat. "Oh, Lang, I'm so sorry."

"Why? We never loved her, damn her," he retorted. "She never loved us, either. We were a nuisance, an inconvenience. She told our father every time they had a fight that she never wanted us in the first place, but he'd worried her to death about wanting kids, so she gave in. We were her greatest regret. She didn't remember a birthday the whole time we were kids, and she never remembered Christmas presents. I made her an ashtray at school in clay and painted it her favorite colors. She threw it in the trash."

Why hadn't he ever told her this? She realized then that Lang had never shared his deepest feelings with her. In all the years she'd known him, he'd never spoken of his childhood at all—until now. And she understood for the first time why he was so reluctant to marry.

"You think it will be the same for us," she said suddenly. "You think I'll be like your mother."

He looked in the rearview mirror before he made the next turn, with smooth ease. "Won't you, Kirry?" he asked with world-weary cynicism. "This is the era of single-parent families. I know all about that. I was the product of one, even if my parents were married on paper. I was a latchkey kid from the age of six. Would you like to hear some horror stories that came from it?"

"I can imagine," she said. Her soft eyes slid over his face. "It's a different world. Life-styles are changing almost overnight. What used to be the norm isn't anymore. We can't go back to the past, Lang. We all have to adjust. With the economy in its present state, most families can't make it on one income, so women have to work. If we did get married, I'd still have to have a job."

He grimaced. He didn't like what she was saying. It was all too true. They could hardly have a decent standard of living and children on just his salary, as good as it was. And what if he became disabled? If Kirry couldn't work, how would she support herself and their family if something happened to him?

"It's not such a bad thing, a woman being independent," she said gently.

"My mother certainly was," he said.

He turned into the parking lot of the building where they lived, closemouthed and quiet. Old memories were hurting him. He didn't like remembering his mother and her single-minded devotion to the almighty job. His father worked as a laborer at a feed mill. He didn't make a lot of money and he worked long hours, so he wasn't home when Bob and Lang got home from school.

Their mother could have had time for them if she'd wanted to. She was pretty much self-employed. Her job schedule could have been rearranged. But she was always gone. And when she was home, she expected Lang and Bob to have the housework done and wait on her because she was tired.

Their father had done his best to accommodate her, and that had made Lang and Bob resentful and angry at the way she used him. When she died in the plane crash, their standard of living dropped radically. But Lang hadn't cried. Neither had Bob. Their father had tried to explain it once, to make them understand that she'd loved them, in her way, but she hadn't wanted to get married in the first place. He'd compromised her, and they'd had to, for her parents' sake. In those days, in a small Texas town, church-going girls didn't have babies out of wedlock.

"My parents had to get married," Lang muttered, staring into the past.

"I'm sorry."

He cut off the engine and turned to her. "Why were you having chills?" he demanded. "Could Connie have been right with that shot in the dark?"

"We used something," she said weakly.

"And nothing is foolproof." He looked haunted. "Tell me!"

"I can't tell you what I don't know, Lang," she replied very quietly. "It's way too soon to even guess yet."

He relented. His hand ruffled his own hair as he leaned back in the seat. "I don't want you to be pregnant, Kirry," he said.

She felt her body stiffen. That was blunt enough. "You can't forgive your mother, so I'm to be punished for her sins, is that it?"

He looked puzzled. "That has nothing to do with it."

"Sure." She opened the car door and got out. Her legs felt shaky. Her self-confidence was on the blink entirely.

He got out, too, and followed her into the building and the elevator. He rammed his hands into his pockets and stared at her broodingly as they went up.

"Don't pretend that you'd be thrilled about it any more than I would," he persisted.

She didn't look at him or answer him.

They got off on their floor and she paused at the door of her apartment. "Lorna said that you didn't want to live here anymore. You denied it, but was it true?"

He frowned as he studied her. Lorna's threat came back full force. She was a vindictive woman, and Lang knew from the past that she didn't bluff.

"What if you lost your job, Kirry?"

"I'd find another," she said. "I'm not hopelessly untalented."

"If you left under a cloud, it might be difficult to find something else as good."

"I'm not going to be fired," she said heavily. "Lorna may not like me, but Mack does, and he can clear me with the Lancasters. It isn't as if I've done something unforgivable."

He looked worried and couldn't hide it. His dark eyes searched her green ones quietly. She didn't know what Lorna had threatened. He couldn't tell her, either.

"Are you sure that there won't be any consequences from what we did?" he asked heavily.

"You're worrying it to death because of one idle remark Connie made! Lang, I'm not pregnant, all right?"

"All right." He laughed at his own concern. He was overreacting. "Then if you're that sure, maybe it would be better if we let the engagement fade away."

Her eyes narrowed. "That's what Lorna wants, I gather?"

He hesitated. "Yes," he said. "That's what she wants." He didn't add why.

She searched his face as if she were saying goodbye. In fact, she was. "Then give her what she wants," she replied. "I don't want to sacrifice my future to your conscience. The only reason you wanted the engagement in the first place was because you felt guilty that we slept together. That's a bad reason to marry someone, especially when there is no possibility of any consequences," she added firmly.

Women were supposed to know if they were pregnant, he assured himself. She sounded confident. Right now, getting Lorna out of the picture before she could damage Kirry's future was the most important thing. Let her think she'd won. Yes.

"Consider the engagement off, then, if that's what you want," he said.

She managed a smile, but it was strained. "It's what you want," she said, pointedly. "You can't let go of the past, can you? I never knew why you really wanted out. You never told me anything about your life, and I didn't even realize it. You wanted me. That's all it ever was."

He didn't deny it, but his face was taut and his eyes unreadable.

She turned away. "That's what I thought," she said quietly, as she unlocked her door.

Lang watched her hungrily, averting his eyes when she looked back at him.

"I'll still be around," he reminded her. "Don't let your guard down where Erikson's concerned. And if you'd rather not keep the lessons going with me, I'll have one of my advanced students work with you. It would be a shame to stop now."

"Whatever you think," she agreed complacently.

His eyes were weary. "Maybe I am living in the past," he said then. "The fact is, I don't want children and I can't settle for half a marriage. I'm sorry. Sex isn't enough."

She knew her face had gone pale, but she smiled like a trooper. "No, it isn't," she agreed. "See you around, Lang."

He nodded. He couldn't trust himself to speak.

She closed the door with a firm click and Lang stood staring at it with his heart in his eyes for a long moment before he turned and went back to his own apartment. It had never seemed as empty in the past.

Kirry lay awake most of the night, thinking about Lang's comments. Somehow she couldn't equate the man who'd said sex wasn't enough with the incredibly tender lover of the other night. It had been much, much more than physical lust. But he wouldn't acknowledge it. And he'd seemed withdrawn the night before, especially when she'd mentioned Lorna. She didn't know what was going on, but it had to have something to do with her job. Was she going to be fired? Did he know something she didn't?

Perhaps he'd made that suggestion about an alternate campaign for a purpose. When she got up the next day, it was with a new resolve. She wasn't going to hang around and wait to be bumped from the company roster. She had some good ideas. Lorna might not appreciate them, but she knew someone who would. She put in her notice that very morning, cautioning Mack not to share it with the Lancasters just yet. He agreed, feeling personally that Kirry had been deliberately dealt a bad hand through Lorna's catty remarks to her friend, Mrs. Lancaster.

Kirry went to see Reflections, Inc., on her lunch hour. It was a new public relations firm, and the owner had a lean and hungry look. He hired Kirry on the spot when he heard some of her ideas, even going so far as to offer her a percentage of the business as well as a salary if she pulled in new business for them. Her feet hardly left the pavement on the way back to work. Marrying Lang would have made her float twice as high, but now the job would have to be her satisfaction. If she allowed herself to think about losing Lang again, she'd go mad.

By the time she got ready to leave the office, much later than she'd planned to, she'd forgotten all about Erikson in the joy of the day. Her mind was on her new position and the delight she was going to feel when she walked out the door for the last time. Her only regret was poor Mack. His ideas weren't pleasing Lorna, and she was taking out most of her frustrations on him. Everyone in the office could hear her displeasure.

"I'll cope," he'd told Kirry, tongue in cheek. "When she's had enough, she'll go looking for another agency. The joke will be on the Lancasters, not me."

Kirry had to agree, and she couldn't help feeling a little sting of pleasure at the thought. Mrs. Lancaster hadn't learned that friendship had to be kept separate from business if she wanted her company to prosper. By allowing Lorna to manipulate her, she'd cost herself a lot of new business. And an employee who could have helped her keep it.

She was thinking about the markets she could help bring to Reflections, Inc., when she suddenly realized that it was dark and she was alone in the parking lot.

Her car was in plain view, and the lot was lighted. She looked around quickly, but there wasn't another car in sight. She was being paranoid, she told herself. Erikson hadn't been seen all day. It was highly unlikely that he'd be laying in wait for her tonight.

She had her keys in her hand, locked in between her fingers to make a formidable weapon if necessary. She walked quickly and her eyes darted around cautiously. She unlocked the car, but before she got in, she looked in the back seat. Then she dashed inside and locked the doors again. Safe!

There was nothing suspicious in the interior, and she checked carefully. Then she started the car and put it in gear. No Erickson. She'd worried for nothing.

She turned the car out into traffic and drove toward her apartment building. It had been a very profitable day. She wondered how Lang had fared, and if Bob and Connie had talked over their differences. It would be sad for little Mikey if his parents divorced. She felt sorry for all of them. She felt sorriest for Lang and herself.

As she pulled into the parking lot of her apartment building and turned off the engine, she looked around cautiously. But there were other people nearby and she relaxed. Nothing to worry about, she assured herself. He was going to give it up. She knew he was. She felt better about everything.

She got her purse and locked the car, pulling her coat closer against the chilly night air. Her eyes sparkled as she thought about her one pleasure, the change of jobs.

She walked into the apartment building and got into the elevator with a couple of other tenants. Nobody spoke. She got off on her floor, wondering as she walked down the hall if Lang was at home. She stared at his door, but she only hesitated for an instant. He'd made his feelings clear. She was no longer part of his life. In fact, he might have even moved out by now. She was just going to have to learn how to live without him.

She unlocked her apartment door, idly aware that it was un- usually easy to get into tonight, and closed and locked it behind her. She turned on the light and walked into her bedroom to change clothes.

As she entered the room, an arm came around her neck and trapped her, hurting.

"Hello, girlie." A familiar voice chuckled. "Did you think I'd forget about you? Not a chance! It's payback time, blondie."

Her heart ran wild. Her knees felt like jelly. He was hurting her and in a minute he'd cut off her wind. She had to keep her head. If she panicked, it was all over.

"Mr. Erikson, you'll go to jail." She got the warning out through dry lips.

"Do you think so? It will be my word against yours. Nobody will believe you." His free hand touched her blatantly over her jacket. "Nice. You feel real nice...."

Now or never, she thought. Now or never. Her heartbeat went wild as she came back with her elbow right into his diaphragm as hard as she could. His intake of breath and the relaxing of the arm around her neck told its own story.

She whirled, acting instinctively, all Lang's training firmly in place as she brought up her knee into his groin and then stepped in, broke his balance and sent him careening down onto the floor.

Get out, she heard a voice in her head, *don't be a heroine.* She ran for the front door. Her hands fumbled with the lock, but only for a second. She got the door open and ran into the hall. Her hands beat on Lang's door, and she screamed, but he wasn't home. The hall was deserted! She heard noises coming from her apartment.

She ran to the elevator, giving way to panic, and pressed the button repeatedly. But the elevator didn't budge. She remembered the warning about the stairwell, but she was too frightened to heed it. It was the only way out.

She ran into the stairwell and tripped going down the steps, straining the muscles in her ankle so that each new step was painful. She was breathing raggedly now, and every breath hurt. A sob caught in her throat as she made it to the ground level and burst out into the lobby.

The security guard frowned as he saw her, and he came toward her at once, with a hand on the gun at his hip.

"Are you all right, Miss Campbell?" he asked quickly. "What's happened?"

"In my...apartment. A man. He attacked me," she gasped.

His face went taut. He took her to the manager's office and handed her over to a concerned clerk, who took her in back while the security guard went into the stairwell.

Kirry knew what he was going to find. Erikson was too savvy to let himself be caught. He'd be long gone, and out for blood now. She'd hurt his pride. It wouldn't be a game to him anymore. He'd want to kill her.

Nausea rose in her throat, making her sick all over. The clerk helped her to the rest room, just in time. She was white and drawn when she went back to the office, to find that the security guard was back, and grim-faced.

"I knew he'd be gone," she whispered unsteadily. "But I hurt him."

"He got out over the balcony. Somebody must have seen him, though," he told her. "Nobody gets away with that sort of thing in my building," he added coldly. "Is there someone you can stay with, Miss Campbell, for tonight? I don't like thinking about you being up there alone."

She laughed bitterly. It hadn't occurred to her before that she had nothing in her life except friendly acquaintances like Betty. She had no family in this country; God only knew where her mother was, and there wasn't anyone else.

"No," she said, choking down tears. "I have no one."

He looked worried. He scowled as he tried to come up with a solution. "We'll have to call the police," he said.

She didn't have the strength to argue. Her willpower was at its lowest ebb in years.

The police came and questioned her. She gave them a description of Erikson, explaining the problem and referring them to people at her office—and to Lang.

"We'll pick him up," a young officer said coldly. "He can't be too hard to find."

"Good thing you knew some self-defense, young lady," his older partner added. "I taught my daughter when she was just a kid. It's handy stuff."

"You can say that again," she agreed with a wan smile.

"I've called in one of our part-time security guards," the apartment security officer said, rejoining them with a taut expression. "He'll be outside your apartment all night long, Miss Campbell. You needn't worry."

She felt tears sliding down her cheeks. "Oh, it's so kind…!" she whispered.

He looked embarrassed. "You're a tenant," he said. "We can't have people upsetting our tenants. Here, now, don't do that. It's all over."

The cluster of people in the lobby piqued Lang's curiosity as he came into the apartment building. He'd had to interview applicants and then there had been a faulty burglar alarm that had to be dealt with. He was worn from the rigors of the day, and from hating what he'd done to Kirry. Damn Lorna, he wasn't going to let her dictate his life or intimidate Kirry. He'd told her so, too. And, he'd added, if she told the Lancasters about Kirry, he'd have something to tell them about her.

She hadn't expected that. Her face had gone pale and she'd blustered around for ten minutes. But in the end, she'd given in. She had other men in her life, she'd informed him. She didn't need to drag up old relationships to keep her warm, and she didn't want him, anyway.

Lang had felt sorry for her. But not sorry enough to hang around. He was guilty over the way he'd treated Kirry, and he'd done some hard thinking about his position on marriage. He was overreacting because of his mother, Kirry had said, and she was right. He'd come back with the intention of telling her so, and suggesting that they might think about starting over one more time. But there would be no more secrets. And whatever problems they encountered, they'd work out.

But the commotion near the manager's office distracted him. He walked toward it, and suddenly saw Kirry's white face and torn blouse. Erikson!

He pushed his way through the crush of police officers to her, and without a word, he pulled her into his arms and wrapped her up there.

"Are you all right?" he asked without a greeting.

She was stiff in his arms, but she didn't push him away. "Erikson was waiting for me in the apartment. I remembered just enough of what you taught me to get away in time. But he's vanished. They're searching for him now."

Lang lifted his head and looked into her eyes. She was putting up a good front, but that was fear in her face.

"Damn him," he said through his teeth.

"We're posting a man outside her apartment," the security guard began.

"To hell with that. I'm taking her to my brother and sister-in-law's home. She'll be safe," he said abruptly.

"That would be the best thing you could do," one of the policemen said. "We'll get him. But she'll be safer where he can't find her."

"I'll take care of her." Lang turned to the security guard. "Thanks," he said huskily.

The other man shrugged and smiled. So that was the way of things. Nice young woman, and that beau of hers was pretty protective. She'd be looked after.

10

Lang waited for her to change and pack in her apartment, while he telephoned Bob and explained what had happened.

"Come on down," Bob said in a subdued tone. "Connie and Mikey came back today."

"And Teresa?" Lang asked.

"I was a fool. Connie isn't speaking to me, but if you bring Kirry, maybe it will help all of us out."

"I'll see you shortly. And thanks."

He hung up. Kirry was still standing in the doorway of her bedroom, in the same clothes.

"You haven't changed," he said gently.

"I don't want to go in there alone," she said with a self-conscious laugh. "Silly, isn't it?"

"Not at all. I think you're pretty brave," he said, smiling.

She smiled back. "I don't feel it. I was sick."

"No wonder." He came into the bedroom with her. "What do you want to wear?"

She laid out some jeans and a top. Before she could move, he did, to begin undressing her.

She looked up at him like a child, her eyes wide, curious.

He smiled at her tenderly. "I could learn to like this," he remarked as he stripped her out of everything except her briefs and bra. "You're exquisitely designed, Miss Campbell."

"I feel weak all over."

"Do you?" He pulled her close and bent to kiss her with breathless tenderness. His hands slid down to her hips and his thumbs spread over her belly. He lifted his head and searched her eyes while he touched her gently. "So do I. My knees buckle when I kiss you."

That made her laugh. "They do not."

He rubbed his nose against hers. "How do you know? You aren't looking down."

She drew in a slow breath and her face was worried. "Did I hear you say that Connie was back with Bob?"

"For the time being. He's come to his senses."

"Maybe she has, too." She lifted her hand to his face and had to fight tears at the hunger she felt for his love. "I wish..."

"What?" he asked softly.

She withdrew her hand. "Nothing. We should go."

"With you like that?" he asked. "We'd be arrested."

"If you'll let me go, I'll get dressed."

"No, I don't like that idea," he murmured. "Covering up such a beautiful body ought to qualify as a crime."

She blushed and laughed. "Lang!"

He tilted her face up and kissed her with slow, sweet ardor. "We could make love before we go," he whispered. His hands moved up to her breasts and teased them, possessed them. "Would you like to?"

"We've already agreed that it isn't a good idea if we see each other," she protested weakly.

"That was before," he murmured against her lips.

"Before what?"

"Before I discovered that I wouldn't mind if we had a baby together."

Her body stilled against him. She lifted her eyes to his and found warm, dark secrets in them. "Wh…what?"

He bent and lifted her into his arms. "You'll still have to work," he said as he carried her to the bed. "I make good money, but we'll have a better life-style with two salaries. Besides that, you need to be self-supporting. We can find a good day-care center, one that we both feel comfortable with, and I'll learn to do diapers and feed him…unless you want to?" he added with a wickedly sensuous smile as his eyes dropped to her breasts.

She shivered with the force of her feelings. "Oh, yes, I'd like…to," she moaned. "Lang, I love you so much," she sobbed. "More than my life…!"

He eased over her and pressed her gently down into the mattress. His mouth covered hers and his hands found fastenings and revealed the soft bareness of her body to his mouth and his hands and his eyes.

"I love you," he whispered back. "It was the thought of a family that unsettled me. I didn't even know why, until you made me realize how badly my childhood had scarred me. But I think I can come to terms with it. The one thing I can't do is walk away from you twice in one lifetime. So we'll just have to cope."

"We will. I know we will." Her heart was in her eyes as she looked up at him. "Lang?"

"Hmm?" he murmured against her throat.

"Could you take your clothes off?"

He chuckled. "I guess so. Want to watch?"

Her breath caught. "Yes," she whispered, her eyes wide and ardent.

He laughed unsteadily as he stood and pulled off everything that concealed his powerful body from her. When he turned back to the bed, she shivered a little in anticipation, because she knew now what pleasure he could give her.

He slid down beside her, his eyes warm and alive with the joy of what they were sharing. "We can use something, if you want to."

She pulled him down with loving arms. "You're so certain that I can't be a wife and a mother at the same time, aren't you?" she asked gently. "Why don't you let me show you?"

"Darlin'," he whispered as he covered her open mouth with his, "I'd love nothing better!"

She opened her arms to him as his body moved down to press against hers. For endless minutes, they lost themselves in the soft caresses that led to the urgent, slow, sweet rhythm of love. There was a new tenderness in the expression of it, but the passion was just as familiar as the upswing of frenetic pleasure that left them shuddering in its exquisite aftermath.

"My God," he groaned into her mouth as his full weight descended on her. "Am I dreaming?"

"I hope not," she whispered, shaken. Her legs tangled in his and she pressed her face into his damp throat. "The world trembled, didn't it?"

He laughed. "And a few other things," he murmured dryly.

"I love the way you love me," she whispered. "I love you."

"Show me again," he said against her mouth, and his hips shifted slowly against hers. "Make me cry out."

"But can you?" she asked uncertainly.

He moved sharply and chuckled at her wide-eyed wonder. "Let's see," he murmured, and pushed down.

It was three hours later when they arrived at Bob and Connie's house.

"We were getting worried," Bob said as they climbed out of the car in his driveway. "Kirry, are you all right?"

"Oh, I'm fine," she assured him with a smile. "I'm a little sore, but that's normal."

"She laid Erikson out," Lang added with pride, glad that his brother couldn't see the flush on his high cheekbones. "I appreciate your letting us come down."

"What are family for? Connie, they're here!"

Connie came out, in a dress, looking subdued and so feminine that Lang actually leaned forward for a closer look. "Connie?" he asked, shocked.

She glared at him. "Yes, it's me, can't you recognize me when I'm not covered in grease?" she asked caustically.

He grinned. "Well, come to think of it, no," he teased.

She had her arms tight over her breasts and she wasn't looking at Bob. She moved them to hug Kirry. "Are you all right, honey?" she asked, concerned.

"I'm fine," Kirry said, smiling helplessly at Lang. "We're engaged," she told them.

"You've already told us, don't you remember?" Connie asked gently.

They hadn't known about the engagement being broken. Kirry and Lang exchanged glances and smiles.

"No use expecting any sense out of you two." Bob chuckled. "Come on in. Mikey's gone to bed. We'll have some coffee and cake."

"My cake, not hers," Connie said sharply to Bob, who looked uncomfortable. "I just baked it. I can cook."

"Honey, I never said you couldn't," Bob began.

"Hmmph!" she muttered, and led the way into the house.

"She's been like that since she got here," Bob said miserably. "She treats me like an adulterer. I swear to God, I never put a hand on Teresa."

"Have you told Connie that?"

"Would she listen?" he muttered.

"If you tell her the right way, she might," Lang mused, his eyes warm and loving on Kirry as she went into the kitchen with Connie.

Bob glanced at his brother curiously. "Are you serious this time about marrying Kirry?" he asked.

Lang paused, sticking his hands into his pockets. "I'm serious," he said. "I guess the way we grew up had a worse effect on me than it did on you, Bob," he added. "I couldn't bear the thought of bringing a child into the world whose mother treated it like a nuisance."

"I can't believe you thought Kirry would be like our mother," he mused. "Kirry's a motherly type."

"Not anymore," Lang told him, with a sense of pride. "She's got a good mind and she should use it. Besides that, she's one of the best karate students I've ever trained," he added with a chuckle. "Erikson attacked her and she laid him out." His eyes sparkled with quick temper. "Damn him, I hope we can put him away forever. If she hadn't known what to do, the least that would have happened is that she'd have been raped. He might even have killed her."

Bob frowned. "What did she do to him?"

"He was a security guard at the office. She objected to being talked to like a prostitute."

Bob's eyebrows rose. "How did he keep his job so long, with that sort of attitude?"

"Women have kept quiet about harassment in the past.

They've started objecting to it, and so they should. You know, in the early days of the century, despite the fact that women weren't permitted the freedom men enjoyed, at least they were treated with respect. A man who insulted a woman, married or single, could expect to be beaten within an inch of his life. These days, you'd be surprised at the language men feel comfortable using around them."

"Listen, have you ever heard Connie when she hit her thumb with a hammer?" Bob mused.

Lang clapped his brother on the back. "Point taken."

Kirry's bad experience was the talk of the evening, but the looks she and Lang were exchanging amused Bob.

"I guess you still haven't set a date," he commented.

"Next week," Lang said easily, smiling at Kirry's surprise. "If you don't want a big wedding, that is."

"I just want you," Kirry said honestly. "A justice of the peace and a simple wedding ring will suit me fine."

"That's how Connie and I did it," Bob said, his dark eyes searching his wife's subdued face. "We used to sit up all hours just talking. We were good friends long before we wanted to live together. And when Mikey came along, he was the beginning of the whole world."

Connie's eyes softened as she remembered her son's birth. She stared at Bob with pain in her whole expression. "And you're willing to throw away ten good years for a little girl playing house."

His face hardened. "At least she likes it."

"For now," Connie agreed. "But she's very young. When she gets a few more years on her, she'll realize that a woman has to be a person in her own right, not just an extension of her husband. Thinking up new recipes isn't enough anymore."

"Keeping a clean house and raising good children who were loved and given attention used to be enough," Bob said angrily.

"Of course it did," his wife replied with a sad smile. "But the world has changed. It's so tough on one salary. When I worked, I could afford so many nice things that we could never have before. I guess I went wild." She shrugged, glancing uncertainly at Bob. "I almost lost my family in the process. I've decided that I want to be a mechanic, but that I don't want it more than I want you and Mikey."

Bob studied the coffee cup in front of him. "I don't want to start getting used to another person this late in my life," he confessed.

She smiled. "I could work for someone…"

He looked up. "You could work at your own shop, in the back," he said stiffly. "But you can close up on Wednesdays and Saturdays, and we'll spend those days, and Sunday, as a family. Meanwhile, having someone to help keep the house clean isn't a bad idea." Before she could speak, he added, "I know a teenage boy who likes to cook and doesn't mind cleaning. Mrs. Jones's son, and he could use the money because he wants to go to one of those French cooking schools when he gets out of school."

Connie was surprised. "But you hate my work!"

"I was jealous of it," he confessed with a smile. He looked at his brother. "I guess Lang and I never talked enough about how we were raised. We were a dysfunctional family and never even knew it. Now we're both having to learn that marriage is what you make of it."

Connie's face had brightened. She flushed when Bob smiled warmly at her, and he chuckled. "It isn't so bad, having a mechanic in the family. Except that my car sure does run rough," he added.

"I can fix it," Connie mused.

"I know."

Kirry felt Lang's hand curving around hers where it lay on the table. She looked at him with her heart in her eyes, and his breath caught.

"Where are you going to live when you're married?" Bob asked them, breaking the spell.

"I like the security where we are," Lang said with a chuckle. "My apartment or hers, it doesn't matter. I'd live with her in a mud hut," he added solemnly.

"That goes double for me," she said softly.

"Until the kids come along," he added very slowly, holding her eyes. "Then I think we might want a house. One with a big yard, so we can have a dog."

There were tears of pure joy in her eyes.

"Will you go on working for Lancaster, Inc.?" Connie asked her.

Kirry caught her breath. "Oh, that reminds me!" And she told them what she'd done, and about her new job.

Lang burst out laughing. "And I thought you weren't listening when I suggested it."

"I was listening. Mack says Mrs. Lancaster is going to be very sorry indeed, because Lorna is already talking about pulling the account."

"That doesn't surprise me in the least," Lang ventured. "I'm sorry that Lorna gave you a hard time. I hope you believe that I was serious when I said there was nothing between us."

"Oh, of course I do," she assured him. It would be impossible to believe anything else, when he looked at her that way, with everything he felt naked in his face.

"What will they do to that man when they catch him?" Connie asked, concerned. "Will there be enough evidence to keep him locked up?"

Lang was remembering the times Erikson had gotten away with what he'd done, and he was worried. "I hope so."

Kirry was thinking the same thing. She clung to Lang's hand and tried not to brood about it. She had visions of a long, drawn-out court case and legal expenses that would bankrupt them.

"Don't worry about it," Lang said softly. He bent and kissed her forehead softly. "We'll work it all out. I promise you we will."

They stayed the night, parting reluctantly as she went to the guest room and Lang bedded down on the sofa. She didn't want to be away from him long enough to sleep. Apparently he felt the same way, because in the early hours of the morning, he picked her up out of the bed and carried her back to the sofa, bundling her up in his arms until morning.

Connie and Bob came upon them like that, and stood looking down at them with indulgent smiles, their arms around each other.

"Remember how that felt?" Bob asked gently. "To be so much in love that you can't bear the agony of being apart even for a few hours?"

"Oh, yes." Connie reached up and kissed him. "I still feel like that. It's why I came home."

He smiled and drew her close. "So do I. I'm glad we both woke up in time, Connie."

"Marriage has to have compromise or it can't last. For Mikey's sake, and our own, I'm glad we're both reasonable people."

He chuckled. "After last night, I'm not sure that I'm very reasonable anymore. In fact, I think I'm loopy." He whispered in her ear, "Did you really do that, or did I dream it?"

She flushed scarlet. "Bob!"

The cry woke Lang and Kirry. They blinked and stared up at their hosts. Lang smiled sheepishly. "This isn't quite what it looks like…"

"Looks like two people in love to me." Bob chuckled. "Come and have breakfast, you idiots."

Later in the day, Lang and Kirry drove back up to San Antonio. Both of them were anxious to see if any progress had been made about Erikson. What they discovered shocked them.

"It was kind of tragic, in a way," the police lieutenant who spoke to them at the precinct said matter-of-factly. "He was going too fast and just shot right off the bridge, through the railing. We found him a few hours ago. I tried to call you both, but no one was at home."

"We were at my brother's house in Floresville," Lang said. He pulled Kirry closer. "It's been a hell of a few weeks."

"Yes, I know. This isn't the only stalking case we've ever had," the policeman replied. "I've talked to one of our legislators, and he's willing to introduce some legislation about it. He'd like to talk to you, Miss Campbell."

"I'd like to talk to him," she replied quietly.

"At any rate, you're safe now," he told her. "Try not to let it scar you. The world is full of people who enjoy hurting other people. It's why I have a job."

"Thanks."

They walked out into the sunlight, and Kirry clung to Lang's hand.

"This is why women put up with it," she said uneasily.

"What?"

"Harassment on the job," she said simply. "They're afraid of something like what happened to me. They're afraid of being the object of gossip by other employees, or being fired, or being discriminated against. Even if you keep your job, people still resent you. Even some women think it's stupid for a woman to cause trouble because a man is vulgar in front of her, or because he makes sexist remarks."

He turned to her. "Nobody ever promised that life was easy. Sometimes it's dangerous to do the right thing. Sometimes it causes heartache. That doesn't change the fact that people have a right to work unmolested."

She hesitated. Then she nodded. "All the same, I don't know if I'd have enough courage to do it again after what happened to me."

He chuckled. "Really? I think you have enough courage."

"You're prejudiced."

"I love you to distraction," he said simply. "Doesn't it show?"

Her eyes sparkled with delight as she looked at him. "Cold turkey and in broad daylight, even! You must mean it."

"Didn't you believe me?"

"Yes," she said after a minute. "I didn't really think I could care so much about you unless you cared about me, too."

"Smart lady. When do you leave Lancaster, Inc.?"

"Monday after next. I got a raise, too, at Reflections, Inc."

He grinned. "Even better. Will it involve as much traveling as you're doing now?"

"No," she replied, her face bright. "Because I told my new boss that I wanted to be home at nights, and he said that he's got two single employees who love to travel, and they'll carry the ball in that respect. I may have to go out of town occasionally, but it won't be every week."

"That I can handle." He pursed his lips. "My job will keep me in town, thank God, so if you have to be away, I can mind the kids."

"Kids? Plural?"

His eyes slid over her with kindling desire and slow pleasure. "I thought a boy and a girl would be nice."

"Did you, now? Boys run in your family for three generations and I'm the first girl in my family in two. The odds are against little girls." He started to speak and she put her fingers over his mouth, smiling. "I like playing baseball, don't you remember? And I never did play with dolls."

He chuckled. "Okay. We'll see what we get."

"Why don't we go home, since we don't have to go in to the office today, and you can see what you get."

He whistled softly. "My knees are going weak."

"So are mine." She pressed close to him as they walked toward the car. She allowed herself a little pity for Erikson. "He didn't have a family, did he?" she asked.

He knew who she meant. "No."

"Poor man. He was sick, Lang. Sick in the mind. I'm sorry for him."

"So am I, in a way. But it was fate, honey. I'm glad you're safe. I'll take care of you."

She liked that protectiveness in him. She nuzzled her face against his shoulder. "I'll take care of you, too, my darling."

He kissed her forehead. "Let's stop by city hall and get the marriage license. Then," he added softly, "we'll see how wicked we can get behind closed doors."

She didn't have an argument with that.

* * *

They were married less than a week later, with Bob and Connie and Mikey for witnesses, and they managed a brief honeymoon trip to Jamaica. When they came back, Kirry started her new job and found it much to her liking. The Lancasters lost the Lorna McLane account in short order, along with the promise of new customers. They apologized to Kirry, once they found out just how Lorna had twisted things to make her look incompetent. Kirry accepted the apology gracefully, but wouldn't return, even though Lang stayed with them. There were no hard feelings, and the Lancasters gave them a handsome belated wedding present of a silver service.

"That was nice of them," Kirry remarked later as she was lying in Lang's big arms in bed.

"I thought so, too." He opened one eye as she propped over him. "You lost your breakfast this morning. Was it something that didn't sit well on your stomach?"

She smiled wickedly. "It's something that probably will sit well on my stomach until it gets too big."

Both eyes opened, with love and soft wonder. "Are we sure yet?" he asked with a glowing smile.

She nodded. "I got one of those kits this morning, and did it twice. I'll go to the doctor to make sure, but there won't be any surprises."

He pulled her down and kissed her tenderly, smiling against her mouth. "Are you sure we're going to have a boy?"

She laughed. "There's absolutely no chance that it will be anything else," she said smugly, and squealed when his fingers dug gently into her ribs.

Seven months later, Lang stood in the hospital room with Cecily Maureen Patton in his arms and one eyebrow lifted with superior irony down at his pretty wife.

"Go ahead," she challenged. "I know you're dying to say it."

He chuckled. Then his face sobered and he looked at Kirry with such love that she flushed. "Thank you," he said gently. "I never knew what life was all about until they put her in my arms."

"I know," she replied with wonder. "Lang, I've never felt like this. To know that we did that, that we created something so incredible between us."

"And had such delight from doing it," he teased gently, loving her soft flush. He looked down at his daughter. "Isn't she a beauty? Daddy loves little girls," he cooed as he kissed the tiny face. "He'll take her on picnics and buy her toys and kill boys who break her heart. Daddy will teach her to shoot guns, and do martial arts, and track spies…"

"And Mama will teach her how to promote people and write brilliant ads," she said with twinkling eyes.

Lang grinned at her. "Guess which things she's going to like learning best?"

Kirry pursed her lips and didn't say another word. Their daughter was going to have a very interesting life, and their marriage got better by the day. She looked back over the rocky road they'd traveled to this day and knew that she'd do it all over again. Her whole heart was in her eyes when she smiled at her husband, and in his when he smiled back.

* * * * *

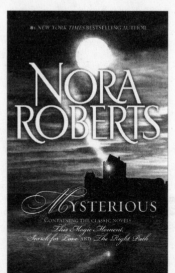

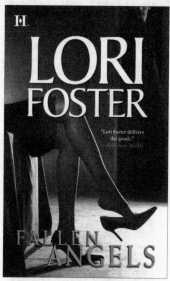

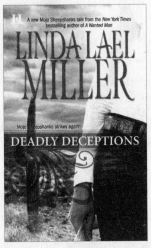

Silhouette® Desire

NEW YORK TIMES BESTSELLING AUTHOR

DIANA PALMER

A brand-new Long, Tall Texans novel

IRON COWBOY

Available March 2008
wherever you buy books.